Jenna's eyes da[...] register to th[...]

It seemed to be lying on the conveyor belt screaming, "Jenna thinks she's pregnant!" She craned her neck down the aisle, and just as she feared, spotted Adam and Ryan on their way back.

By the time the checker turned her attention to Jenna's purchases, it was too late to ask her to ring up the pregnancy test separately. Adam and her son were within hearing distance. Maybe they wouldn't notice it, she prayed, but lost all hope of that when the checker tried to run the package through the scanner and it wouldn't beep. Frowning, the woman picked up her microphone. "Johnny? Would you get me the price of the First Choice Pregnancy Test? Aisle 9, I think."

Jenna took a gulp of air and held it as Adam's jaw dropped and his eyes flew to her face. She gave an uncomfortable laugh. "Where did that come from?" she asked. "That's not mine."

The checker blinked at her. "You don't want this?"

"No, it's not mine." Jenna could feel her cheeks burn with embarrassment. "Maybe it belonged to the person in front of me."

"Mrs. Jones?" The checker scoffed outright. "She must be sixty-five. I don't think so, honey." She shoved the pregnancy test off to one side.

Jenna wanted only to get out of the grocery store and away from the First Choice box as soon as possible.

Dear Reader,

I can't tell you how happy I am to be a new Superromance author and to be able to share *Expectations*, my first contemporary romance, with you.

Not long ago, when I visited the picturesque town of Mendocino along the northern California coast, I knew I wanted to set a book there. *Expectations* is that book. It's a story about coming home, about two people who are, for very different reasons, eager to leave the small, close community where they grew up. One ventures into the world and meets with success; the other must come to terms with a failed marriage. But they're both searching for something when they come home again—and what they find, surprises even them.

I'd love to hear what you think of *Expectations* or answer any questions you may have. And I hope you'll look for my next book later this year. You can contact me at P.O. Box 3781, Citrus Heights, CA 95611, or via my web site at www.brendanovak.com where the dates and titles of my upcoming books will be listed, along with current book-signing information.

Happy reading!

Brenda Novak

EXPECTATIONS
Brenda
Novak

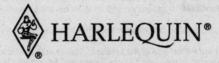

HARLEQUIN®

TORONTO • NEW YORK • LONDON
AMSTERDAM • PARIS • SYDNEY • HAMBURG
STOCKHOLM • ATHENS • TOKYO • MILAN • MADRID
PRAGUE • WARSAW • BUDAPEST • AUCKLAND

ISBN 0-373-70899-8

EXPECTATIONS

Copyright © 2000 by Brenda Novak.

This edition published by arrangement with Harlequin Books S.A.

® and TM are trademarks of the publisher. Trademarks indicated with ® are registered in the United States Patent and Trademark Office, the Canadian Trade Marks Office and in other countries.

Visit us at www.romance.net

Printed in U.S.A.

To my editor, Paula Eykelhof.
For her open heart and open mind.
For treating authors with patience and respect.
For listening to me when I was an unpublished writer
fumbling through my first verbal pitch, and seeing the
potential in spite of the nerves.

I would like to acknowledge the assistance
of René Stwora-Hale, criminal prosecutor, for her advice
on matters legal. And I would like to thank Kim Grace
for giving me those precious few, guilt-free hours to write
without distractions. Thanks also to my sister,
Tonya Schmidt, for her interest in and excitement
about my work.

CHAPTER ONE

WAS SOMEONE BREAKING IN?

Jenna Livingston stiffened beneath the fluffy comforter of her bed. The Mendocino house, which she helped run as a bed-and-breakfast, was more than a hundred years old. It had its share of nighttime settling noises. And the sea was never silent. Less than a half mile away, surf pounded constantly against the tall black rocks of the Northern California coast, a life rhythm for the small community.

But this noise...this was different. She might have thought Ryan had awakened, but her son's room opened off her own and the door between them was still closed.

Straining to hear beyond the rasp of her own breathing and the thump of her heart, Jenna waited.

There it was again. Scratching against the side of the house. A bump. Coming from downstairs.

Had Mr. Durham heard it? Jenna listened for movement in the room across the hall.

A snore loud enough to reach through two doors answered her. Lyle Durham, the seventy-year-old owner of Victoriana Bed-and-Breakfast, was obviously sound asleep. His sixty-nine-year-old wife, Myrtle, probably snored right along with him. She wore hearing aids, which she removed at bedtime along with her teeth. And there were no paying guests tonight. Tourist season was over. Except for the occasional weekend when visitors again swelled the local population, the advent of autumn left the small town of Mendocino quiet and close.

Creeping out from under the covers, Jenna pulled on a robe over the tank top and bikini underwear she wore to bed. If her own troubled thoughts hadn't kept her awake, she doubted she would have heard anything, either. But these days she spent more time tossing and turning than she did sleeping, and the effects were beginning to show. She was jumpy, not yet at peace with the recent changes in her life.

Another thump led Jenna to the top of the stairs, where she squinted into the darkness below. Running a hand through her long tangled hair, she considered waking the Durhams, then decided against it. Mrs. Durham would call the police, Mr. Durham would insist on going alone to investigate, and if Ryan got up, he'd find himself in the middle of another frightening episode.

A lot of unnecessary fuss if the trouble turned out to be nothing more than an alley cat getting into the garbage again. Besides, if it came to facing a burglar, Jenna trusted her own skills more than she did the old man's bravado. She felt almost as protective of the Durhams as she did of Ryan. They had taken her in at a time when she badly needed someone; they treated her like a member of the family.

The stairs creaked as Jenna descended, one hand on each wall to help keep her balance. The moonlight, which had filtered easily through the sheer curtains of the upper bedrooms, struggled to reach the dark interior of the lower level. Heavy draperies and blinds covered the tall thick-paned windows, but Jenna wasn't about to give her presence away by turning on a lamp. Not when she already knew where each and every piece of furniture was. After her arrival at the end of August, she'd helped redecorate the place and had selected and arranged its many antiques.

Tiptoeing past a Louis XVI settee with matching chairs, Jenna paused to listen.

A muttered curse, very definitely human and very definitely male, broke the silence.

The kitchen. The man, whoever he was, sounded as though he was climbing through the kitchen window.

I should call the police. Jenna looked up the stairs, once again tempted to wake the Durhams. Breaking and entering wasn't kid's play. Mendocino had a low crime rate, especially during the fall and winter, but that was no consolation if she, Ryan and the Durhams joined the few who'd been victims.

Judging from the movements she heard, however, the thief was nearly inside. By the time the police arrived, whatever he planned to do would be done.

Jenna had a better idea. Pressing herself to the wall outside the swinging kitchen door, she tightened her robe and calmed her mind, seeking her karate instructor's voice in her head. After three years of lessons and intense training, she'd earned her black belt—and she'd proved herself capable of handling even a large man the last time her drunken husband had come after her. Drunken *ex*-husband.

The sound of the refrigerator door opening and the clink of bottles came from within. Then the crackle of cellophane, water running in the sink and a cupboard being closed.

What was he doing? Stealing food? Snooping? *Or looking for a stash of money?*

Finally she could hear him crossing to the door. Jenna's heart skidded and bumped as her taut nerves threatened to leave her in a quaking heap on the carpet. During her encounter with her husband, her emotions had sustained her, but long-smoldering anger was quite different from fear.

She raised her hands in a defensive stance. Whoever it was wouldn't expect her. She'd have the element of surprise on her side. Except that this housebreaker seemed to think he had all the time in the world, which was partly what frightened her. Only a bold thief would be so careless. *Or a thief with a gun.*

The door swung open, and Jenna reacted, refusing to give the man a chance to use any weapon. Slicing the air with her right hand, she landed a blow to the neck. Her foot rose almost in unison, kicking him squarely in the groin.

He grunted and collapsed to the floor, curling into a fetal position.

Jenna grabbed the vase from the table at her side and lifted it high. "Who are you and what do you want here?" she demanded, prepared to bring it crashing down on his head.

For a moment the intruder didn't speak. At last he wheezed, "I'm Adam Durham. My grandparents own this place. What the hell is going on?"

Jenna's blood turned to ice. Adam Durham! She hadn't seen Adam since high school—and she didn't want to see him now. Especially not rolling on the floor because she'd kicked him.

Or maybe he deserved it for ruining her life all those years ago.

"What's happening down here?" Jenna squinted as

the lights flashed on. Lyle Durham stood at the foot of the stairs, a concerned scowl on his seamed face.

"Jenna, girl, you all right?"

Jenna realized she was still holding the vase. Setting it back in its rightful place, she nodded and followed Mr. Durham's gaze to the man at her feet.

"Adam, what are you doing here? And what the devil's the matter?"

"Kung Fu here just kicked the shit out of me. What does it look like?" he groaned.

The old man's scowl deepened. "What did you do to her?"

Adam didn't answer. He rolled to his back and tried to catch his breath, giving Jenna her first glimpse of his face. He'd changed—she saw that right off—and all for the better. The rangy reckless boy she'd known had grown into a well-built man in a tailored business suit. With slick black hair that shone almost as richly as his leather loafers, he looked the consummate business executive. Except for his eyes, which still sparkled with mischief.

Myrtle Durham, wrapped in a fuzzy pink bath robe that complemented her husband's gray terry-cloth one, came down the stairs and peeked over Mr. Durham's shoulder. "Oh, my! It *is* Adam. And he's hurt."

"I thought he was a burglar," Jenna explained.

"And she didn't stop to ask any questions," Adam added with a glower.

Jenna lifted a challenging brow. "Most men who climb through windows in the middle of the night aren't paying a social call."

"But why didn't you use the key?" Mrs. Durham asked. "I always leave one out for you."

Adam shook his head. "It wasn't where you usually keep it, and I didn't want to wake you."

"Nothing gets past our new manager." Mr. Durham winked at Jenna. "Come on, boy. You can't be too badly hurt. Jenna's not big enough to cause lasting damage." He offered Adam a hand.

"Unless you don't know she's lying in wait for you." Adam accepted his grandfather's help. "A man with a Twinkie in his mouth isn't exactly prepared for attack."

His voice, full of the same wry humor she remembered so well, made Jenna wince. She'd spent fifteen years trying to forget Adam Durham.

It felt as if it hadn't been a day.

"Look at you," his grandfather said when Adam stood, towering half a foot above the older man. "You grow taller every time I see you. What's it been, two years?"

Frowning, Adam slapped the dust off his suit pants. "I've been six-two for ten years, Pop. You say that every time I come here. Besides, you know it's only been four months since my last visit."

"Four months, two years—it's the same to an old man with no other family. Did you get tired of all that talking in court and decide to move home, like you should've done a long time ago?"

Seeming to recover his aplomb, Adam chuckled and ran a hand through his thick hair. "No, Pop. I'm still a lawyer, still living in San Francisco. I just had some time this week and thought I'd come for a stay."

"That means you'll be on the phone till you leave."

"Lyle!" Myrtle brushed past her husband to give her grandson a hug.

Adam returned the hug, lifting the short plump

woman off her feet. Then he released her and pulled off his already loosened tie. Jenna assumed his jacket had been removed before his climb through the window and pictured it draped across the passenger seat of—what kind of car would he own now? Certainly nothing like the beat-up Chevy they used to drive everywhere, back when they were high-school sweethearts.

"I won't make a single call. Promise." He crossed his heart, drawing Jenna's attention lower. She'd tried not to notice the other marked changes in him, but now she couldn't stop looking. Adam was no longer a gangly eighteen-year-old. He was a man, and he had the body to prove it. The white shirt he wore, unbuttoned at the neck, covered shoulders broad enough to fill a doorway, a lean waist and arms contoured with well-defined muscle.

"What's she doing here? And where's my old buddy *Dennis?*" he asked.

His use of the third person and his emphasis on Dennis's name told Jenna he hadn't yet forgiven her for the kick to his groin. And that he felt as uncomfortable around her as she did him. They hadn't parted on the best of terms. The minute he'd graduated from high school, he'd broken up with her, saying he wanted the freedom to pursue a career. She'd retaliated by saying she was going to marry his best friend, who had chased her for years. They'd fought, Adam had gone off to college, and she hadn't seen him since.

Unfortunately, when she graduated a year later, she'd followed through with her threat to marry Dennis.

"*She* has a voice," Jenna answered, telling herself she wasn't the same person she'd been back in those

days—lost and vulnerable because her mother and stepfather had just died in a car accident and her real father
had rejected her yet again. She'd been through a lot to
toughen her up since.

"Dennis and I are divorced." She stated it matter-
of-factly, as though she didn't care about conceding
their last argument to him. But she did. She hated admitting the divorce to anyone, Adam most of all. According to the Durhams, who had raised him after his
mother died of a drug overdose, he'd gone on to accomplish all he wanted. He'd become a huge success
in the big city; he was rich, powerful, happy.

She couldn't even keep her marriage together.

"Mom?" A sleepy-eyed Ryan hovered behind the
Durhams. "What's wrong? Is it Dad?"

Jenna hurried to her eight-year-old son and, putting
a reassuring arm around his shoulders, brought him into
the light. "No, honey, it's the Durhams' grandson,
Adam. You've heard them talk about him before,
haven't you?"

Ryan scratched his tousled head of wheat-blond hair.
"Yeah. He's the real busy guy from San Francisco,
right?"

If Ryan's words implied an accusation, Jenna knew
her son wasn't aware of it, but the adults shifted uncomfortably.

"I'm a defense attorney," Adam explained. "With
the number of bad guys running around these days, not
to mention the wrongly accused, there's a lot of work
to be done."

Ryan nodded and covered a yawn. Had Adam said
he was a football player or a cop, the boy might have
been more impressed. Jenna doubted he knew what a
defense attorney was.

"This is my son, Ryan," she explained, proud of the one good thing her years with Dennis had given her.

Adam focused on the boy, an unreadable expression on his face. "I went to school with your parents," he said. "Used to play ball with your dad."

That he had played far more intimate games with Jenna went unsaid, but the look he gave her indicated he hadn't forgotten.

Neither had Jenna. The memory of his kiss, warm and insistent, skittered through her mind, creating the same old flutter in her stomach. How could so much time pass without changing anything?

Then again, those same years had changed everything.

Suddenly Jenna wanted to get away—and stay away—from Adam Durham. The history books were closed. She wasn't ready to think about the old times, the *good* times.

Mr. Durham lifted one gnarled hand to smooth back the gray hair above his ears, the only place he had any, just as Mrs. Durham waved them all toward the kitchen.

"I've got a fresh pumpkin pie—"

Adam grinned. "I know. I found it."

Jenna remembered the sounds she'd heard coming from the kitchen and blushed. While Adam had been raiding his grandmother's refrigerator, she'd thought he was searching the freezer for a juice can full of cash. "I thought you were eating a Twinkie."

"I went easy on the pie, in case Gram had big plans for it. The Twinkie was just to finish me off." He stretched, accentuating his size. "I'm a growing boy, after all."

Hardly a boy, Jenna thought. "Well I wouldn't want

to keep you from your second piece of pie. You three go ahead.'' She began pushing Ryan up the stairs in front of her. ''I'd better get this boy back to bed.''

Yes, the Durhams had always made her feel like part of the family, but Jenna knew she wasn't part of this. As soon as Adam appeared, she'd become the intruder—understandable, considering their history and what had just occurred, but awkward all the same.

''Jenna, wouldn't you like a slice of pie? You're getting far too thin,'' Mrs. Durham said.

''She looks good to me,'' Adam muttered.

Jenna felt Adam's dark eyes on her like the heat of a campfire, and again she tightened the belt of her robe before turning back to face them. ''Go ahead and enjoy yourselves. There's school in the morning, and Ryan agreed to tidy up the woodpile afterward. I've got to be up early to interview waitresses if we want to replace Gayle before the holidays.''

Adam smiled, his teeth glinting against his darkly shadowed jaw. ''Maybe I'll help Ryan. When I was a kid, I used to collect the spiders I found out in that old woodpile.''

Ryan brightened. ''Great! I found a tarantula once when we visited the Grand Canyon.''

''We'll see if we can find another one tomorrow, though we'll probably have better luck coming up with a black widow.''

''Black widows are cool.'' Ryan resisted his mother's hand long enough to add, ''Hey, save me a piece of pie, okay?''

''You got it, kid.'' Adam winked at Ryan, and Jenna shooed her son on his way.

''I'm sorry about your, um, neck,'' she said to Adam, then followed Ryan up the stairs.

"OKAY. WHAT'S JENNA doing here?" Adam took the milk from the stainless-steel restaurant-style refrigerator and set it on the large oak table. Taking a seat, he crossed his legs at the ankle and angled them out in front of him, trying to appear patient as he waited for the explanation. He'd never dreamed he'd see Jenna again. Not here. Not after all these years. And certainly not minus his old friend.

What was more, he'd never expected the sight to land him a blow in the gut with twice the impact of those she'd landed elsewhere on his body tonight.

Grandma Durham busied herself uncovering the pie she'd reclaimed from the fridge. "She's working here, dear. She's our new manager. Didn't you know? I could swear I mentioned it on the phone a time or two."

She stood on tiptoe to reach the cupboard where the plates were stored, and Adam swiftly stood and retrieved them for her.

"You said nothing of the sort—and you know it." He leaned down to see her face, which was worn and lined and pleasant to look at, like a treasured old book. "Why? What's going on?"

With a smile and a shrug, she sent a glance her husband's way. Pop Durham sat across from Adam's seat, rattling the pages of yesterday's paper as though absorbed in what he read there. But Adam wasn't fooled. Pop listened to every word they said, all the while pretending his grandson's visit wasn't that important to him, just the way he did whenever Adam came home.

"In August, I think it was, she moved back to town to sell her stained glass—"

"Her what?"

"She makes the most beautiful windows and lampshades, dear, in stained glass. You really should see them.''

"That's how she was planning to earn a living?" Adam couldn't keep the skepticism from his voice, and Gram reacted with a dose of defensiveness.

"She could, you know. She's good enough. She's just getting her business set up. So it was perfect that she could come and work here. We needed the help and she needed the extra income.''

His grandmother gestured him back to his seat, and Adam stretched out again. "What, exactly, does she do for you?"

"Oh, whatever we need, actually. She fills in if the maid doesn't show up, or the waitress, or she helps Mr. Robertson in the kitchen if the restaurant gets busy. She does some bookkeeping for a few hours the first part of the week, then basically manages the restaurant and inn from Thursday to Sunday.'' Gram frowned. "I told you we were going to hire someone, that Pop and I are getting too old to handle this place alone.''

With a twinge of guilt, Adam loosened his collar by unfastening another button. Her meaning was clear. His grandparents wanted him to come home and work, and eventually take over the place when they passed on. They had never understood his desire to make something more of himself, and he couldn't seem to explain it to them, though he'd certainly tried. As the illegitimate son of a drug addict who'd abandoned him when he was only five and then killed herself, he knew what a psychologist would say. He'd dated one once who'd sent him her analysis of him after he'd broken it off. She'd said he was an overachiever, acting out of a desire to prove himself valuable to society. Because he'd been rejected at such a young age he had no faith in his intrinsic worth. He feared losing control, which was why he never did, and why he worked himself nearly to death to fill his life with things, instead of people.

For all the confidence with which that letter had been written, Adam wasn't sure he agreed. He was a simple man and not prone to blame his faults on anyone, least of all his parents. His mother, when she was alive, had enough troubles of her own, and no one knew who his father was. Besides, he wasn't about to lay that psychological mumbo jumbo on his poor grandparents. They'd feel as though they'd failed him in some way, when they'd always been the best part of his life— along with those three years with Jenna.

"You told me you were going to hire *someone,* but you didn't say *who,*" he said.

"Does it matter?" Pop Durham glanced at him over his paper as the scent of cinnamon and cloves wafted through the kitchen. The smell brought back the autumns of Adam's youth: the crisp sea winds, the crackle of a warm fire, melting butter on homemade bread and, most of all, the safe haven the Victoriana had provided him under the loving care of his grandparents.

He owed them so much, yet he couldn't give them the one thing they wanted. He couldn't move back home.

Using his fork to draw designs in the whipped cream his grandmother had ladled over his warm pie, Adam lifted his gaze to meet Pop's. "I think it matters. You both know Jenna and I were once close."

"That was fifteen years ago," Gram asserted, pouring him a tall glass of milk. "I wasn't sure you'd even remember Jenna."

Adam took a bite of his pie, savoring the spices and

the smooth texture of the filling. How could he ever forget Jenna? She was his first love and, in some respects, his last. "So what happened between her and Dennis?"

"She told you. They got divorced," Pop said. "It's over."

"When?" Adam wasn't about to let his grandfather put him off. He'd suffered through too many years of imagining Dennis with Jenna, in every way *he* had once been with her, to settle for just "It's over."

"'Bout six months ago."

"That boy's got problems." Gram shook her head. Her hair, now dyed a harsh black, was flat on one side, where she'd been sleeping on it. "But it's none of our affair. You'd better let Jenna tell you about Dennis."

Adam downed his pie, wondering how Jenna had managed to claim so much of his grandparents' esteem and loyalty in the short time she'd lived with them. "Does he come around?"

"Not yet, and he'd better not show up while I'm here," his grandpa said, finally folding the paper and setting it aside to accept his own pie.

Adam opened his mouth to ask another question, but the ringing of the telephone cut him off.

He glanced at Gram in surprise. Who would be calling the Victoriana at nearly one o'clock in the morning?

His grandmother clucked her tongue, but neither she nor Pop made any move toward the phone, so he reached over and picked up the receiver himself. Before he could say hello, he heard Jenna's voice. She sounded...wary.

"Hello?"

"Jen?"

"Dennis? Why do you keep calling me? I've asked you not to bother us here."

"You think I'm going to let you get away that easy, Jen? You're my wife, and that's my boy you got there." Dennis's words were slurred and difficult to understand, and Adam realized immediately that he'd been drinking. Reluctant to intrude on Jenna's privacy, Adam started to hang up when her shaky response made him pause.

"Dennis, the divorce has been final for months. I've got a restraining order against you. If you don't leave me alone, I'll call the police. Besides, I won't have you bothering the Durhams. They're old and they need their rest."

Dennis gave a throaty laugh. "It's not the Durhams I plan to bother. You go ahead and call the police, Jen. That karate shit won't help you this time. They'll need to bring a body bag by the time I'm through with you."

Then the phone clicked and the line went dead.

CHAPTER TWO

JENNA SAT ON THE EDGE of her bed, trying to stop the tremors that racked her body. Dennis had rattled her, which was exactly what he'd intended. She shouldn't have let him, but there was a craziness about her ex-husband that frightened her, for Ryan more than herself.

Dennis had been getting worse since she and Ryan had left him. Would he, one day, follow through with his threats?

"Mom? Was that Dad?" Ryan's voice came from the other room, where his light had just snapped off.

Drawing in a deep breath, Jenna wondered what she should say. She didn't want to blacken Dennis's name. Ryan was only eight. He needed a man in his life, a healthy role model. But the boy's father was far from healthy right now, and Ryan had, no doubt, already heard her responses to the caller.

"Yes," she told him.

"Was he drunk again?"

Jenna squeezed her eyes shut, hating the truth and the pain it caused her son. "I think so, honey."

Ryan didn't answer. The springs of his bed squeaked and, in a moment, he shuffled into her room. "I know he scares you." He stared at her, his large brown eyes as earnest as his words. "I wish I was big enough to protect you."

Smiling, Jenna beckoned him to her. "Ryan, it's not your job to protect me, especially from your own father." She blinked back tears brought on by her son's sweet devotion—and aggravated by her own raw nerves. "Dennis is...just confused right now. When he gets a handle on his drinking, he'll be the fun dad we once knew."

"Will we go back home, then?"

Jenna searched her son's face for any sign of hope and found none. "I don't think so. Why?"

"Because I don't remember him being any fun."

Standing, Jenna rested her hands on her son's thin shoulders. At four foot five he was only a foot shorter than she was.

"That's a real shame, Ryan, because your father was...*is*...a wonderful person. He's just got a big problem." She didn't add that their troubles had started long before his drinking. That piece of information wasn't relevant, anyway, because Jenna would have stayed with Dennis, for Ryan's sake, had he not become abusive.

Ryan nodded. "I'd better get back to bed."

"Okay." Jenna gave him a squeeze. "We're doing just fine on our own, don't you think?"

He smiled. "Yeah. I like it here."

"So do I."

"Do you think that Adam guy will really help me catch a black widow tomorrow?"

Adam. Another sensitive subject. Refusing to dwell on the man she'd just kicked—hard—Jenna looked at the clock next to her bed. Nearly one-thirty. What a night.

"I think so," she said. "Now hop into bed."

Ryan gave her a quick kiss on her cheek and headed

to his room, leaving Jenna to climb back into her own bed and stare at the ceiling. She listened to the ocean, hoping it would calm her, soothe her mind into sleep, but she was still awake when the Durhams went to bed. As they passed her door, she heard Mrs. Durham ask her husband if he'd taken the medication for his high blood pressure.

Then Adam's sure step sounded in the hall. If she wasn't imagining things, he paused by her room, and she half hoped he'd knock so they could talk the rest of the night away. Over the years she'd wondered countless times about his life. Was his career as fulfilling as he'd thought it would be? Did he still like motorcycles? Was he in love?

She knew he'd never married. Occasionally Mr. Durham grumbled something about how quickly Adam went from one woman to the next, but neither of them had said much more than that. They were disappointed that he hadn't settled down and started a family. And they hadn't forgiven him yet for moving away.

Jenna yanked the comforter over her head, well aware that the desire to spend time catching up with Adam was a crazy notion.

She hadn't forgiven him, either.

ADAM LAY AWAKE long after the rest of the house grew quiet, his head swimming. The evening had been an eventful one. Not only had he discovered his high-school sweetheart living with his grandparents, he'd heard the voice of his old friend, Dennis, for the first time in fifteen years.

Only he hadn't liked what Dennis had to say. *They'll need a body bag by the time I'm through with you.*

Adam's hand flexed with the urge to connect with

Dennis's face, even though Dennis and Jenna's problems had nothing to do with him. He was just visiting for the weekend. Monday would see him whizzing back to San Francisco in his new Mercedes coupe, with the top down if the weather was warm enough—his hometown and the friends he'd left there easily forgotten.

No, purposely ignored, maybe, but not forgotten. He remembered the hurt in Jenna's eyes the day he'd broken up with her and the regret that had weighed on his heart at odd moments since. She might have married Dennis, but she'd haunted Adam's life like some elusive ever-present ghost. She was the standard by which he measured all other women.

Blocking out the sadness of their final month together, he shifted his thoughts to better times and settled eagerly on the day they'd first made love. They'd already been dating for two years and knew each other better than Adam had ever known another human being. That day, they'd gone swimming in the ocean, as they often did. But this time Jenna hadn't stopped him from removing her swimsuit when they left the water and stretched out on the beach.

Giving in to the smile that tempted his lips, Adam closed his eyes and relived the moment of seeing Jenna naked for the first time. She'd been beautiful, with the wind whipping her dark hair about her face, her blue eyes gazing up at him with complete trust, nipples drawn tight and hard with desire.

When he touched her, his hand shook as it did now, just remembering the feel of her silken limbs entwined with his own. He felt again the grit of the sand on his palms, the warmth of the sun on his back, the sound of the sea in his ears—and Jenna beneath him, tight and warm and willing.

After the initial pain she'd experienced, she had matched his eagerness and his passion with an honesty and an intensity that would never fade from his mind. Since then, he had searched for that same responsiveness, those same feelings, but he'd never again achieved what he'd had with Jenna. Maybe he never would, as punishment for pledging her all his tomorrows and then breaking that promise.

As much as he'd wanted her, loved her, some inner devil had urged him to leave Mendocino before he became an innkeeper like his grandparents. He wanted to see the world, challenge himself, and eventually become part of the stiffly competitive legal world in San Francisco.

A year after he left Jenna, he'd winced at the news that she'd married Dennis, but he'd forged ahead. A law degree, a prestigious practice, becoming one of four partners in a firm of sixteen. Two hundred thousand a year, then three hundred, and finally half a million turned his beat-up Chevy truck into a Buick, a Lexus and now his first Mercedes. He drove one of the most expensive cars on the market. He had a big home on the bay, powerful friends, important clients. He'd made it to the big time, hadn't he? He should be glad of the path he'd chosen.

And he was. He'd had no real doubts until he'd seen Jenna tonight. The sight of her wide sky-blue eyes had pulled him up short. The curves of her body beneath the robe, the body he'd once known so well, had made him wonder what he'd missed—and if it wasn't better than what he'd had, after all.

At the sound of someone in the bathroom, Adam

checked his alarm clock in surprise. He'd feared it was morning and he hadn't slept at all, but according to the clock it was only two-thirty. *Only.* He'd be exhausted in the morning.

He went back to the pleasant memories of his days with Jenna, remembering her carefree laugh that time he'd given her a ride on his buddy's motorcycle. Afterward, she'd insisted on driving, gave it too much gas and popped a wheelie. They'd gone down the street on one wheel, then two, again and again, until she finally crashed and bloodied his knees, as well as hers, and they'd limped home, laughing and pushing the bike before them.

Chuckling, he wondered if she still remembered ruining her new pair of jeans that way. Fortunately holes at the knee became fashionable after that, so he still got to see her in those great-fitting jeans.

And then there was the day she'd baked him a strawberry dessert, which she spilled in her aunt's car when she tried to bring it over to him. They'd spent the better part of the night trying to clean it up....

Whoever was using the bathroom was sure taking a long time. He could hear his grandfather's snores throughout the private part of the inn and knew that Pop, at least, was sleeping soundly. It could be Gram or Ryan in there, but after overhearing Dennis's call, Adam suspected it was Jenna.

Slipping out of bed, he put on the pajama bottoms he usually left in his leather bag and headed out into the hall. A light glimmered beneath the bathroom door, but the occupant seemed to be sick, not merely upset.

He knocked softly.

"I'll be out in a moment." Jenna's voice sounded oddly breathless.

"Are you all right?" he asked. "Is there something I can get you?"

A few seconds passed before she answered. "No, thank you. I'll be fine in the morning."

In the morning? What about now? He paused, wondering what to do. Considering how she must feel about him, he figured she could be seriously ill and still not let him help her. "Do you want me to get Gram?"

Another long pause. "No. Please don't bother anyone. I'm sorry if I woke you."

Adam smiled to himself. She *had* kept him awake, but not in the way she thought. "I couldn't sleep, anyway. Would you please unlock the door so I can see you're as fine as you say you are?"

"No." This time her response came quickly and the toilet flushed right afterward. To cover the sound of her retching?

"Jenna? Are you throwing up?"

No answer. He rattled the knob. "Jenna, open this door, or I'm going to wake the whole damn house."

"Just a minute."

He heard the tap water turn on and off. After another lengthy silence, she opened the door and flipped the light off at the same time.

"I'm fine, see?"

Blinded by the instant flood of light and then the sudden darkness, Adam couldn't see anything. He thought he glimpsed a tired and unusually pale face, but her voice sounded better.

"What was wrong in there? Have you started throwing up when you get upset?"

Forced cheer edged her words. "No. Why would I be upset?"

Because your ex-husband just threatened to kill you. Adam nearly blurted it out before he caught himself. He had no right to barge into her personal affairs. No right to hear as much as he had. But damned if he didn't want to help Jenna in some way, if only to make up for hurting her so long ago.

He changed tactics. "I was about to go down and make myself some tea, thought it might help me sleep. Would you like a cup?"

"No. I've got a big day tomorrow. I'd better go back to bed."

That's what you said two hours ago, but it doesn't look like you've gotten much sleep.

"Sure." He moved aside, catching a trace of her perfume as she slipped past. He didn't recognize it as one of the more expensive brands he'd smelled on some of the women he'd dated, but it was perfect for her: spicy, warm, rather exotic.

"Jenna?"

She turned back when she reached her door.

"I was sorry to hear about you and Dennis."

She stepped into her room and he wondered if she was going to answer him.

"Divorce is never pretty," she said at last. Then, with a decisive click, she closed the door.

JENNA BROKE OUT in a cold sweat as Adam's steps receded. She couldn't even move. She stood in the middle of the floor, hugging her body, rocking back and forth.

She'd felt nauseated, she'd thrown up, she'd felt better—just the same as last night. But that cycle was exactly what worried her. The flu struck for at least a day. With food poisoning, you threw up until your system cleansed itself. Her nausea hit about the same time each night and always occurred on an empty stomach.

Just like it had when she was pregnant with Ryan.

Dropping her head into her hands, Jenna began to knead her temples. *Oh, God, please, I can't be pregnant.*

After Ryan, she and Dennis had tried and tried to have another baby. When she hadn't conceived after four years, they visited a doctor, who told them Dennis's sperm count was too low. They were given the name of a fertility specialist, whom they'd never called, partly because Dennis seemed to lose interest—he had his boy and was satisfied—and partly because he'd started drinking.

Jenna took a deep breath and managed to stumble back to her bed. Climbing under the covers, she shivered and wondered if she'd ever be warm again. Just when Dennis and the divorce were almost behind her, she could be pregnant.

A new baby. A huge responsibility. Dennis's child.

A sob escaped her as she tried again to count the days since her last period, but she couldn't remember exactly. Dennis had forced himself on her almost three months after the divorce was final. She'd submitted because she hadn't wanted to wake Ryan with another of their fights, and after sharing her bed with Dennis for thirteen and a half years, she hadn't thought one more time would make a difference.

But if she was pregnant, it made a huge difference.

She thought of Adam asking her if she threw up when she was upset, and tried to calm down. He'd unwittingly offered her an alternative explanation. Stress did strange things to the body, causing headaches, stomach ailments, insomnia, all kinds of things.

Besides, her symptoms could result from fear. What she needed was to buy a pregnancy test at the grocery store and find out for sure. If it turned out negative, she could relax.

If it turned out positive...

Jenna closed her eyes. *Sleep,* she ordered herself. Ryan was depending on her and so were the Durhams.

But who could *she* depend on?

Adam. His name leaped into her mind, and for one sweet instant she let herself pretend. Then reality doused her like an icy ocean wave.

"I can only depend on myself," she whispered to the moonlit ceiling, and settled herself sternly between the cold smooth sheets.

CHAPTER THREE

JENNA STOOD in the kitchen, staring out the large bay window that overlooked the side yard. If she leaned close enough to the wall, she could see Adam and Ryan stacking wood along the back fence. She'd been watching them for several minutes already, as she drank her morning coffee. After the disruption during the night, she hadn't made Ryan get up for school. He got good grades and she figured one day off wouldn't matter much.

"They making any progress?" Mrs. Durham came into the room and opened the refrigerator to survey its contents. She held a pad, on which she wrote various groceries they needed to purchase, but she paused to glance at Jenna.

"I think they've spent more time squirting each other with their water bottles. Can you hear Ryan squealing?" Jenna smiled; Ryan and Adam had been running around the yard, wielding their water bottles like pistols. Periodically they took aim and fired, only to have the other duck behind the house or shed. By the time their bottles were empty, they were both laughing so hard they could barely stand.

She felt relief—and pleasure—at seeing Ryan laugh again. He needed to do more of it. He was a sober responsible boy, a wonderful child, but Jenna sometimes worried that her problems with Dennis had made their son older than his years. To see his carefree spirit revived lifted her own somber mood, and she knew she had Adam to thank. Ryan wouldn't be having such a grand time if he was out in the yard alone.

"Adam never could set his mind to a task and simply do it. He made everything into a game, remember?" his grandmother said.

Jenna looked away from the scene beyond the window to focus on Mrs. Durham. "I remember. But he's not the same person now. I mean, he's just the opposite, isn't he? So intense..."

Mrs. Durham finished her inventory and shut the fridge. "He's certainly driven. I don't know what happened to him. When he was young we couldn't keep him in school. The principal was always calling to say he'd cut class again. Once he graduated and started college, that all changed."

Looking back at Adam, Jenna took a sip of her coffee. "I guess he decided it was time to grow up." *Grow up and leave me...*

"I'm not so sure he wasn't better off before," Mrs. Durham muttered. "Anyway, I'm going to the store now. Anything I can pick up for you, dear?"

Jenna's thoughts instantly reverted to the gnawing worry that had claimed her attention for most of the morning. She needed a pregnancy-test kit, but she wasn't going to ask Mrs. Durham to get her one. She'd have to go to the store at some point herself.

"We could use some more turkey for Ryan's lunches, if you wouldn't mind." Crossing to the counter where she'd set her purse, Jenna pulled a ten-dollar bill out of her wallet, but Mrs. Durham refused to take it.

"Lunch meat is part of your room and board, you know that."

"But you pay me a good salary besides. I can't help worrying that I'm not pulling my weight around here—enough weight for me *and* Ryan, that is. You and Mr. Durham always encourage me to finish my glasswork, even at the expense of my duties."

"Nonsense. You handle all the PR, work with our vendors, take care of the bookings. We couldn't get by without you. All I do is a little bit of shopping and the cooking on Mr. Robertson's days off. But your stained glass is going to make you rich someday, mark my words. Louis Comfort Tiffany could do no better." Mrs. Durham nodded toward the window, where Jenna could see Adam and Ryan bent over some new object of interest. "You don't have to worry about doing anything extra for Ryan's keep, anyway. It's been too long since we had a boy in the house."

Their boy. Adam.

"How do I look?" Mrs. Durham grabbed her own industrial-size bag. "Is the back of my hair okay?"

"You just need it ratted a bit right here." Jenna used the comb Mrs. Durham fished out of her purse to lift the flat spot at the back of her head, just as she did every morning of the week except Thursdays, the day she went to the hairdresser. "That's better," Jenna said, handing back the comb.

"Thank you, dear." Mrs. Durham retrieved a tube of bright red lipstick from her bag and liberally applied it. Then she ran a finger along each painted eyebrow, patted her nose with powder and snapped her compact shut before slipping it back into her purse. "I should be back in an hour or so."

Jenna followed her to the door in the wake of the

gardenia fragrance that trailed behind her. "Do you want me to go with you?"

"No. I spoke to a young girl earlier on the telephone who wants to interview for the waitress position. I told her she could come any time this morning, so you'd better stay, just in case. Now that Gayle's moved away, she won't be able to fill in again, and I don't like it all falling on you. See what you think of this girl, if she shows up."

"Okay."

Jenna watched Mrs. Durham back her beige Cadillac down the driveway, then walked to the sink with her cup. She'd interviewed three people for the position and thought she'd found a good candidate, but it didn't hurt to talk to a few more. Only the Durhams, Pamela, the maid, and Mr. Robertson, the cook, worked with her at the Victoriana. Jenna wanted to be certain that the person she hired fit in.

"Can we get a drink?"

Adam's voice startled her. She turned to see his arms and face glistening with sweat despite the cooler weather. His T-shirt and faded blue jeans clung damply to his body.

Jenna could smell the slight tang of his sweat as he brushed past her to claim a glass from the cupboard. She tried to forget the times she'd tasted the salt on his skin after they'd been swimming in the ocean or running or...

Ryan followed Adam in, carrying a jar with a huge spider inside. "Look, Mom! Isn't this cool?"

Stifling her initial revulsion, Jenna forced a smile. "It's great. What kind of spider is it?"

"Adam's not sure. It looks like a tarantula, but it's not. See the babies crawling on its back?"

This time Jenna couldn't quell a shiver as Ryan shoved the jar right up to her face. Inside, she could see hundreds of tiny spiders squirming on their mother's back. "Don't you think you should let it go?" she asked.

"I'm not going to hurt it. I just want to keep it as a pet."

"I think it would rather be free."

Ryan rolled his eyes at Adam. "My mom's trying to turn me into a sissy."

"Going soft in her old age, is she? She didn't feel too soft last night. She nearly ruined some equipment I consider very valuable." Adam rubbed his neck where she'd chopped him and grinned.

Glad he hadn't put a hand to his other injury, as well, Jenna resisted the urge to smile back at him. They'd been angry with each other for fifteen years. She might be soft on children, animals, even insects, but he was a full-grown man, and she wasn't about to go soft on *him*. Soft got you hurt, especially if it involved his "equipment."

"Could be poisonous," she replied, keeping her eyes on the jar with the spider, where, fortunately, Ryan's attention remained.

"It can't bite me when it's in a jar, Mom. You're just afraid it'll die or something, and you don't like to see anything get hurt."

"Just rattle a few pans in the middle of the night and send it through the kitchen window. She'll smash it quickly enough," Adam said, and downed his glass of water.

Jenna narrowed her eyes. "You look pretty healthy to me."

He cocked one dark eyebrow at her. "You haven't seen my bruise."

"And I'll thank you not to show it to me." Jenna's quick response drew Ryan's interest.

"What bruise?" he asked.

Adam gave Jenna a slow smile, letting her stew. "It's right here—on my neck."

He tugged his T-shirt down until Jenna saw more chest than she wanted to. She glanced away, but Ryan said, "I don't see anything."

"Just give it a few days," Adam told him.

"Or give me one more clear shot," Jenna muttered under her breath.

Adam hooted with laughter, but she ignored him. To Ryan, she said, "You can keep the spider for a day or two, then turn it loose in the woodpile."

The doorbell sounded, and Jenna felt a profound sense of relief. She hated being in the same room with Adam. He kept her off balance, scowling at her one minute and teasing her the next.

At the same time she had to admit that his presence at the Victoriana excited her like nothing had in a long time.

"That must be my applicant." She dropped a kiss on her son's sweaty brow. "Are you all finished with the wood?"

"Yeah, but Pop wants Adam to weed the garden. There's only pumpkins and squash left, but I said I'd help, too."

Jenna blinked in surprise. *Pop?* What had happened to "Mr. Durham"? "I'm glad you're making yourself useful," she said. "I'd better get the door."

The girl on the front step was young, maybe eighteen. She seemed eager enough to work, but tattoos on her arms and neck and extensive body piercing didn't create the best impression. The Durhams were conservative, and their business was intended to re-create the aura of Victorian days. This girl's appearance was hardly consistent with that.

Still, Jenna asked her a few questions, just to be sure she wasn't making a mistake. As they stood in the hall talking, Adam and Ryan came past them to head outside.

The girl's eyes rounded and her gaze stayed on Adam until the door shut behind him. Then she stared blankly at Jenna. "What? What did you ask?"

Jenna repeated the standard question about prior experience, but while she waited for an answer, her eyes strayed to her own reflection in the cheval mirror across the room. If they hadn't known each other before, would Adam find her as attractive as this young woman had just found him? Could she catch his eye? Make it follow her across a room?

For the past five years she'd felt invisible to Dennis, and throughout her marriage she hadn't bothered to notice any other men who might have given her some indication of her attractiveness. She'd been too busy trying to make her world right. Adam had said she looked good, but she'd been in her robe, with her hair a mess. He couldn't have meant it.

"Mrs. Livingston?"

It was Jenna's turn to be jerked back to the conversation. "Yes?"

"I was wondering how many days a week you need someone."

"The restaurant is only open for dinner Thursday through Saturday, and Sunday for brunch. Boyd Robertson is our cook. He comes from a military background and runs a pretty tight ship, so we've always called him by his last name. He's lived in Mendocino as long as I can remember, and his culinary talents pull in a lot of locals in addition to our guests. If we get busy, Mrs. Durham, one of the owners, helps cook, and I help waitress."

"So how many hours would that be?"

"About twenty a week."

The girl glanced through the front window, and Jenna wondered if she was hoping to catch a glimpse of Adam, who had disappeared around the side. "I'm afraid that wouldn't be enough. I really need something full-time."

"You might try some of the restaurants in Fort Bragg if you can't find a position around here," Jenna told her.

"Thanks." With a fleeting smile, the girl left, and Jenna decided to hire the applicant who was pushing fifty years old. The last thing she needed was a waitress who followed Adam around with stars in her eyes— not that another woman's admiration of him bothered her, she told herself.

ADAM WHISTLED as he helped his grandfather weed, wondering why he felt so carefree this morning. An avalanche of letters and legal documents awaited him at the office, and though he hadn't checked his voice mail, he knew it was loaded with messages. He'd told his grandparents he had some extra time this week, but in his world there was no such thing. Still, here he was, pulling out weeds with Pop as if at least thirty people didn't need to get in touch with him.

It must be the change of pace, he decided. His work was grueling, all-encompassing, a hundred-hour-a-week investment. Mendocino represented home and family and was, in its comfortable way, refreshing.

Adam stood up and drew a deep breath of the salty air gusting in from the sea. He saw Jenna through the window, talking to the heavyset Mr. Robertson, the Durhams' cook. She wasn't sixteen anymore, but she looked better at thirty-two. Her body hoarded no un-wanted pounds. Karate, or some other type of exercise, had kept her muscles toned, and her eyes, which had always been her loveliest feature, hadn't changed.

Except, perhaps, for the expression in them. Now a wiser Jenna gazed back at him, instead of the romantic girl who used to love him. He wondered what her life with Dennis had been like and when their marriage had turned bad.

She caught him watching her and drew the shade, leaving him with no distraction but his thoughts.

"How's the herb garden, Pop? Do you need me to weed that, too?" Adam asked, bending back to his work.

His grandfather leaned on his rake. From beneath a straw hat, great drops of sweat ran down his weathered face, and he wiped them away with his forearm. "Cook takes care of that. He won't let me near the place. Says I don't know a weed from a dirt clod—" he chuckled "—and I'm happy to let him think so."

Ryan approached, squinting up at them from beneath an Oakland A's hat, the gold in his eyelashes sparkling in the sunshine. He'd given up on the weeds shortly after they'd started in favor of playing with his new eight-legged pet, but he never strayed far from Adam's side. The kid seemed starved for male attention. "Hey, what do you think this spider eats?" he asked.

"I bet it eats flies, just like most spiders," Adam told him.

Ryan frowned. "Where can I find a fly?"

"Well, we'd have better luck if it was barbecue season, but—"

"Ryan?" Jenna stood on the porch, shading her eyes with one hand. She'd changed from the professional-looking wool slacks she'd worn all morning into a baggy pair of jeans, an oversize sweater and leather sandals.

"I have to pick up something at the store. I'll be back in a few minutes, okay?" she called.

Ryan nodded, still studying his spider, but Adam stopped Jenna before she could leave. "Maybe we'll go with you," he said. "Ryan needs something to feed his new pet."

A frown flickered across her face. "From the size of that spider, a large rodent would do."

"Fresh out of those, I'm afraid."

Jenna's smile turned devilish. "Then how about a defense attorney from San Francisco?"

As Pop cackled from his corner of the garden, Adam gave Jenna his darkest scowl. "Enough lawyer jokes already. You're revealing your eagerness to be rid of me. It's not polite."

Jenna shrugged. "This is your home, not mine."

"For the moment it looks like we both live here. So how about it? Will you give us a ride to the store?"

The expression on Jenna's face said she didn't want them to go, but her reluctance only made Adam push harder. "Well?"

"Actually I was going to walk. My van's in the shop," she said, and winced visibly when Ryan added,

"It's a junker. My dad bashed up one whole side of it."

Adam leaned his rake against the nearest tree, acting as though this piece of information didn't surprise him—but it did. After Dennis's call, his grandparents had admitted that his old friend had become an abusive alcoholic, but Adam couldn't picture the somber boy he'd once known beating up on Jenna. Dennis had been so lovesick he'd dogged Jenna's footsteps all through high school. His infatuation with her had destroyed his and Adam's relationship—and they'd been friends since Little League. It was difficult to believe someone as devoted as Dennis had been could turn on the object of his affection. Had his drinking really gotten that out of hand? And if so, how badly had Jenna and Ryan suffered?

Adam peeled off his gloves. "We can take my car," he told her. Nodding at Ryan, he added, "As long as arachno-lover here doesn't mind sitting on your lap. There's no back seat."

Ryan's eyes lit up. "We get to ride in *your* car? Cool!"

Jenna fidgeted with the strap of her purse as though she was about to protest again, but Adam didn't give her a chance. "The spider stays behind," he said, taking the jar from Ryan and setting it under the tree next to his rake. With a hand on the boy's neck, he guided him to the parking lot on the other side of the house.

Jenna met them at the car. Her eyes widened slightly as she took in the sleek contours of the black Mercedes coupe, but she made no comment.

"Isn't this great, Mom? Have you ever seen a car like this?" Ryan asked.

"Only on *Miami Vice*," she muttered, sliding onto the black leather seat when Adam opened her door.

"Miami what?" he asked.

She chuckled. "Never mind. It was before your time."

Adam climbed in and started the car. "Don't pretend you'd be more impressed if I drove a station wagon," he said.

Jenna threw him a playful look, reminding him of the girl he used to know. "If you really want to impress me, you'll let me drive."

He dropped his jaw in mock surprise. "This from the person who wrecked my friend's motorcycle in high school?"

"Mom wrecked someone's motorcycle?" Ryan echoed.

Jenna's delicate brows drew together, creasing her forehead. "You can't still hold that against me. It happened more than sixteen years ago."

Adam pinned Jenna with a level stare. "I'll let bygones be bygones if you will," he said softly.

Jenna turned toward the window, but Adam could see the stubborn tilt of her chin reflected in the glass. "I didn't want to drive, anyway," she said.

A FEW LOCALS milled about the grocery store eight miles up the coast. Mrs. Trumbill, the chiropractor's receptionist, looked over the painkillers and allergy-relief medicines. Mr. Francis, the town pharmacist, thumbed through the latest issue of *People*. Jenna acknowledged them both on her way to the produce aisle, wondering what she was going to buy, now that she couldn't purchase her pregnancy test.

"What is it you need to get?" Adam asked, hefting

two good-sized oranges in his hands. Jenna watched his fingers curl around the fruit and remembered his touch on her body. He'd driven her crazy with those hands, those lips...

Making an effort, Jenna pulled her gaze and her thoughts onto safer ground and picked out six golden delicious apples. "Just some fresh fruit for Ryan's lunches." Although Jenna had carefully timed her departure from the Victoriana so that Mrs. Durham would be finished with her shopping and on her way home, she couldn't calculate the other woman's movements with any accuracy. She was afraid they'd run into Adam's grandmother and then Mrs. Durham would say something about the teeming drawers of fresh produce they already had at home.

"It's not like Gram to run out of that sort of thing," Adam said.

Jenna glanced at him, but his face held no suspicion. He bagged the oranges and dropped them in the basket as Ryan tugged him toward the ice-cream aisle.

"Hey, do you think we can talk Mom into buying us some ice cream?"

Jenna knew Adam hadn't dampened Ryan's enthusiasm for treats when they came back with ice cream, fudge and caramel toppings, M&Ms, a container of popcorn and whipped cream.

"We're going to make sundaes and watch movies tonight," Adam explained when Jenna raised a questioning brow.

"Great." She didn't ask who made up the "we." At the moment she didn't care. She was too busy looking for things to put in her cart that would constitute more than a waste of money. She managed to remember the new toothbrush she'd been wanting to purchase for at least a month, but when they got in line at the checkout, she still didn't have what she really needed. And that was when she decided to get it.

"Adam? Would you mind taking Ryan to pick out a package of lunch meat? I forgot to get some," she said.

A refrigerated section at one end of the store contained lunch meat. Shelves at the opposite end displayed feminine hygiene products. With any luck she'd have just enough time to grab a pregnancy test and have it rung up and bagged before the two of them returned.

Fortunately Adam agreed to do as she asked. Unfortunately, by the time Jenna retrieved what she wanted and raced back, another customer had engaged the checker in conversation.

"Are you going out of town for Thanksgiving this year, Mrs. Jones?" the checker was asking an older white-haired woman dressed in an expensive velour jogging suit.

Having already paid, Mrs. Jones paused in wheeling her groceries away. "Not this year, Karen. We usually go to a cabin at Lake Tahoe, but I think I'm ready to have the family out here. The grandkids are getting older, so I don't think it'll be too hard on me. Say, did you ever try that stuffing recipe I gave you?"

The checker propped a freckled arm on the back of her booth. "No, but I tried one off the bag of bread crumbs I bought here, and it wasn't too bad. I thought this year I'd add a bit of celery, even though my husband doesn't really like celery. It's my Thanksgiving, too, and my mother always put celery in her stuffing."

Jenna's toe tapped, and her eyes darted from the cash register to the pregnancy test. It seemed to be lying on the conveyor belt, screaming, "Jenna thinks she's pregnant!" She craned her neck to see down the aisle and, just as she feared, spotted Adam and Ryan on their way back.

She cleared her throat. "I'm sorry...um, I don't mean to interrupt, but I'm kind of in a hurry."

The checker smiled with forced tolerance. "Sure. I'll be right with you." She pushed away from the back of the booth. "Well, Mrs. Jones, tell your husband I said hello. And maybe I'll try that stuffing recipe of yours this year."

By the time Mrs. Jones said her goodbyes and the checker turned her attention to Jenna's purchases, it was too late to ask her to ring up the pregnancy test separately. Adam and Ryan were within hearing distance, and the sight of it, right there in front of them both, was almost enough to give Jenna heart palpitations. She didn't want Ryan to get his hopes up about having a sibling unless it was true, and she didn't want Adam to know, period. He'd already made her feel like a fool, appearing out of nowhere in his flashy car and his expensive suit, while Dennis had ruined their credit and lost them their 1996 Oldsmobile, which wasn't much of a car to begin with, as well as their house.

Besides, the whole thing might be a false alarm.

Jenna's eyes flicked over the pregnancy test again. Maybe Adam and Ryan wouldn't notice it, she prayed, but lost all hope of that when the checker tried to run the thing through her scanner and it wouldn't beep. Holding it almost at eye level and frowning, she said, "I wonder why this isn't in our system." She brought the microphone to her lips. "Johnny? Would you get me the price of the First Choice Pregnancy Tests? Aisle nine, I think."

Jenna took a gulp of air and held it as Adam's jaw dropped and his eyes flew to her face. She gave an uncomfortable laugh. "Where did that come from?" she asked. "That's not mine."

The checker blinked at her. "You don't want this?"

"No, it's not mine." Jenna could feel her cheeks burn with embarrassment, but she tried to act as natural as possible. "Maybe it belonged to the person in front of me," she said, because there was no one behind her.

"Mrs. Jones?" The checker scoffed outright. "She must be sixty-five. I don't think so, honey." She shoved the pregnancy test off to one side, where the smiling woman on the box stared at Jenna.

The next few minutes stretched into what felt like an hour. Jenna kept her eyes on her checkbook until it was time to pay, then Adam gently nudged her aside and threw two twenties on the counter. She didn't fight him. She only wanted to get out of the grocery store and away from the First Choice box as soon as possible.

"Thank you, sir, and come again." The checker smiled at Adam, her thick makeup creasing as she handed him the receipt.

Adam gave the lighter bag to Ryan and carried the other out himself. He didn't say anything as they walked back to the car, but Jenna didn't have to look at his face to know he wasn't smiling.

CHAPTER FOUR

THE BRINY SMELL of the sea wafted through the cracks of the old building, permeating the entire room Jenna used as her studio. She sat staring at a half-finished stained-glass window portraying a small lake surrounded by great willowy trees. Natural light, which flooded the square room through a series of skylights, passed through several of the finished pieces hanging from the rafters and made small rainbows of color on the cement floor. Shortly after she'd moved in, the Durhams had hired their contractor to turn one of the old gardening sheds into a small studio for her, and there wasn't another place on earth she felt more at home.

Outside, Adam and Ryan were talking and laughing as they tossed a football, but Jenna felt no inclination to join them. She'd fled to her studio as soon as they returned from the store and hadn't come out since. Though normally she would have spent some of her day with Ryan, working on a school project due next week, he seemed to be occupied well enough without her. That her son already adored Adam, her nemesis, after only one day in his presence annoyed her—even more than Adam catching her trying to purchase a pregnancy test.

Allowing herself a deep heartfelt sigh, she picked up her carbide glass cutter, determined to finish the lake or to sit up all night until she did. She was using antique glass, one of the most delicate and expensive kinds, to make the water, but it varied in thickness by almost three-quarters of an inch. She couldn't get a clean cut, couldn't get the feel of her medium. Normally her hands worked almost independently of her mind, somehow sensing just how much pressure to use to score the glass without breaking it, how to tap gently near the cut and separate the two pieces. But not today.

After ruining yet another section that was supposed to be a lapping wave, Jenna slouched onto her stool. At this rate, she would be buried in broken glass by sunset! She couldn't concentrate. Not with Adam just outside.

Standing again, she skirted the waist-high worktable and walked to the back of the studio where utility cupboards lined the wall. Taking out a large rectangular window she'd finished shortly after returning to Mendocino, she lifted the fabric she'd used to protect it and gazed down at a secluded cove—the stretch of beach where Adam had made love to her the first time.

She kept this piece hidden, as though someone else might guess its history, but really there was no need. With tall black cliffs and a green, tempestuous sea, it could depict almost any part of the Northern California coast. Except for the house she'd put in the background. She'd seen the same house over Adam's shoulder that day sixteen years ago; she'd gone back to look at it since and had created a perfect likeness.

Closing her eyes, Jenna drifted back in time and felt the sand of the cove radiating heat beneath her naked body, the wind stirring her hair. When she thought of how Adam had touched her, his voice from outside the shed made the memory that much more real. She shivered as she relived it, feeling his hands move over her flesh, raising goose bumps along their path, as they curled around her limbs with the strength of the sea.

Moving in unison with the water that lapped at their feet, he'd covered her body with his, gently coaxing her to succumb to him like the pull of the tide. *Let go...let go...*

She'd wrapped her arms around him and relinquished control, and soon Adam began to pound into her with the rhythm of the waves against the rocks. Then her nerves tightened and leaped, like the spray flinging itself freely into the air, and she seemed to burst into a million fragments of brilliant light.

Opening her eyes, Jenna stared numbly down at her own representation of that day. It reminded her of what it felt like to be loved.

To be loved by Adam.

"Incredible."

Jenna jumped and nearly dropped the window, but Adam's sure hands grabbed hold of it.

"Damn, don't you believe in knocking?" she snapped.

Adam's gaze didn't falter from the stained-glass depiction of the cove. "I did knock. You didn't answer."

Jenna's eyes moved guiltily to his face. Maybe she hadn't heard him. She'd touched an emotional memory so deep it had eclipsed all else. Like the actual event.

"Does Ryan need me?" Seeing him looking at the cove made Jenna feel as if he was reading her journal. Exposed, she wanted to distract him, but he didn't answer her question. And he resisted her efforts to pull the window away.

"When did you learn to do stained glass?"

"I started about six years ago when I took a course at a community college. But I'm just an amateur, really. I've sold a few pieces to the tourists who come through here, nothing more.''

Did he know what he was looking at? Did he guess Dennis had never been able to replace him?

"Gram told me you were good. But I never imagined anything like this. You've definitely got more than your share of talent."

The space heater that hummed a few feet away was making the place unbearably hot. Jenna yanked out the plug, wishing Adam would stop looking at the cove. "Thanks. There's more over there if you'd like to see them. This one's actually not my best," she lied, relinquishing her own hold on the piece as if it meant nothing to her.

Retrieving a little broom hanging on a hook inside another cupboard, she began to clean up the glass splinters at her worktable.

He circled the room, carrying the window with him, then paused at the partially finished lake. "They're nice, really nice." He held the cove up again for closer inspection. "But I like this one best." He turned to look at her for the first time since he'd made his presence known.

Did he know?

No! How could he? It was sixteen years since they'd been on that beach. And she'd been the one to stare up at the house in a dreamy half doze as he slept facedown on her breast.

Still, Jenna couldn't meet his eyes. She finished sweeping up the glass chips, then glanced beyond him to the subject of their conversation. "It's a fairly good rendition of the coast, I guess."

He studied the window, a thoughtful frown on his face. "I think I've been there."

"Then you know how beautiful it is."

"I do." He smiled at her. "In fact, I've never experienced anything like it."

Jenna gave a shaky laugh and stepped back to avoid the scent of his cologne. "Sounds like you need to travel more."

"Or purchase this window. How much?"

She shook her head. "It's not for sale. I'm trying to accumulate some inventory for a spring show. Maybe when that's finished—" *or when hell freezes over* "—I'll let you know."

"Sure." Carefully setting the stained-glass cove on her table, he turned away. "Gram wanted me to tell you dinner's ready."

"Great." She kept her smile casual, as though Adam hadn't just reached inside her and cradled her heart in the palm of his hand. "You go on in. I'll be right there."

DURING DINNER Adam received a call from his secretary. Though Pop frowned when he got up from the table to accept the receiver from Gram, he ignored his grandfather's disapproval. He'd promised them he wouldn't make any calls, and he hadn't. But he was a big boy now, and if Cheryl needed him, he wasn't about to turn her down. Though Pop hated the thought of him living and working anywhere other than Mendocino, he had a life in San Francisco and a practice to run.

"Cheryl? What are you doing still at the office? It's past seven on a Friday night."

"Adam, I'm so glad I got hold of you! Why haven't you been checking your voice mail?"

He could hear her popping her gum as she talked,

and pictured her leaning on her desk with both elbows, her glasses and her short blond hair falling forward as she stared at the phone. "What's the emergency? I've only been gone one day."

"That's all it takes with Mr. Whitehead."

Recognizing the name of one of his biggest and most difficult clients, Adam took the cordless phone into the living room where he could talk without interrupting the meal. "So what's new?"

"He's frantic, that's what. The DA has subpoenaed his files, and he's convinced we have to do something to block it right away."

"Monsoto's going to get the records because they're evidence. I've already explained all this. There's no legal way to stop him."

"I don't think Whitehead cares about legal. I tried to tell him that, too, but he started swearing and demanded I put him through to Mike."

"There's nothing Mike can do."

"Except make your life miserable. He still owns more of this practice than anyone else and he wants this guy mollified."

"What does he want me to do? Destroy evidence? Because short of doing that, there's no way to stop Monsoto, at least no honest way."

Cheryl's voice dropped to a whisper. "Honest isn't in Mike's vocabulary, you know that. And I get the impression he's tired of it being in yours. He's been giving all the questionable stuff to Roger, who's more than willing to do whatever it takes. Money is God to that guy."

The loyalty in his secretary's voice felt good, but not good enough to offset Adam's anger. "Roger's going to have to learn his own lessons. Whether Mike makes him a partner or not, I won't risk my reputation for an ambitious developer who's bribed half the city council.''

''Don't you mean *allegedly* bribed?''

''We both know the answer to that.''

''Then maybe you should turn him over to Mike or Roger.''

''I've tried. They want my clean-cut mug to be the one in front of the jury. And I don't have any problem with that, as long as they let me do things my way.''

''Uh-oh…''

''What?'' Already feeling the old tension mounting, Adam stretched his neck. Mike was getting greedy in his old age and was starting to make him uncomfortable. The question was, how far would he go? And how far would he push Adam?

''Mike wants to talk to you.''

The words had scarcely left Cheryl's lips when Adam heard Mike's gruff voice.

''Where the hell are you, Adam? We've been trying to reach you all day.''

''I'm out of town. Cheryl says we've got trouble with Whitehead.''

''Those records will put him behind bars.'' Mike paused to blow his nose. ''We've got to come up with a way to keep the district attorney from getting his hands on them.''

''You mean a legal way, don't you, Mike?''

Mike cursed. ''Adam, you gotta get with the real world, buddy. No one plays fair anymore. You insist on that, you'll lose every time.''

''My record is pretty good so far.''

''Things are changing.''

''What's that supposed to mean?''

Mike grunted. "It means we gotta be flexible. I should fire that secretary of yours for trying to start trouble between us. Look, this is a competitive business. You don't need me to tell you what'll happen if you fall from the top. It takes money to live the way we're accustomed to living."

"What's going on, Mike? My stand on this should come as no surprise. I've told you before that I'm not willing to bend the rules."

"Dammit, do you picture yourself wearing a suit of armor and riding a white horse? Everybody's entitled to a defense. Who are you to say where that responsibility begins and ends?"

Adam sighed and rubbed his temple. "Last check, I was your partner. Listen, we've been over this before. I'm no saint, Mike, but I don't break the law. I'll give Whitehead the best honest defense there is. You can't ask me for more than that."

Angry frustrated silence.

"Mike?"

"Don't worry about Whitehead, Adam. Roger will take care of it."

Adam opened his mouth to protest, but the line went dead. He didn't want the case, but he hated letting Mike make him feel like a schoolboy who couldn't handle a tough assignment. Things *were* changing. Mike had been his mentor for years. Only now, the more closely Adam looked at the firm's senior partner, the less he liked what he saw.

"Is something wrong, dear?" his grandmother called from the dining room.

Adam propped his elbows on his knees and tapped his forehead with the phone. He needed to get back to work. He was losing his edge. The political machina-

tions of the sixteen lawyers who worked at the firm
had always provided an exciting challenge for him. He
hadn't minded Roger and others like him, struggling to
climb the power ladder, stepping on anyone in their
way. Adam had eagerly pitted his wits against theirs
and had come out as one of Mike's three junior partners. But he was getting tired of the grind. Now office
politics seemed just another distraction, an irritant.

"It's nothing," he replied at last, shoving himself to
his feet. Jenna was still in the dining room, drawing
him back. When she was around, the last thing he
wanted to think about was San Francisco or his career.
"Are we ready for ice cream yet?"

AFTER DINNER, Jenna made Ryan do some reading at
the table while Mrs. Durham helped her with the
dishes; Adam went to pick up a video. Dinner had been
delicious, but she hadn't been able to eat more than a
few bites. The roast beef, carrots and potatoes with
gravy she'd swallowed churned in her stomach as a
bout of nausea visited her early tonight.

"Mom, what's this word?"

Jenna took a deep breath and looked down at the
book her son held out to her. She helped him sound
out *familiarity,* read the word in context, then kissed
his cheek.

"You like Adam, don't you?" she asked.

"He's cool. I can see why Dad would hang out with
him when they were kids. Adam says they used to go
bodysurfing in the ocean all the time."

All the time before she and Adam got together. After
that there was nothing but enmity between the two
young men.

"I'm sure you'll do plenty of that yourself in a few years," she said.

"So we're going to stay in one place for a while?"

Jenna mussed his hair. "I've told you we're going to be here until I'm old and gray. What, do you want me to sign a blood oath?" She gave him a reassuring smile. Her son had experienced enough emotional distress in his eight years. She wouldn't uproot him again. Dennis had moved them five times in the past twenty-four months. Each time he lost his job he dragged them to another Oregon city to "start over."

"Thanks, Mom."

"It's no sacrifice, love. I like it here, too."

Adam returned with the video, and Jenna lost her son to his innate charm, which was surpassed only by the promise of an ice-cream sundae.

"Mom? Do you want one?" Ryan asked, helping Adam dish it out.

The thought of more food, of any kind, was almost enough to send Jenna running for the bathroom. "No, thanks. I ate too much at dinner."

Adam glanced up and caught her eye, giving her a searching look, but she dried her hands on the towel, hung it under the cupboard and excused herself.

"I'll spend another hour or so in my studio, then I'll go to bed early," she said.

Ryan's face registered disappointment. "You're not watching the movie with us?"

"Not tonight, honey."

"Mom, are you all right? Are you sick or something?"

Jenna shook her head. "I'm fine. Just tired."

"You go and get some rest, Jenna dear," Mrs. Durham said, carrying a dish of ice cream to her husband, who was already sitting in front of the television. "And don't worry about getting up early. We have no reservations for tomorrow night. I've given Pamela the day off, and Mr. Robertson will be coming in later than usual, just in time to start dinner. I was hoping Adam would take us all for a drive along the highway. It's been months since I've been anywhere fun. Would you like to come along?"

Jenna declined politely. Highway 1 followed the coast and made her carsick even when she wasn't feeling nauseated to begin with. "It will be nice for you to get out. I'll look after the place while you're away. Sorry to miss out on the movie tonight," she added, and hurried upstairs to get her sweater before going to her studio through the back door. She needed to escape her son's hero worship of her old boyfriend—and from that same man's unsettling presence.

A ROILING STOMACH woke Jenna long after everyone else had gone to bed. She darted across the hall, stopping only long enough to lock the door behind her, and bent over the toilet just in time.

Damn. She had to be pregnant. What other reason could there be for this regular sickness?

Remembering the incident at the grocery store earlier, she groaned and smacked her forehead with her palm. She'd been tempted to invent another excuse to get away later in the day, but she feared Adam would guess what she was doing. So she'd made herself wait. He would leave in a day or two, probably on Sunday, and she'd be free to do what she wanted. Certainly she could wait that long.

The shrill ring of the telephone broke the silence,

and Jenna stiffened. Dennis! It had to be him. Only he would call so late.

She got to her feet and tried to launch herself from the bathroom before he could wake the whole house, but the ringing stopped before she unlocked the door. She waited, wondering if he'd call back, but heard nothing more. Slumping down to sit on the floor, she stared miserably at the yellow-and-blue-flowered wallpaper with its contrasting border until she felt strong enough to stand again.

Was she safe to leave the bathroom and go back to bed now?

She thought so.

Using the lip of the counter to help her rise, she brushed her teeth and washed her face, taking the time to rub some peach-scented lotion on her arms and legs. Then, switching off the light, she opened the door and headed to her room.

A male voice at her elbow startled her. She tried to scream, but a hand clamped over her mouth, and she felt herself being pulled against a solid chest. "Shh, you'll wake Gram and Pop. It's only me."

"Adam, what are you doing up?" she whispered as soon as he released her.

With a hand on her arm, he propelled Jenna into her room. "Are you the only one with a night-owl permit? Shut the door and turn on the light."

Confused, Jenna closed the door behind her and did as he asked, belatedly realizing her near nakedness. Crossing her arms in front of the spaghetti-strap tank top that did little to conceal her breasts, she glared at him. "You nearly scared me to death!"

He grinned. "Since I'm not wearing any athletic protection, that could have been very dangerous."

Jenna's eyes glided over him. He wasn't wearing much of anything. A thatch of dark hair covered his broad chest and narrowed down to his navel, disappearing beneath the pajama bottoms that hung low on his hips. His feet were bare. "Are you going to tell me what you're doing?"

He lifted something for her to see. "Don't look at me like I'm some kind of stalker. I was just trying to give you this. I didn't think you'd want the whole house to know."

Jenna's eyes dropped to the square object he held in one hand. She blinked. It was the First Choice Pregnancy Test she'd tried to buy at the grocery store.

CHAPTER FIVE

COULDN'T ANYTHING go right? Jenna stared at the box for several seconds before working up the nerve to accept it with a simple thank you. She tried to smile, to ease the awkwardness of the moment, but she didn't have it in her and could only hope she didn't look as miserable as she felt.

"Dennis?" he asked.

Jenna almost nodded before she pictured Adam counting back the months—and wondering why the hell she'd slept with her ex after their divorce was final. Rape by someone she'd lived with for years wasn't an easy thing to explain, and she had no intention of trying. She was enough of a pity case already.

"No," she said. "I met the guy not long after Dennis and I split up. It was...just a one-night stand. It didn't mean anything."

Adam's brows drew close. "You had unprotected sex with a stranger?"

Jenna raised her chin. "I didn't exactly plan it, all right? It's not like I carry something in my purse, hoping to get lucky. Are you saying you've never done anything like that?"

"No, I haven't." His steadfast gaze was difficult to meet, making Jenna wonder if the truth wouldn't have been less painful, after all.

"Besides, even if I took a different woman to bed every night, it wouldn't be the same," he added.

"Oh, yeah? Interesting you think so." Jenna heard her voice rise and carefully lowered it so she wouldn't wake Ryan, grateful for the anger that surged through her body, because it replaced humiliation and embarrassment. "Maybe you'll enlighten me. I've always wanted to hear the rationale behind the old double standard."

"I don't have an eight-year-old son to explain this to, and I don't have a deranged ex who's going to go ballistic as soon as he learns."

"No, you don't have either of those because your precious practice and your own personal success are more important." She forgot about trying to cover herself and clenched her hands at her sides. "Your responsible-parent act is convincing, but the truth is, you can't even imagine what it's like to look at the child you helped create and know that regardless of all the other shit that happens in your life, you've done one thing right. Because you're too scared to love that much." She tossed the pregnancy test on her dresser and flounced into bed, pulling the blankets up to her chin. "Now, if you'll go, I need to get some sleep."

He stared at her, eyes narrowed, and Jenna was afraid he'd make a rejoinder. She prayed he'd leave her in peace. Her strength was ebbing, and the nausea, the worry and her lack of sleep combined to make her feel like an emotional wreck.

To avoid letting him see the tears swimming in her eyes, she rolled over and presented him with her back. He had the life he wanted. What difference did her problems make to him?

"Damn," he swore, and stalked out.

TOO ANGRY TO SLEEP, Adam prowled around his room for the next thirty minutes. Part of him wanted to wring Jenna's neck for getting herself into such a tough situation; another part wanted to race back to San Francisco and avoid the whole mess.

In any event, he couldn't help feeling he owed her *something*. Jenna would never have married Dennis if he hadn't broken his promise and left her behind. But she could only blame herself for this pregnancy. She might not be as sophisticated as those women who routinely protected themselves against pregnancy and STDS, but she was old enough to understand the consequences of her actions. She had one kid already, for hell's sake!

A soft knock at the door stopped Adam in his tracks. Knowing it was probably Jenna, he moved as far away from the entrance as he could before calling, "Come in."

She'd been crying. He could tell the minute he laid eyes on her, and he felt the ice around his heart melt a little, despite his best efforts to keep the temperature down. Fortunately the stab of jealousy he'd felt when he first suspected Jenna might be pregnant returned, keeping his voice gruff. "What is it?" he asked.

She cleared her throat. "I...I wanted to make sure I could trust you to keep what you know a secret. Just for now."

"About the baby?" With one arm, Adam braced himself against the wall and stared out the window at the landscape lights in the garden below. "Are we sure there *is* a baby?"

"I'm afraid so." She pressed her palms to her eyes. "I need a few days to decide what to do."

Evidently she'd already taken the test he'd bought

her, and the results had shaken her. Her voice was soft and sounded nearly as frightened as her enormous eyes looked. Adam could understand why. He felt shell-shocked himself, and the baby wasn't even his. "How far along are you?"

"About three months." She fiddled with the belt of her white terry robe, then sighed. "Listen, I have Ryan to think about and, well, I regret saying what I did about the, um, baby's father. It would only confuse Ryan to think Dennis wasn't—"

"I won't say anything, to anyone." Adam cut her off, hating the thought of a total stranger getting past barriers Jenna would never let him cross again. He remembered the stained-glass window he'd seen in her studio and wondered, for the first time, if he was wrong about it being "their" stretch of beach. Just because their years together still meant something to him didn't mean Jenna held them with the same sacred regard. It was egotistical of him to even think so.

She smiled a little, and he felt another tug at his heart. What would it have been like to marry Jenna and to watch her grow big with his child? To have a son like Ryan?

"I guess you'll be heading back to San Francisco soon," she said.

"Yeah. I've got to get back. Some things have happened since I've been gone..."

"Sure, it's hard to get away when you've got so much going on." She spoke quickly and started toward the door, obviously expecting him to take her words at face value, but he couldn't ignore the undercurrent. She knew he was running away from her again. He hadn't been able to fulfill his promise to her fifteen years ago.

And he hadn't gotten any better at making commitments since.

"Dammit, Jenna," he said, catching her by the arm. "What do you expect me to do? Walk away from my practice?"

"What do *I* expect?" She frowned. "I don't expect anything. I couldn't hold you here once, I wouldn't try again. Any demands you feel are simply your imagination. Or maybe they're reflections of your grandparents' hopes, not mine."

"Liar." He could feel her shaking under his hand, a natural reaction after learning about the baby, he supposed, but he wanted to believe that part of her still responded to him.

She released a bitter laugh. "God, Adam, what do you want from me? If you want to hear me say it nearly destroyed me when you left the last time, I will. But if you think I'll give any man the chance to hurt me like that again, you're a bigger fool than I thought."

"Didn't Dennis hurt you, Jen?"

"The truth?" Defiance flashed in her eyes. "In some ways," she admitted. "Fat lips hurt. Broken bones hurt. Worrying about Ryan because of Dennis and me hurt. Living in fear hurt. But Dennis could never really reach me. Not in here." She tapped her chest with the knuckles of one fist. "This is locked up tight, and the key was lost a long time ago. A divorce is a huge wake-up call, Adam. We're not kids anymore. Every decision I make affects my son, and even if I wanted to, I couldn't take another emotional risk, at least not now, and not with you. Ryan needs me to be strong and consistent. So that means you're safe. Get it? I don't want anything from you, and to be completely honest, I wish you'd do us all a big favor and go back to San

Francisco. That's where you want to be. That's where you belong. So go, okay?''

The phone on the nightstand jangled. As Jenna jerked away to answer it, a shadow of apprehension entered her eyes. Dennis again, Adam thought. This time of night, it had to be him. And Jenna knew it.

Instinctively he skirted past her to grab the receiver. "All right, Dennis," he barked into the phone, "you want to threaten somebody, try threatening me. I won't stand still for your harassing Jenna anymore, do you understand?"

"Well, if it isn't my old buddy." A harsh chuckle sounded on the line, then the soft *pop* a bottle makes when it loses its seal. "I thought so," Dennis said, his words barely recognizable amidst the slurred syllables. "Jenna might think my brain's pickled, but I'm not stupid. I knew what was happening all along. As soon as you snapped your fingers, she packed up and left me to run right back to you, eh?"

Adam didn't like the sound of Dennis's crazed voice. Neither did he like the accusation that he'd been responsible for the divorce. "I didn't even know you two weren't together until I came home last night, but you've had too much to drink to believe that. So believe what you want. It doesn't matter, anyway. You guys are divorced. You got that, Dennis? That means you leave Jenna alone."

Again the grating laugh. "You getting all you want, friend? Because she was sure a stingy bitch with me."

Adam clenched his teeth. "Just leave Jenna alone."

"And if I don't?"

"I won't bother calling the cops. It'll be just you and me, and a lesson learned the hard way."

"That sounds like something I won't want to miss.

Maybe we should sell tickets. Jenna would love that, wouldn't she? To have us fighting over her again? It'll be just like old times." And the line went dead.

Jenna stood staring at Adam, her face chalky white, her hands over her mouth.

"If he calls or bothers you again, Jen, I need you to tell me—"

"No! Thanks for the infusion of testosterone, Adam, but it won't help me protect Ryan or your folks when Dennis comes here, raving drunk, and you're in San Francisco. Don't you understand? Dennis lived in your shadow our whole married life. Nothing could bring him here quicker than to think we're together. So next time don't do me any favors."

She slipped from the room and into the hall, and Adam resisted the urge to go after her; instead, he rammed a hand through his hair. Jenna had had one hell of a night, and because of his own scrambled emotions, he hadn't done much to make things better. But it was high time someone stopped Dennis from harassing his ex-wife. Jenna thought Adam's involvement might cause Dennis to do something rash, but Dennis was already a ticking bomb, ready to go off. And most women didn't understand something boys learned at a very young age: the only way to stop a bully was to beat him at his own game.

"ADAM! ADAM, wake up!"

With a groan Adam rolled over and squinted bleary-eyed at a blond head— Ryan's. "Hey, squirt," he mumbled. "What you doing up so early?"

"It's not early, Adam. It's almost seven o'clock. Grandma Durham sent me to tell you we're ready to go."

"Go?" After the almost sleepless night he'd spent, Adam felt as if he'd been hit by a truck. He rolled over and snuggled deeper into the blankets, but any hope of going back to sleep ended when Ryan's small fist knocked gently on his head.

"Hello? Is anybody home?"

Chuckling, Adam scrubbed the sleep from his face. "All right, wise guy," he said, "the lights are going on, but slowly. We're traveling up the coast. Am I right?"

"Yep! Grandma Durham packed us some snacks to eat in the car. Her blond brownies, which I hate—" he grimaced, then brightened "—but there's chocolate-chip cookies, too, and fudge, almond roca, deviled eggs, Jell-O jigglers—"

"Whoa, I haven't even had breakfast yet."

"You gonna take as long to get ready as my mom?" the boy asked.

Adam perked up. "Jenna's going?"

"No. She just takes a long time to comb her hair and do all that girl stuff."

"Oh, I see the connection. You think I look like a girl."

The boy rolled his eyes. "No, I just don't want to wait while you spend an hour in the bathroom."

"So it's a baseball-cap day, huh?"

Ryan grinned. "Yeah, just wear a hat!"

The prospect of a long drive without Jenna dimmed Adam's enthusiasm. After what had happened last night, he didn't want to leave her side until he knew what Dennis was going to do. But Oregon was nearly a full day's travel away. She should be safe until some time after noon, and he, Ryan, Pop and Gram would be back by then.

Adam was surprised to realize that he wasn't upset about the possibility of postponing his return to San Francisco. Spending more time in Jenna's company appealed to him, despite the knowledge that it would probably be better for both of them if he kept his distance.

Humans were so perverse, he mused. The more they knew they shouldn't have something, the more they wanted it.

"All right, squirt. Out you go, so I can dress."

Ryan ambled to the door, tossing a baseball a foot or two into the air and catching it with a stiff new glove.

"You think we can play catch later on?" he asked as the ball landed with a satisfying plop.

"Sure. Looks like we need to get that glove oiled up and broken in."

"Yeah." Ryan's grin widened at the prospect, and Adam wondered how a father could let anything come between him and a boy like this.

And a woman like Jenna.

For a moment he actually pitied Dennis. His old friend had lost a lot. Granted, it was his own fault— but what did he have left in his life?

As soon as the door closed, Adam threw off the covers and started digging through his suitcase.

"Adam? You ready? The day'll be half-gone before we get out of here if we don't go now," Gram's voice called from downstairs.

"Half-gone! It's not even seven o'clock, and it's Saturday," Adam muttered, buttoning his faded jeans and pulling on a 49ers sweatshirt. His grandparents would never change. They got up at dawn every day, even when it was only to have fun.

"After dragging me from my bed, I hope you at least have a cup of coffee waiting for me," Adam called back, settling a baseball cap over his sleep-tousled hair.

There was no answer, but he knew Gram well enough to expect more than a cup of coffee. She'd probably fixed him a ten-course meal. Remembering the quick bowl of cold cereal or occasional Pop Tart he tossed down before rushing off to the office in San Francisco, he thought he could get used to the pleasures of living in Mendocino again. Then he realized something—until that very moment, he hadn't known how much he'd missed it. Small town, slow pace. Home and family.

"Hey, this is what I went to San Francisco to get away from," he grumbled, then opened the door to find Ryan waiting in the hall. "Come on, kid. Let's go."

AFTER GETTING a couple of rooms ready in case they had some drive-by business that evening, Jenna went to her studio, planning to spend the morning finishing her stained-glass window of the lake and trees. Pamela, the maid, had the day off, and Mr. Robertson wouldn't be in until four o'clock to start dinner, so she was alone, and grateful for the solitude.

Flipping on the space heater to get rid of the chill, she studied the glass she'd cut before bed the night before and decided to start leading the window. She had a penciled drawing of the finished work on the table under the glass. But the telephone interrupted her before she could begin.

"Hello?"

"Hi, Jen. It's me." Laura Wakefield was the one friend Jenna had grown up with in Mendocino who hadn't married or moved away. She still lived with her parents, just a few miles down the highway, and helped her mother care for her father, a victim of Alzheimer's.

"Laura, what are you doing up this early? It's only eleven o'clock. You never roll out of bed before noon."

"A fringe benefit of working the late shift."

"You manage a seafood restaurant that closes at ten. That's hardly the late shift."

"Well, it's not the early shift, either, which means I can sleep in if I want. Anyway, today I thought I'd drive over to Fort Bragg to see a matinee. Feel like coming with me?"

Jenna considered the work in progress waiting on her table. "I'm working on the lake piece. Then I've got to see about ordering more brochures for the Victoriana. And I promised Mrs. Durham I'd finish their website. So I'd better pass for today." She considered telling Laura about Adam's being in town, then decided against it. Her friend would want to know exactly how she felt about seeing him for the first time in fifteen years, and Jenna didn't want to identify her feelings, let alone talk about them.

She realized that if she spent much time with Laura, she'd end up telling her anyway, but that didn't stop her from extending the usual invitation. "Want to come over for a cup of coffee before you go?"

"No. I'm going to have a shower and color my hair."

"You are? You've never colored your hair before."

"I know, but my dad's sister is in town. She's helping take care of him and I'm ready for a change, and one of the waitresses at the restaurant said I should go blond."

"As in bleach blond?"

"Is there any other kind for a brunette?"

"Oh, no, Laura, think of the roots."

"It'll be a hassle, but if I do it often enough—"

"You'll ruin the texture of your hair."

"I take it you don't like the idea."

"I think you'll regret it."

"Hmm. Maybe I will. Anyway, my stomach's a bit queasy. I should probably just go back to sleep."

Reminded of her own nausea, and the baby, Jenna put a hand to her stomach. "I've got something to tell you," she said.

"So tell me."

"I'm pregnant."

"What?"

Jenna held the phone away from her ear, but she was too late to avoid the blast of Laura's exclamation.

"I'm pregnant," she repeated.

"Oh, my gosh! And I thought you led this chaste little life. Where have you been going without me?"

Jenna couldn't help chuckling. "Nowhere. It's Dennis's."

"But you haven't seen Dennis for, what, three months?"

"Yeah. It happened just before I left Oregon, and it's a long story, one I really don't want to go into right now. I just…I don't know. I wanted the support of someone who might understand how frightened I am, that's all."

"Oh, Jen! You poor thing. I'm so sorry. What are you going to do?"

"Do I have a choice?"

"You could give it up."

"Ryan's brother or sister? Are you crazy?"

Silence. "It's Dennis's baby."

"It's mine, too. I'll raise it."

"And what are you going to tell Dennis? A baby will only give him one more link to you and Ryan, one more reason to beg you to come back or punish you for not coming back."

Jenna stretched the phone cord with her so she could reach the back of the studio where she retrieved a box of lead came, the metal compound she used to hold her windows together. "I know."

"What if you keep the baby a secret? As long as Dennis never comes around, he'll have no way of knowing."

She sighed. "Except I still have a glimmer of hope that Dennis will get well. Ryan needs a father." Taking a long metal rod out of the box, Jenna put one end in a vise and began to stretch the came to firm and tone the lead that would surround each small piece of glass.

"Do you really think that might happen?"

"I can only hope so, for Ryan's sake. Besides, it wouldn't be fair to anyone involved if I claimed the baby belonged to another man." Jenna winced at her words, unwilling to admit to Laura that she'd already made that mistake. "I want my children to know they're full-blooded siblings."

"Okay, but what if Dennis doesn't believe you, anyway? Didn't you tell me he questioned you about Ryan once? When that doctor told him he wasn't likely to father another child?"

"Yeah, he accused me of cheating on him." Tempted to resume her old habit of biting her nails, Jenna kept her hands busy. Now that she was pregnant, she had to be extra-careful around lead.

"I know another pregnancy must sound scary," Laura said, "but you've been doing really well since you got here. You'll handle this, too, Jen. I know you'll handle it just fine.''

Jenna gave a weak smile, even though Laura couldn't see it. ''Thanks for the vote of confidence. I knew I could count on you to say what I needed to hear, Laura.''

''I'll help you. I'll baby-sit whenever you want me to.''

''Thanks.''

''Uh-oh!''

''What?'' Jenna exclaimed.

''I feel like I'm going to throw up.''

''Go!''

Jenna heard a click and a dial tone, and Laura was gone. She hung up, the mere suggestion of vomiting enough to make her queasy. Remembering that she hadn't eaten much for breakfast, she headed over to the house for some crackers.

Unlocking the back door, she made her way to the kitchen and rummaged through the refrigerator, but ended up digging a box of crackers out of the cupboard as she'd originally planned. She wanted a cup of coffee but knew caffeine wasn't really good for the baby, so she poured herself a large glass of milk, instead.

She *could* handle this pregnancy, she thought. And Ryan would love a sibling. The next few years wouldn't be easy, but she'd come this far. She'd fight the discouragement and the disillusionment and keep on fighting until—

The sound of glass shattering reverberated through the house.

Jenna froze, the milk halfway to her mouth. Then her heart plummeted to her knees because it was Dennis's voice she heard calling, ''Jenna! Guess who?''

CHAPTER SIX

"DENNIS?" JENNA WILLED away the falter in her voice and hurried to the living room to find her ex-husband standing on the porch, grinning at her through the broken front window. Spidery cracks spread out from a hole just right of center, distorting his face and making him look more pitiful—and more sinister—than the last time she'd seen him. Thick whiskers covered his jaw, his eyes were bloodshot, and his hair, prematurely gray, stood up in places, looking as if it hadn't been combed in a week. He wore nothing more than a pair of dirty jeans and a T-shirt, despite the cool weather. A rock the size of a baseball lay at Jenna's feet.

"What do you think you're doing?" she asked, staring at the shards of glass on the carpet winking like new-fallen snow in the late-morning sun. "That's an expensive window you broke. You can't just go around destroying other people's property!"

Still grinning, he put a hand to his chest. "You think I did that? Some kid rode by on his bike just as I drove up. Tossed something through the window. Damnedest thing I ever saw."

Jenna watched him carefully. He'd broken the window in the perfect place to reach a hand through and unbolt the door. And she hadn't locked the back door behind her.

"What do you want?" she asked, cutting to the

chase. Dennis didn't appear drunk, but he could be hungover. And mean. In their years together any mention of Adam sent his temper soaring. And now Dennis believed she'd gone back to her high-school sweetheart.

He dragged a hand through his hair, and this time when he spoke his voice had lost its mockery. "Is it too much to ask to see my son?"

"Do you really want him to see you like this?" Jenna studied the man she'd married and marveled at how much he'd changed. Heavy lines around his eyes and mouth made him seem at least ten years older than he was, and his stomach, once taut, now hung soft and flabby over his belt. He smelled as if he hadn't had a bath in weeks. Worse, he didn't seem to care. "How did you get here so fast, anyway?"

He shrugged. "I wasn't coming from Oregon. But then, you wouldn't know anything about that. You don't give a damn where I live anymore."

As long as it's far away from me. "Listen, Dennis, Ryan isn't here, and we have nothing to say to each other. We've been through everything—"

Slamming his fist into the door, he shouted, "Not enough, we haven't!"

Jenna backed away and sent a glance at the telephone. Could she get hold of the police before Dennis got inside?

As if reading her intentions, he breathed deeply through his nose and stood straighter, trying to regain control. His hands, the brutal power of which Jenna knew all too well, flexed but remained at his sides. "Come on, Jen. I don't want trouble. I just want to talk to you about Ryan. I'm better now. I want to come around sometimes, see my son. Let me in so we can talk. I'm not some worthless piece of shit!''

"Dennis, you're nuts if you think you're any better. I can see you still need help. And I don't want you in here, not with all that talk about body bags."

Chuckling, he turned to gaze out over the front lawn, which was perfectly manicured and green and sloped down to a white sign with "The Victoriana" written in fancy script. Jenna could see Billie, the owner of Billie's Bath and Body, inside the house-turned-retail establishment across the street and wished she'd call the police. But their neighbor had no way of knowing Jenna was in trouble.

"Lover boy's not home, eh?" Dennis said, turning back.

"Adam's not my lover. Regardless of what you may think, we have no interest in each other. He just came home to visit his grandparents. It's the first I've seen of him."

"Well, he's not much of a protector if he's always running off. I guess that macho crap last night was just big talk. And here I thought he was ready for me."

"Leave Adam out of our problems, Dennis. He's going back to San Francisco and his own life. He's got nothing to do with us."

"He's the one who stuck his big nose in, Jen."

Jenna shook her head. "You shouldn't have been calling here so late. He's got his grandparents to worry about."

"Didn't sound too upset about the old folks. Sounded like he was worried about you. What's he doing? Banging you a few times while he's on vacation? At least I was willing to marry you. Support you and raise a family. What's he ever done?"

The old rage bubbled up inside Jenna. She'd supported their little family more years than Dennis had. She'd worked full-time and been Ryan's mainstay. She'd taken care of their house and cars and taxes. She'd lied for Dennis, carted him around, cleaned up his messes, sat through more Al-Anon meetings than she could count and pretended everything was okay for so long that the mere memory was enough to send her blood pressure through the roof.

But she bit her tongue to avoid falling into the same old argument, and raised her hands. "I give up, Dennis. Blame me for everything. Call me any name in the book. Tell everyone you meet how terribly I treated you. Send all our old friends letters and e-mails. You can publish it in the paper. Just go away, all right? Ryan and I are happy here, and I'm going to do my best to make sure we stay that way."

"The two of you are happy? And what about me, Jen? Seems you've forgotten something. What about 'till death do us part? In sickness or in health'?" Shoving his hand through the hole in the window, he tried to unbolt the door. Before he could manipulate the latch, however, Jenna grabbed the brass bunny that held the front door open during the summer and used it like a hammer to smash Dennis's hand.

With a cry he pulled his injured fingers back.

"Now go away," she said again, "or the next time you stick your hand in here, you'll draw back a bloody stump!"

Cursing, he shook his hand as if to ease the pain, and his face twisted with rage or hate or both. "I'm gonna kill you, bitch," he said. "Just you wait and see. When you least expect me, I'll be here. Then Ryan will come to live with his daddy."

Dennis lifted his head at the sound of a siren in the distance. Then he whirled around and stalked down the porch, climbed into a battered Ford Escort Jenna had never seen before and peeled out of the drive.

Jenna stared at a drop of blood rolling down the window from a jagged piece of glass that must have cut Dennis's arm.

And then she ran to the bathroom and promptly threw up.

"WOW! WHAT HAPPENED?" Ryan looked up at the cardboard Jenna had taped to the inside of the broken window. Her son had raced inside ahead of the others. Mr. and Mrs. Durham followed, and Adam brought up the rear.

Jenna kept her voice as neutral as possible, considering she'd barely had time to clean up the mess and tape the cardboard in place before the Durhams' Cadillac turned into the drive. "I was on my way to get the mail and tripped. Put my hand right through the glass. I'm sorry. I'll pay for it to be replaced."

Mr. Durham took her hands in his larger ones and peered at them. "You didn't get cut?"

"No. I don't know how I avoided it, but I feel terrible about the window."

"That's why we have insurance," Mrs. Durham piped up. "Accidents happen. We're just glad you're safe."

Only Adam seemed to doubt Jenna's story. He raised an eyebrow and turned to study the window with a frown.

"Mom, you wouldn't believe what we saw!" Ryan said, the window quickly forgotten, at least by him. "Whales! A big bunch of them—"

"A pod, dear," Mrs. Durham corrected, gathering up the basket she'd set on the floor and trailing Mr. Durham to the kitchen.

"—swimming south to warmer waters. That's where Adam said they were going. It was so awesome. Wasn't it, Adam?"

Ryan looked at Adam with such naked adoration that Jenna had to take a step back and find a seat before her shaky legs crumpled beneath her. As if an insane ex-husband wasn't enough of a problem, now her son worshiped Adam. The man who was so good at telling bedroom lies. The man with No Commitment stamped on his forehead.

"Adam knew just the place to pull over," Ryan went on. "And Pop took binoculars so I could get a good look. Whales have a blowhole, you know. I saw water shooting out of it!"

"Is that so?" Jenna folded her arms and refused to meet Adam's probing eyes. She hadn't fully recovered from Dennis's visit yet; she was afraid that her anxiety showed.

"Adam said next time he comes he'll take me mountain biking," Ryan announced.

It was Jenna's turn to cock an eyebrow at Adam, but she responded to Ryan. "Honey, you don't have a mountain bike, and besides, Adam is a busy man. He rarely has time for a visit, you know that. Maybe he can take you on a hike come spring."

"Spring?" Adam disarmed her with a boyish grin. "How do you know I won't be back next weekend?"

"Because I know you," she said simply. *And I think I know what you've come to like—a fast pace, a sophisticated woman who asks for nothing more than you're willing to give, stiff professional competition and the excitement of winning a case. Not an old girl-friend who once loved you more than life, or an eight-year-old boy who already thinks you're the next best thing to a super hero.*

"Maybe you don't know me as well as you think. I'm not eighteen anymore, Jenna."

She smiled back. "Coulda fooled me."

"Did you hear that, Ryan? I think your mother's asking for the old tickle torture."

"No!" Jenna swatted at Adam's hands, but he lifted her easily out of the chair and had her on the ground, rolling in a fit of laughter in seconds.

"Say uncle," Ryan advised, laughing as he watched. "He has to let you up if you say uncle."

"Say uncle," Adam echoed, straddling her waist and pinning her arms above her head with one hand.

"Uncle means…I surrender," Jenna said breathlessly amid her efforts to escape, "and I'll never surrender, at least not to you!"

Adam stopped tickling. "That sounds like a challenge."

Jenna could smell spearmint on Adam's breath and feared he was going to kiss her right there in front of Ryan. Or at least that was all *she* could think about—his kiss.

Instead, Adam angled his head to look up at her son. "Next week, squirt," he said. "I'll be here Friday night, and we'll go mountain biking Saturday morning. Consider it a date."

"Yippee!" Ryan set off in a circling gallop that gave Jenna the opportunity to voice her displeasure.

"I tried to get you off the hook," she said, her voice barely audible, "but you don't know when to quit. Now he's got his heart set on next week."

"And you think I'll leave you both behind and not look back." Adam's thumb gently followed the line of her jaw.

"That's exactly what I expect—based on experience. But Ryan doesn't know any better." She tried to free her hands so she could get up and put some space between them, but Adam was too big, too powerful. His hat had come off during their scuffle, revealing a head of tousled hair, and the whiskers on his chin made him look more rugged than usual. In spite of her tart words, Jenna itched to bury her hands in his hair and draw him closer. But she wasn't about to ask for that kind of trouble.

His gaze lowered to where her breasts strained against the fabric of her blouse. "Like I said, I'm not eighteen anymore."

"Neither am I," she replied, but the hunger in his eyes made her nipples tighten until even she could see them standing out through her shirt.

He gave her a slow sensuous smile, and she knew he'd noticed when he said, "Oh, yeah? Well, *some* things haven't changed."

"YOU OKAY?" Adam approached Jenna on the narrow street fronting the inn and waited while she collected the mail from a white Victorian-style box. He'd showered and shaved and now looked more like the suave lawyer she'd seen the night he arrived, although he was dressed casually in a pair of jeans and a button-down shirt.

"I'm fine. Why?"

"Because you look like a scared rabbit."

Jenna pretended to be fully absorbed in checking

through the stack of envelopes. "I'm just tired. We were up late last night."

He leaned against the mailbox, blocking her retreat to the house. "And?"

She finally gave him her full attention. "And what?"

"Tell me what happened with the window."

A strong wind, carrying the scent of eucalyptus and redwood, nearly yanked the mail from Jenna's grip. She tucked the letters in the pocket of her thick corduroy jacket, then used one hand to keep her hair out of her face as she gazed into Adam's dark eyes. "I already did. I fell."

He studied her, but didn't press. Instead, he approached the subject from a different direction. Lawyer tactics, Jenna guessed. "I figure it would take Dennis eight hours or so to get here from Oregon. That means he could arrive anytime. Is that what has you so jumpy?"

"I don't think he's coming."

"What makes you so sure?"

Jenna shrugged. "What can he hope to accomplish? I have a restraining order against him."

"That hasn't stopped him from calling."

"He gets drunk, he calls. I doubt he has the money to get here, anyway. He hasn't worked in months, and his family's getting tired of helping him since he refuses to go into detox."

The memory of Dennis looming through the broken window rose in Jenna's mind, making the lies taste bitter in her mouth. She longed for Adam to pull her to him and hold her tightly against his chest until the shakes went away—because sometimes it seemed they never would.

But she was determined not to frighten Ryan or

worry the Durhams or involve her old boyfriend in her problems again. Adam seemed to think he couldn't go home until he knew she was safe, but she'd been dealing with Dennis for years without a protector. She could handle her ex-husband. It was Adam who frightened her.

"So you're going to stick with your story. You fell?"

She shrugged. "Sorry, nothing more exciting than that. You said yourself that Dennis couldn't have gotten here any sooner than now."

Adam nodded but didn't look convinced. "I told Ryan I'd take him out for a burger tonight. Any chance you'd like to come along? Just to make sure I don't make any more promises you've already decided I won't keep?"

"Is that your way of asking my permission to take Ryan somewhere?"

"Would you rather I didn't?"

Jenna could think of no good reason to deny her son the adventure of a night out. "He can go, I guess."

"Does that mean you won't join us?"

"I can't. We've had three late bookings. They'll be here any minute. But please don't think I'm being overprotective in worrying about Ryan. His father's already been a big disappointment. He doesn't need another one."

"What makes you so sure I won't deliver, Jen?"

"I guess I'm just trying to figure out why you're bothering to take an interest. You have a lot waiting for you in San Francisco. I don't want to keep you from your work."

His face grew stubborn, pensive. "Enough of that. I'm tired of your trying to get rid of me. I'll go when

I'm ready, and not until I'm sure Dennis is minding his manners.''

''You'd better send for your things, then.''

''That bad, huh?''

Jenna raised her brows. ''There's no way to be sure he'll ever leave us alone. That's a fact I have to live with, but it has nothing to do with you. And Dennis isn't to blame for everything.''

''Oh, yeah?'' Adam slid his hands in his pockets and hunched against the wind.

''Yeah.'' Jenna heard her voice soften with the pain of admitting the truth. ''I couldn't give Dennis what he needs. I couldn't love him enough to make him whole. Maybe if he'd married someone else, things would have turned out differently.''

Adam opened his mouth to say something, then seemed to change his mind and settle for, ''So the trouble started early on?''

''The trouble started before I even married him. I just wasn't smart enough to walk away then.'' How could she say she'd been lost without Adam? That she hadn't had the confidence to take life solo? It was so pathetic—and true. But the years had a way of strengthening people, of ameliorating weaknesses. What Jenna had once thought unbearable—being alone—she now found a relief.

Adam squinted at a gray sky that looked like rain, an odd expression on his face. ''You were young. I bet if you'd met Dennis later in life, you'd have chewed him up and spit him out, just like you're doing to me.''

Jenna tucked her hair behind her ears. ''What's that supposed to mean?''

''Only that you won't give me a chance to be your

friend. You're determined to shut everyone out. To shoulder this on your own.''

"So after three years of dating in high school, no contact for fifteen years, and a brief reunion, the man who took my virginity wants to be my friend?''

He smiled, charm so natural to him he wore it like a second skin. ''So you do remember.''

"How could I forget?'' She looked past Adam to where the dark rich earth sloped downward to meet the sea. Black rocks jutted out of the water. Seagulls wheeled above the white foaming waves, their cries lonely against the deserted beach. Trees grew sideways, like stooped old men carrying the burden of the wind on their backs.

"Then you also remember that I lost my virginity at the same time,'' he murmured.

But for me it meant something. Jenna swallowed the words before they had a chance to pass her lips. She'd come home to Mendocino knowing, even before Adam had returned, that he'd always be part of this place. "All right,'' she said. ''Let's be friends. Friends are supposed to keep your secrets, anyway, and you already know one of mine.''

"The baby?''

She nodded and he stepped closer, lowering his voice even though there wasn't anyone else around. ''Some of your secrets I've kept for years, Jen.''

She swallowed hard. ''Like?''

"Like how your breasts felt against my chest. How you'd wrap your legs around me and pull me so deep inside you that I didn't know where I stopped and you began—''

Unwilling to hear more, Jenna shook her head and put up a hand to stop him. ''On second thought, I don't want to be friends, Adam. I don't want to be anything.''

CHAPTER SEVEN

WITH A CURSE, Adam watched her hurry inside. Where had he been going with *that* little routine?

Jenna was driving him mad. He'd only been with her for three days, but already he longed to soothe the hurts he knew she'd suffered and protect her from whatever blows might come. Beyond that, he wanted her to welcome his touch as much as she had when they were teenagers. He didn't want to look in her eyes and see the wariness he saw now. He wanted to win back her trust.

Why? He still wasn't ready for a serious relationship—especially with a woman who was having another man's baby. Who knew what complications that might entail? The father could suddenly appear and demand a paternity test, decide he wanted to be part of the child's life. It was even possible that Jenna had some feelings for him.

Besides, Jenna seemed completely uninterested in the life he had built for himself.

So maybe it was for the best that he'd scared her off. Now she'd double-board her heart against him, and once he'd taught Dennis a thing or two, he could go back to San Francisco knowing he didn't have the slightest chance with her, no matter how hard he tried. Maybe then he could get on with his life.

"There you are. I've been looking all over for you."

Ryan came skipping around from the back, carrying Adam's leather jacket. Just as the boy reached him, a minivan drove down the street, creeping along. The man and woman inside swiveled their heads, checking addresses. Probably the Victoriana's first guests for the evening.

Eventually this was confirmed when the van paused in front of the sign, then swung into the drive.

"Come on, squirt, we're outta here," Adam said, taking his jacket and shrugging into it. "Your mom and the others will be busy, so we'll grab a burger and stay out of their way." He winked. "Guys' night out."

"Do you think we could get a chocolate shake, too?" Ryan asked as they headed up the drive.

"What good's a burger without a shake?" Adam took his car keys from his pants pocket and unlocked the passenger side of the Mercedes. Ryan hopped inside. "While we eat, you can tell me a little about Oregon and where you grew up," he added. *And what it was like to know your mom through most of the years I missed.*

THE SOUND OF POUNDING woke Jenna while it was still dark. At first she thought she was banging the brass bunny against Dennis's hand, that he was trying to get to her again. Then reality intruded, and she opened her eyes to stare at the alarm clock.

"Three o'clock," she muttered. Who could want in at—

Dennis! Was he back? Already?

Throwing off the covers, Jenna slid out of bed and wrapped her robe around her. Nights were turning into a circus around here, starring her as the Amazing Insomniac. She'd slept only a couple of hours after tossing and turning, trying to forget Adam and the way he'd looked at her outside at the mailbox, the intimate words he'd spoken.

There was more pounding on the door as Jenna scurried to the top of the stairs. She didn't want Dennis to wake the hotel guests, or Ryan and the Durhams, but as she stood there, gazing into the darkness of the front parlor, she lost the nerve to go down and confront him. The memory of his vile threats, even the violence of her own defense, curdled her blood and made her doubt she could handle another encounter with him so close on the heels of the last.

Despite her desire to keep Adam out of her life, she turned and hurried into his room. As he lay sleeping, she could see his profile silhouetted against the moonlight—the straight nose, narrow at the bridge, his full lips. His torso was bare; all the blankets, except for the sheet that rose as far as his hips, had been kicked away. One arm was thrown carelessly above his head.

As Jenna moved closer, her presence—and probably the insistent knocking below—must have disturbed his sleep. He lifted his head to blink at her. "Jen? Is that you? Are you okay? What is it?"

She pressed the heels of her hands to her eyes. "Someone's downstairs."

"Dennis?"

"I think so."

Adam sprang out of bed, seemingly without a thought for his nudity, and grabbed his pajama bottoms off the chair next to the closet. Jenna tried not to watch him, but the sight of his muscular body, still taut and trim but broader and fuller than it had been in his youth, worked like a magnet.

"Do I pass muster?" he asked, giving her a devilish grin as he finished tying the drawstring on his pants.

To her relief Jenna didn't have a chance to respond before he said, "Stay here," and left.

Instead of waiting behind as he'd told her to, Jenna followed Adam down, too afraid Dennis might have brought some kind of weapon this time. Her ex wasn't the same man she'd once known, and she had no idea how far he would go to carry out his threats. Especially when he saw Adam. The last thing she wanted was for Adam to get hurt trying to defend her.

When he reached the front entry, he threw open the door and flipped on the porch light at the same time. Jenna braced herself, expecting to see Dennis's rage-filled face in the doorway, to smell the booze on him even from several feet away.

Instead, two police officers waited on the porch. They identified themselves, flashed Adam their badge and nodded toward the drive. As Jenna came up behind Adam, she could see a black-and-white patrol car with the shadowy figure of a man sitting in the back seat.

"Todd, it's been a long time," Adam said, recognizing one of the officers, as Jenna did, from high school. "I didn't know you'd gone into law enforcement."

"I was still in school when you left. It's good to see you again, Adam." He nodded at Jenna. "You, too, Jenna. I heard you were back in town. I'm sorry to wake you, but Billie from across the street called in, said there was a Peeping Tom in the neighborhood. When we drove by, we found an unfamiliar car parked at the end of the street and caught a man prowling around your yard. Won't give his name or his reason for being here, and he's not carrying any identification. Thought you might know him.''

"I could probably wager a good guess,'' Adam said. He gave Jenna a look that said he'd take care of this and stepped outside.

Their voices dimmed as they walked down the porch and descended the three steps to the gravel drive. Jenna followed them as far as the swing so she could hear. They stopped next to the police car, and Adam bent to peer through the window.

"Yep, that's Dennis Livingston, Jenna's ex. He's been harassing her ever since she moved in with my grandparents in August. She's got a restraining order against him, but he doesn't let that bother him.''

Adam's presence and his words acted on Dennis like a lit match to a can of gasoline. Her ex-husband shouted something Jenna couldn't make out, then leaned back and started kicking the window.

Todd's partner smacked the door with his palm. "You keep that up and you'll do time for damaging police property.''

Dennis stopped kicking but continued to shout obscenities and glare at Jenna as though he wanted to choke the life out of her.

Adam bent closer to the window. "Leave her alone,'' he said simply.

The shouting and thrashing stopped, and Dennis started to laugh, but Adam ignored him.

"So this is what's become of Dennis Livingston,'' Todd said. "I knew him in school, too, but I didn't recognize him. He looks bad.''

"He's been living in the bottom of a bottle. Calls here every now and then, threatening to kill Jenna.''

Adam rubbed his bare arms against the chill wind. "What'll happen to him?"

Todd jotted a few notes in a pad he took from his pocket. "Probably not enough. Violating a restraining order is only a misdemeanor, but since it's Saturday, we can hold him until he's arraigned, which happens Tuesday morning in Fort Bragg."

"After that it depends on the judge," Todd's partner added.

Adam looked back at Dennis. "What do you think the judge will do?"

Todd shrugged. "Who knows? Mr. Livingston could be fined or required to do community service. I doubt he'll do any real jail time, maybe a couple of weeks. Depends on how he behaves. If he bothers Jenna after this, though, he'll be asking for trouble."

Adam turned his back to the car and lowered his voice. "You'll keep an eye out and make sure that doesn't happen, won't you, Todd?"

Todd put his pad away. "Sure. Won't you be around?"

"No, I just came for a visit. I live in San Francisco and I'll be going home soon."

With a quick glance at Jenna, Todd's voice dropped, too, but she could still hear what he said. "I'll look after her. I used to have a crush on her, you know. I think a lot of boys did, but she only had eyes for you. If all that's truly in the past, maybe I'll come by sometime and take my protective duty a step further by asking her out to dinner or a movie. You know, two divorcés whiling away some time."

Adam was a few inches taller than both officers; to Jenna, he seemed to use the advantage of his height to emphasize his words. "She's not interested in a date. Just make sure she's safe."

Jenna's mouth fell open at the curtness of Adam's response. He had no right to interfere in her love life, and she would have told him so, except she didn't want to go out with Todd, anyway.

Todd chuckled. "I guess it's not over. That tells me what I wanted to know. Didn't mean to step on any toes." He headed to the passenger side of the car.

"Thanks for taking care of things tonight, Todd," Jenna called, and for Adam's benefit she sent the officers a beaming smile. "It was good to see you again."

"You look great, Jenna," Todd replied.

Adam didn't say anything, but Jenna could see his scowl, despite the distance and the darkness, and felt a moment's satisfaction. He might have left her fifteen years ago, but it still bothered him to think of her with someone else.

Todd waved and got in the car while his partner climbed behind the wheel. "We'll let you know what happens."

The slamming of their doors reverberated above the sound of the surf only fifty yards away, and Adam turned to her. "It was good to see you again, Todd," he mocked in a high-pitched voice as he strode toward the porch.

Jenna hurried inside and tried to make a dash for her room, but Adam's hand closed over her elbow and spun her back to face him. "Tell me about the window," he demanded. "The truth this time."

An angry glint shimmered in his eyes, and Jenna flinched, feeling a twinge of guilt. "I didn't want to…to involve you. I shouldn't have dragged you into it tonight, but I…I just—''

''Dammit, Jenna, I'm trying to help you!'' His other hand came up to grasp her upper arm and give her a little shake. ''You're pregnant and sick, and you've got a boy upstairs who has a right to feel he and his mother are safe. Why are you fighting me? Why am I the enemy?''

His face was only inches above her own, forcing her to tilt her head back to see his eyes. She tried to put some space between them under the pretense of adjusting the messy hair she'd tied in a ponytail before going to bed, but he held her fast.

''The enemy?'' she repeated. ''Why wouldn't you be? I told you before—I don't want to be friends,'' she said when she realized he wouldn't let her go until he was good and ready. ''Although I appreciate your help tonight, my problems shouldn't concern you. And how dare you tell Todd I'm not interested!''

''He's not your type.''

''And you know this because…''

''I am.'' His arms went around her, bringing her against his chest, and when he spoke, she could feel the warmth of his breath on her ear. ''I'm sorry, Jen. I know the past few years haven't been easy for you.''

Jenna stiffened. She didn't want Adam's sympathy or his kindness; they made it too hard to protect her heart against him. But she did want him to hold her, because when she was in his arms, nothing else mattered. ''I'm okay,'' she whispered, closing her eyes and burying her face in his neck.

''What about the baby?''

She breathed deeply, smelling the musky scent of

his skin, wishing she could taste it. "I'll take care of the baby just like I do Ryan."

"And who will take care of you?"

Jenna felt her body softening, melting into his. He felt so good. Why not let herself hold him again, just once, just for a moment? "I don't need anyone to take care of me," she whispered. Head back, she looked into his eyes...and watched his gaze drop to her lips.

He wanted to kiss her. She could feel it. Standing on tiptoe, she pressed her lips to his mouth, and that single action seemed to snap his restraint like a rip cord. Holding her more firmly against him, he moved his lips over hers with a hunger that easily matched her own.

Jenna told herself to pull away, to break off the kiss, but the rivulets of pleasure that ran from one nerve to another kept her clinging to him. Fifteen years was a long time to miss a man....

"Remember this?" he asked when she didn't resist. "It feels like coming home, doesn't it?"

Jenna shook her head in denial, but it was a feeble unconvincing effort.

"Evidently you need more proof." With a smile he kissed her again, gently this time. Sucking her bottom lip between his teeth, he nipped at it. Then he deepened the kiss, using his tongue to meet hers and stroke the soft inside of her mouth until he simulated a motion so primitive Jenna could think of nothing else. She was no naive teenager anymore. She knew what she wanted, and she knew Adam could give it to her.

Her heart pounded and Jenna could feel the rush of blood through her body. It made her light-headed and dizzy; at the same time, the rest of her grew heavy and began to throb, wanting more. "Adam..."

His name was a sigh that spoke more of longing than reproach as he trailed kisses down her throat. Then he pushed her robe and the straps of her top off her shoulders to expose her breasts. ''Jenna, you're beautiful,'' he said, drawing back to study what his hands had revealed. ''I've never seen a more beautiful woman.''

It was too much. It was sensory overload—the smooth skin and male muscle beneath her hands, the smell of his aftershave, so uniquely and appealingly Adam, his words of admiration ringing in her ears. Jenna thought she'd burst from the heat radiating inside her, and that was before he lifted both her breasts in his palms and brought first one, then the other to his lips.

She thought it might hurt, her breasts were so tender. But Adam seemed to sense that she needed him to be extra-gentle. He nuzzled his face between her breasts, then sucked with just enough pressure to send sparks flying through her veins to meet and collide somewhere in her womb.

Shaking, Jenna clung to his shoulders, knowing if he let her go, she'd fall. He was everything she'd imagined, better than she remembered. The shiny thickness of his hair created anchors for her hands as she arched toward him, abandoning all hope of resistance.

''Tell me you want this,'' he whispered, needing her consent from somewhere besides her body's response.

''You mean say uncle,'' she murmured.

He raised his head. She gazed back at him from beneath half-closed lids framed with thick black lashes—the sexiest pair of eyes he'd ever seen. The creamy whiteness of her breasts spilled over his hands, and the feel of her, along with the peach scent of whatever lotion she'd used, had his mind so befuddled he couldn't think straight. He shook his head to clear it. "What?"

"You want me to say uncle."

He smiled. "Uncle's not so bad." Lowering his hands, he cupped her bottom and pressed her against him so she could feel how badly he wanted the same thing she did. If only she'd give him some sign that she wouldn't regret it in the morning.

She drew in a ragged breath. "I won't wave the white flag, Adam. Not again."

Adam felt her stiffen in his arms and knew he'd lost her even before Ryan's voice reached them from the top of the stairs.

"Mom, are you down there?"

CHAPTER EIGHT

JENNA FLED up the stairs to answer Ryan's call with a soothing murmur, leaving Adam feeling cold and empty. Gram's worried voice floated down to him, too, and he heard Jenna assure her that everything was okay. Soon, Gram went back to bed and only Jenna and Ryan's muted whispering reached him while he stood in the middle of the living room, his heart slowly softening its hammerlike blows as other parts of his anatomy began to ache in disappointment.

Damn. He reached up to massage his temples, wondering what the hell had just happened. One minute he thought he'd found the other half of himself. The next he felt as though he'd been leveled by an ax.

A creak drew his eyes to the darkness that pooled near the stairs where there were no windows to let in the moonlight. Jenna appeared, sparking the hope that she'd come back to him. They needed to talk. But she didn't even glance his way. She hurried to the kitchen. A cupboard slammed and the water went on just before Ryan, closer now, called Adam's name.

"What's the matter, squirt?" he asked as the boy stepped into the half light.

"I had a bad dream."

"You did? Come here." Adam sat in one of the more comfortable sofas arranged near the fireplace and waited for Ryan to take the seat next to him, but the boy surprised him by climbing into his lap. Thin arms went around Adam's neck as Ryan pressed a wet cheek to his chest.

"I'm glad you're awake," the boy said, his legs dangling over Adam's thigh. "I heard something down here and I was afraid my dream was coming true."

Adam put one arm around him and ran the fingers of his other hand through the boy's hair. "Tell me about your dream."

Ryan shook his head, squeezing his eyes shut as though he still saw an image that frightened him. "It was too scary."

"Was it monster kind of scary?"

When he answered, Ryan sounded far older than his age. "There's no such thing as monsters, except people who turn into monsters."

"Who was the monster in your dream, Ryan?" Adam asked, even though he could guess the answer. He wanted the chance to tell the boy he was safe from Dennis and to let him express whatever fears he still harbored.

"Just someone we used to know," Ryan murmured.

"Your father?"

The boy pressed his fists to his eyes as though trying to staunch fresh tears. He nodded, and Adam thought his heart would break. The memory of Dennis's enraged face taunting him from the back seat of the police car made it easy to imagine some of what the boy must have experienced over the years.

"I couldn't protect my mom," he sobbed suddenly. "I tried, but I couldn't help her. It happened again, and I tried to stop him, but he only threw me away and..." Sobs choked off his words.

"And he hurt her again?" Adam finished the sentence, wanting to get the worst of it out into the light so they could face it together.

Ryan nodded, obviously trying to control his emotion. "When I get big…" he managed, his words broken. "He better not try that when I get big."

Adam felt Jenna's presence behind them and wondered if she'd take Ryan away. Holding the child in his arms evoked a powerful protective instinct that surprised him. Adam knew she'd be bothered by the fact that he'd involved himself in her life again, but this kid… Jenna was right. Ryan was special. So courageous and trusting and loving, even after everything Dennis had put him through.

"It's not your fault your dad hurt your mom."

The boy didn't respond.

"Some people make bad decisions, and those decisions make others suffer. We can't always control what other people do, even when we're big."

He nodded slightly.

"Not all men are like your dad, you know that, Ryan?"

"I know. You're not like him. I can tell you're not."

Swallowing the lump in his throat, Adam continued to stroke Ryan's hair until the boy's tears disappeared and his breathing evened. He expected Jenna to interrupt them at any moment, but she stayed where she was, a silent bystander. When he glanced down to see Ryan's lids drooping over his eyes, he spoke softly to her.

"Go ahead and get some sleep. I think he's okay now. I'll tuck him in bed in a few minutes."

"You could probably put him there now if you want," she said, setting the glass of water she'd brought from the kitchen on the side table.

Adam shook his head. "I like this. I'll carry him up in a bit."

She paused for a moment and Adam thought she was going to say something. Then he heard her light tread on the stairs.

JENNA WATCHED as Adam passed her bed carrying her son to the room off her own, a room that used to be a small nursery for whomever had lived in the house when it was first built. She'd been waiting for them, wondering how long Adam would continue to hold Ryan, and was surprised when nearly twenty minutes went by.

Through the open door, she heard Ryan mumble a good-night, then pictured Adam pulling the covers up to her son's chin. In another moment he reappeared in the moonlight that streamed through the window, and with a lingering glance in her direction headed back into the hall.

Swallowing hard, Jenna summoned the courage to speak to him. "Thank you."

He turned back. "You don't have to thank me. I can see what a great kid Ryan is, Jenna."

"I know. You've been good to him, and I'm grateful. Ryan needs a healthy role model. But I wasn't thanking you for that. Knowing Ryan is its own reward."

"Then what?"

"For...before. For making me feel so...alive again."

Facing her, he propped himself against the doorjamb. "You want to explain that?"

She leaned up on one elbow. "When you held me...when you kissed me—" Jenna felt her cheeks burn with embarrassment but wanted to get the words out ''—I haven't felt anything like that for a long time. I grew to hate it when Dennis touched me, and I think I was letting him make me old before my time.''

''And now?''

''Now I know I have a lot of life to live. That I can still want a man. And even though I'm not ready to involve myself in any emotional entanglements right now, I know I'll be able to love again someday.''

''What are you going to do in the meantime? Wait for Mr. Right?''

She thought she detected a note of bitterness in his voice. ''No, Mr. Right will have to take care of himself for a while. I'm going to stop telling myself that I don't have enough talent to make a business out of my stained-glass work, and I'm going to go for my dream.''

She saw white even teeth as he smiled. ''I did that?''

''Yeah.''

He looked at her for a few moments. ''Then maybe you could find it in your heart to forgive me.''

''For…?''

''You know what for. Leaving you.''

''That was fifteen years ago.''

''That's what your head says. It's your heart I'm trying to convince.''

Jenna stared across the distance, wanting to tell him she held nothing against him. But she knew it wasn't the truth. She couldn't let go of the past because it was the only thing that protected her from falling a second time. ''How about a stained-glass window for your office?''

He chuckled and pushed off the wall to stand up

straight. "A consolation prize, huh? Well, I won't complain so long as I can take my pick."

"Be my guest." At the moment Jenna was so thrilled with seeing a better future for herself and Ryan, with feeling the stirrings of confidence again, that she wouldn't have cared if Adam took everything in her studio.

He turned to go. "Good night, Jenna."

Smacking her pillow to get it just right, Jenna snuggled under the covers. "Sweet dreams."

"They will be," he said. "You're not the only one who enjoyed what happened downstairs."

The door closed behind him, and Jenna smiled to herself. Things were about to change for the better.

THE WIND RUSHED through his open window as Adam tore along the narrow two-lane highway back to San Francisco. He was cold, but he wanted to be; it cleared his head and kept him from nodding off. He was going to be tired in the morning, but he hadn't wanted to postpone his return any longer. Besides, seeing Jenna and not touching her would only prolong the torture.

After putting Ryan to bed, he'd gone straight to his own room to pack. Then he'd hauled his leather duffel bag down to his car and let himself into Jenna's studio for the window she'd promised him, returning only to leave his grandparents and Ryan a quick note. He and Jenna had already said their goodbyes. And Ryan? Well, he figured Jenna would explain...and he'd see the boy next weekend. The Durhams might not approve of his sudden departure, but he hoped his note would suffice. It explained what had happened with Dennis, and asked them to keep an eye out for Jenna in case Dennis got out of jail right away.

Glancing back, he shifted Jenna's window to better protect it from being damaged and wondered again about what she had told him as he was leaving her room. She'd said she hadn't felt desire for a man in a long time, that Dennis hadn't been able to reach her. But what about the father of her baby? She must have been pretty worked up to go for a one-night stand. Jenna had never been easy; she wasn't now, he thought with a rueful smile.

"Uncle," he muttered, driving with one hand slung over the wheel while he ran the other through his hair. He'd lost the best sex he could imagine over a simple word.

Well, maybe it wasn't so simple. He turned the radio up and thumped the wheel to the beat. He understood what Jenna was telling him. She wouldn't let him get close to her again in case he left the way he had before. And he wasn't sure he could promise her that next time would be different. He loved his work. He loved the city. He still didn't want to run the Victoriana and feared the guilt would eventually trap him into doing just that, if he ever moved back. But when he was with Jenna, he wanted her, too. It was a stalemate.

He gunned the Mercedes, loving the way it hugged the turns, accelerated at the slightest touch of the pedal, stopped on a dime. Maybe he'd be able to forget Jenna now that he was safely away from Mendocino.

He turned his thoughts to Whitehead and Mike and the problems that awaited him at the office. Heaven knew he already had enough to occupy his time, without her.

JENNA SIPPED some herbal tea and watched Ryan pick at his breakfast. He'd been pouting all morning, ever since he'd raced to Adam's room to find him gone.

"He didn't even say goodbye," her son repeated for the third time.

They were sitting in the restaurant portion of the downstairs, near the sideboard that held the remains of the Victoriana's Sunday buffet. Jenna and the Durhams usually ate in the kitchen, but on weekends, they joined their guests. In the backyard Jenna could see Mr. Durham bending over a sprinkler head, but it looked like it was about to rain, so she supposed he'd come in soon. Mrs. Durham had just left for church. "You knew he had to go home sometime, honey," she said, setting her cup in its saucer. "He has a job in San Francisco."

"But he didn't tell me he was leaving. Is he still coming back next weekend?"

Jenna sighed. It was only ten o'clock, but she'd been up since six to oversee breakfast for their guests and any local patrons. Despite her newfound optimism, the lack of sleep was starting to wear her down. Fortunately she'd had a twenty-four-hour reprieve from the nausea. "I can't say for sure. I know that he likes you as much as you like him and that he'll come if he can, okay?"

Ryan nibbled on a piece of toast. "Yeah, he'll come," he announced, suddenly confident.

Tempted to caution her son not to raise his hopes too high, Jenna opened her mouth, but the slamming of the side door turned her attention to Mr. Durham. "Is it raining?" she asked.

"Just started."

"Can I get you some coffee?"

He hung his yellow rain slicker on the coatrack. "I'll take a cup. All the guests gone?"

"We have some late risers in the Ocean View room." She stood and went to the sideboard, where muffins, bacon and scrambled eggs were starting to grow cold and poured him a cup of coffee from a white thermos.

"In the winter breakfast only runs till ten, even on Sundays."

Smiling to herself at Mr. Durham's gruff manner, Jenna brought the coffee back to the table. "They passed on breakfast. I was just about to gather everything up. They might check out after noon, but it doesn't matter if they're a little late. Pamela's cleaning the other rooms already, and we only have one reservation for tonight."

He nodded. "It's been slow. Is Mr. Robertson finished, then?"

The stout cook came through the door just in time to answer the question himself. "The kitchen's nearly clean, but I still have a pan out. Can I make you some eggs?"

Mr. Durham shook his head. "Coffee's enough."

"Jenna, you still hungry?"

"No, thanks. I think Pamela will want her usual toast, though. I'll make it if you're too busy."

"I'll have it waiting for her. No trouble." He surveyed the room as though verifying that breakfast had gone smoothly, then returned to the kitchen. Mr. Durham took his coffee cup and started to follow, but Ryan called after him. "Mr. Durham?"

Adam's grandfather turned and put a work-roughened hand on the boy's shoulder. "It was Pop a few days ago. And what's that frown all about, young man?''

"Adam left," Jenna said.

"So Adam's got us all moonin' over him, eh?" Mr. Durham's eyes crinkled at the corners as he gave Jenna a knowing wink. "He always had a way of making himself the center of the universe. If he knew what was good for him, he'd stay right here where he belongs, but I suppose he'll be back. He comes every now and then."

Ryan propped his chin on his hand. "Did he say goodbye to you?"

Mr. Durham laughed. "He left a note for us, same as you."

"A note?" The possibility that Adam hadn't simply disappeared without a parting word seemed to revive the boy's spirits. He dropped his fork and scrambled to his feet. "I didn't see a note. Where is it?"

"Gram set it on your bed while you were taking your bath."

Jenna looked sternly at her son. "If you'd made your bed like you're supposed to, you'd have found it right away." She winced, realizing how much she sounded like the stereotypical mother.

Ryan didn't seem to hear her, anyway. He dashed up the stairs at the same time the bell above the front door jingled. Expecting someone interested in renting a room or checking out the inn, Jenna rounded the corner to see Laura Wakefield setting a dripping umbrella in the stand by the door. The smell of salt air and moist dark earth accompanied her.

"Laura! What a nice surprise!" Jenna crossed the room and gave her old friend a hug. "I thought you had the flu. What brings you out in the rain? You make me feel guilty. I should be visiting *you* with chicken soup, and here you are.''

Laura smiled. ''I'm better now. Besides, I heard something that would have gotten me up off my deathbed—'' she waggled a finger at Jenna ''—something I thought you would've told me yourself.''

''About me?'' Jenna gazed into Laura's face, wondering how she'd already heard that Dennis had been picked up by the police, when the sparkle in her friend's eye let her know it was something else entirely. ''Oh, you heard Adam was back.''

Laura's highly arched brows rose in unison. ''Don't say it so casually, Jen. There has to be more to the story than, 'Oh yeah.' You guys were the hottest thing back in high school.''

To avoid having Laura spout something she'd rather Mr. Durham or Mr. Robertson not hear, Jenna dragged her through the hall to the back door, which wasn't difficult. Laura weighed less than a hundred pounds and felt more like a cardboard tilt-up than a solid human being. ''Come on,'' Jenna said. ''Let's go to my studio.''

When they reached the old gardening shed, Jenna turned on the light to compensate for the lack of sun, closed the door and waved Laura onto a stool. ''I guess I should have offered you breakfast or a cup of coffee first...''

''I'm only hungry for the juicy details. With my sorry love life, I'm hoping to live vicariously through you. Why didn't you *tell* me Adam was here when we talked on the phone?''

''I didn't want you to think I cared about him.''

''You knew I'd see right through you, you mean! Of course you care. I ran into Adam in town when he was here a couple of years ago, and I have to tell you, those tight buns of his would make any woman drool.''

Jenna smiled in agreement, picturing the straight back that went with those buns, and the long muscular legs. ''No one looks better in a pair of jeans.''

''What I want to know is, does he look as good out of them?'' Laura pushed her Ralph Lauren glasses up on her nose. Despite her angular features and bony limbs, she was attractive in a clean fresh sort of way. She had shoulder-length brown hair with red highlights, gold-flecked eyes and a wide expressive mouth.

''He does,'' Jenna admitted, feeling wonderfully wicked at the memory of him dressing in front of her. ''Actually he looks even better.''

''Oh, my gosh, you guys did the deed again!'' Laura jumped off her stool. ''What was it like after all these years? Is he the same?''

Jenna put up a hand to slow her friend. ''We did not *do the deed*. I don't want to get involved with anyone right now. I saw him getting dressed—by accident. And he kissed me once. That's all.''

Crossing her arms over her flat chest, Laura frowned and settled back on her seat. ''That's disappointing, Jen. Just a kiss? You didn't give him anything else?''

With a shrug Jenna let her gaze wander to the stained-glass pieces hanging from the ceiling or resting on easels. She trusted Laura like a sister, but she still wasn't willing to admit that her attraction to Adam was as strong as ever. Right now her plans didn't include any man. She was going to pour all her energy—all the energy this pregnancy would allow—into her craft. ''I gave him one of my windows. Does that count?''

Laura made a noise resembling a snort. ''Some of us don't know how to make the best of the opportunities that come our way. You guys were meant to be. Even I could see that.''

Jenna was going to tell her friend about the latest developments with Dennis when something she should have noticed the moment she stepped into the studio distracted her.

Laura snapped her fingers in front of Jenna's face. ''What are you thinking about, Jen? You're not with me anymore.''

Jenna frowned. ''I'm sorry. It's just that, well, nothing's missing. I told him he could take his pick of things out here, but... Wait!'' Hopping to her feet, she hurried to the back cupboards where she kept the flannel-wrapped piece she called *The Cove*.

It was gone.

Turning back to Laura, she let the smile that tempted her lips go wide and turn into a laugh. ''Damn! He took my favorite.''

''What?''

''My favorite window. He remembers it!''

Laura was beginning to lose patience. ''He remembers what?''

''That it's our beach. I bet he knew all along.''

CHAPTER NINE

THOUGH THE OFFICES in the expensive high-rise on Montgomery Street were officially closed on Sundays, Adam recognized several cars in the parking garage as those belonging to other attorneys in the firm. Fortunately, he didn't see Mike's blue BMW. After the days he'd spent in Jenna's unsettling company, he was in no mood to deal with his partner. He would have avoided the office until tomorrow, except that he needed today to sort through what had piled up in his absence—without the distraction of ringing telephones, staff meetings, court dates or client demands.

Briefly he'd stopped off at home to eat and rest. Then he'd showered and shaved and donned something more comfortable than the suit he normally wore to work and headed off again. But he still felt a little rough around the edges. His eyes were bloodshot and gritty; his head ached.

Juggling the stained-glass window, he reached into the pocket of his khakis for the key card that would let him into the building. Behind him car exhaust hovered over the busy street, a horn sounded, and someone cursed a pedestrian.

Adam smiled. San Francisco. City by the bay. It was good to be home.

He stepped into a lobby of elegant beige marble, which echoed like a vault when the door closed behind him. The squeak of his rubber-soled shoes accompanied him to a bank of elevators along the far wall, where gleaming silver doors whooshed open almost as soon as he pressed the button.

On the sixteenth floor, Adam used another key to open the tall heavy door to his firm's offices. Decorated in mauve, gray and black, the reception area was furnished with black leather chairs arranged near glass tables. Modern prints lined the walls. The desk that sat in the center of the room, polished to a high gloss, was empty, waiting for the receptionist who answered phones during the week.

Knowing he'd find most of his messages on his voice mail, he gave his slot behind the receptionist's desk only a cursory check and found a small envelope addressed simply "Adam." He stuck it in the flap of his briefcase and made his way through the maze of corridors, past the cubicles where the paralegals and other support staff worked.

When he reached his expansive corner office, he stood at the threshold, eyeing the towers of files, law books and thick stapled documents piled on the walnut desk he had purchased from an antique dealer more than a year ago. He shouldn't have taken more than a day off. He'd probably have to spend all night catching up.

Then it occurred to him that something was different.

Pivoting to scan the anteroom that served as Cheryl's office, he realized immediately what it was: her workspace was cleaner and emptier than the receptionist's desk out front. No neat printouts in the plastic cradle of her printer. No case files stacked next to the phone. No personal items whatsoever. The picture of Cheryl's son in his baseball uniform was gone, along with her glass jar filled with Hershey's Kisses and the pathetic plant he usually watered because she never remembered to do it herself.

What had happened?

Leaning Jenna's framed window carefully against the wall, he crossed to Cheryl's desk and checked the drawers to find nothing more than a few paper clips, a box of staples and blank paper with the company letterhead.

"Hi, Adam. I thought it was you."

Adam glanced up to see Roger standing in the outer doorway. Wearing his tie loose and a wrinkled shirt unbuttoned at the collar, he looked like he'd spent the night at the office and worked all day, besides. "What happened to Cheryl?"

Roger squeezed the back of his own neck. "You'll have to talk to Mike about that."

"Mike's not here. And I want to know *now*."

Roger's brows rose almost as high as his receding hairline. "I think she quit. That's my guess, anyway."

"Guess, my ass." Adam slammed through the rest of Cheryl's drawers, but saw nothing to indicate what had happened to his secretary of nearly ten years. "You keep track of everything that goes on around here. What happened? Did Mike fire her?"

The smaller man shrugged narrow shoulders. "You know how Mike can be, Adam. Maybe she wasn't doing her share. She was always the first to head home come five o'clock."

"That's not true, but even if it was, she's a single mother. She needs to spend time with her kid."

"Still, it's been a long time since I put in a mere forty hours. I'm married to this shit."

"And you're compensated for doing it. Cheryl wasn't."

"Maybe, but now that I've got the Whitehead case on top of everything else…"

Adam heard the accusation in Roger's voice, despite the false humility, and felt his muscles tense. "Don't play games, Roger. You wanted the Whitehead case. It was one more way to score some points with Mike. What I don't understand is where you think you're going with all your ass-kissing. If you're looking at partner, you should know there are no empty seats. By Mike's own decree, the limit is four. We won't take on anyone else until someone either dies or retires."

For a moment Roger let the congenial facade slip, and Adam glimpsed raw ambition. "Or is asked to leave," he said calmly, and walked away.

Adam stared at the empty space beyond the door for several seconds, his hands bunched into fists. He wanted to chase the little prick down and kick his ass the way he deserved. But the other man didn't have the brainpower to be much of a threat, and Adam wouldn't give him the satisfaction of provoking a fight.

Glancing back at Cheryl's empty desk, he sighed heavily and remembered the note he'd retrieved from the receptionist's desk. Taking it out of his briefcase, he tore open the envelope and pulled out a sheet of his secretary's monogrammed stationery. It said simply, "Call me."

IT WAS DARK before Adam looked up from the Thompson file to check his watch. He'd put in a good eight hours of reading correspondence and preparing court documents, and he was hungry and tired. He glanced at the telephone, considered trying to get Cheryl again, then decided eleven o'clock was too late to bother her. He'd left several messages on her answering machine already.

Rolling back in his chair, he stood and stretched his aching muscles. The stained-glass cove faced him from where he'd propped it against the coffee table not far away, and in the quiet of the near-empty building, he could virtually hear the splash of the ocean as he stared at the blue and green of the waves. Did Jenna have talent?

Adam wasn't a stained-glass expert, but to his untrained eye, she did.

He was surveying his own tall windows, trying to decide where to hang Jenna's work, when the telephone rang.

He leaned over and snatched up the receiver. "Bernstein and Lowe."

"Adam? It's Cheryl."

Adam sat on the corner of his desk. "I've been trying to reach you all day."

"I know. I just got back. I took my son to see his grandparents in Santa Clara."

"I got your note. And I saw your desk. If Mike fired you, Cheryl, I'll make arrangements to hire you back. You don't have to worry about anything—"

"No, Adam. No one fired me."

"What?" Adam changed the phone to his other ear.

"I left on my own. I just couldn't take it anymore— the long hours, Mike's short fuse, the office politics. Life's too short, you know what I mean?"

Adam fingered the crease in his khakis. "What if I promised you things would be different, ensured a strict forty hours and gave you a raise?"

"I knew you'd offer to make things better, but I've

thought it all through and decided I've already waited too long to tell you something you ought to know.''

"What's that?"

"I only stayed at Bernstein and Lowe the number of years I did because of you. I watched you date other women, but nothing long-term ever developed—'' she drew what sounded like a bolstering breath ''—and I hoped one day you'd think of me.''

Adam ran a self-conscious hand through his hair. "You mean, in a romantic sense?"

She laughed. "Don't sound so surprised. You're attractive, available, intelligent, and you're great with my son. He still talks about you from the last office party we had, and while I may not be a raving beauty, I know I'm not bad. I think we have a solid foundation for a relationship. We like each other, respect each other. So I decided I was being stupid to hang on at Bernstein and Lowe when it wasn't really what I wanted. And as long as I sat behind that desk outside your office, I knew you'd continue to look right past me. So I did what I've wanted to do for a long time and quit.''

Adam struggled to think of an appropriate response, but it took a few seconds for the pendulum of his emotions to swing all the way from blaming Mike for Cheryl's dismissal to believing his secretary had actually abandoned her post for very personal reasons, reasons that centered on him. "Cheryl, I never had a clue.''

"I left tons of clues. I baked your favorite cake every year for your birthday, bought you ties for Christmas, shopped for your grandmother's Mother's Day gift, picked up your dry cleaning…''

"You said you were going there, anyway.''

"That's not the point. The signs were there if you wanted to see them."

Letting his breath seep out, Adam pinched the bridge of his nose. What could he say to avoid hurting someone he cared about? "I'm sorry, Cheryl. I think you're a smart sexy woman…"

"But? And don't tell me you're gay. I've seen you with too many women to believe that."

"No, I'm not gay. And you're great. I've just never thought of you in that light."

"Because I'm a single mother? Does the responsibility of my son frighten you?"

Adam thought of Jenna and Ryan, and the new baby in Jenna's womb, and knew he answered honestly when he said, "No. I love kids. I'd like to have a few of my own someday."

"Then if you're okay with my situation, why don't you come over?"

"Tonight?" His voice cracked on the word and he had to clear his throat because something about Cheryl's tone told him she wasn't interested in watching television together.

"It's not like we don't know each other, Adam. We've been friends for longer than most marriages last. What do you say?"

That I feel like you just leveled a shotgun at me and fired both barrels. "It's late. I don't think that would be a good idea, Cheryl."

"We don't work together anymore."

"True, but—"

"Adam, if you're not interested, then come over for *me,* all right? I'm feeling like a fool after confessing what I have. Don't reject me on top of it." She drew another audible breath. "God, listen to me. I'm not *that* repulsive, am I?"

"No. Of course you're not. That's the last thing I want you to think."

"Then come over. Please. I'll be waiting for you."

RYAN PRESSED a cool rag to Jenna's neck as she slumped dejectedly over the toilet. The nausea was back. She'd tried crackers, pickles, ice cream—any and all food even jokingly recommended for pregnancy— but it was no use. Nothing stayed down and everything tasted worse coming back up.

"Mom, what's wrong with you?" Ryan's eyes reflected his worry as he stood over her, wearing his pajamas. The two of them had fallen asleep on Jenna's bed while reading together around ten o'clock, and a couple of hours later, when Jenna had had to make a dash to the bathroom, Ryan had stumbled after her. Now he looked wide awake and positively frightened.

"It's nothing, honey." She knew she couldn't lie to him forever. She wanted to explain her situation to him and the Durhams, but part of her still couldn't believe she carried a baby. So she was waiting. For what, she didn't know. To make sure. To see what happened.

"With my luck I'd tell everybody and then have a miscarriage," she muttered to herself. Wincing at the cowardice of that statement, she quickly replaced the negative thought with the tender vision of holding her new baby. This was the child she'd prayed for, the one she'd wanted for so long. She'd just never expected the pregnancy to come at such an awkward time in her life.

"Did you say something?" Ryan hovered nearby, offering her a glass of water.

"No, nothing." She took the water and rinsed her

mouth, then pushed away from the toilet to sit back against the wall. She was just over three months along. Many women reported feeling better during their second trimester. She had with Ryan and could only hope she would this time, too. But, God, she was growing to hate the bathroom wallpaper.

"There's something I need to talk to you about, honey," she said. Ryan had school in the morning and needed to get some sleep, but Jenna decided the truth would be kinder than sending him to bed fearing something worse.

Soberly he put the glass on the tile counter and sat down next to her, cross-legged.

"Mommy's not sick, Ryan. I mean, I am sick, but it's nothing serious. It's just that I'm...we're going to have an addition to our little family."

"What?" He blinked at her in confusion.

"I'm going to have a baby."

His brown eyes opened wide, and Jenna tried to decide exactly what was going on behind them. She was about to lay a hand on his arm and try to explain just how this amazing event had come to pass, with no man in their lives, when a huge smile broke across her son's face. "Is Adam the daddy?" he asked excitedly. "Does this mean he'll be my dad, too?"

Jenna gulped at the unexpected question. *No, Adam is only the man I wish was the daddy.* "Adam's not the father. Adam is only our friend. This baby was made a few months ago. It has the same daddy as you."

Ryan slumped as his gaze lowered to her belly. "Is my dad going to come back for the baby?"

"No. The baby will live with us. Dennis doesn't know about it, and I don't want to share the news with him yet, okay? I didn't realize I was pregnant until I started getting sick. Sometimes moms don't feel so great when they're going to have a baby. It was the same way when I was carrying you.''

"Are you happy about the baby?" he asked, as though trying to decide how he should feel about this new development himself.

Jenna put her arms around her son and pulled him close. "There's nothing more wonderful in the world than having a child to share your life with. I found that out with you, right?"

Ryan nodded, but absentmindedly. "Will it be a boy?"

Jenna shrugged. "Would you like a brother?"

"A sister would be just as good. When will she get here?"

"Not for six months or so, probably sometime in April."

"Oh." He continued to consider her, then finally asked, "How do moms get pregnant?"

The inevitable question. At least it wasn't, "How did *you* get pregnant?" At eight Ryan was just old enough to understand the basics, and Jenna knew it was time she told him. She went through an edited version of human mating, building on the little bits she'd told him in the past and trying not to do such a thorough job that he immediately tied this baby to the last time Dennis had shown up at their rental house drunk.

But she shouldn't have worried. When she finished, Ryan merely scrunched up his nose and said, "Yuck."

And Jenna smiled in relief.

ADAM SHOVED HIS HANDS in his pockets and stared at the phone. Cheryl had hung up after telling him to

come over, and he'd been left pacing the floor in front
of his desk, wondering what to do. Minutes were slipping by. It was now nearly midnight. If he delayed
much longer, she'd have reason to be offended even if
he did show up.

What's my problem? he wondered.

He hadn't been lying when he told Cheryl she was
an attractive woman. And he knew he wasn't the only
man to think so. He'd seen plenty of clients and other
attorneys do a double take when they saw her. He'd
teased her about the attention before; he'd just never
felt the romantic spark that would cause him to look
at her in quite that way.

Still, he cared enough about Cheryl to do almost
anything to avoid hurting her. He particularly hated the
idea of humiliating her.

His poor secretary was lonely enough to lay her feelings out on the table. He could certainly give her a
little pleasure and security, couldn't he? What was
wrong with him? After his sexually frustrating weekend with Jenna, he should jump at the chance.

Yet something kept him from leaving the office. He
told himself it was the emotional entanglements that
were sure to follow, but deep down he knew he had a
bigger reason for holding back. He wanted another
woman. One with dark hair and blue eyes, breasts just
large enough to fill his hands, a warm responsive
body—and another man's baby in her belly.

Was he a fool? Jenna had more than her share of
problems right now, problems that would be his if he
pursued any kind of relationship with her. And beyond
the issues of Dennis and the baby, Adam wasn't sure
she'd ever be willing to trust him again. She'd made it

abundantly clear that she didn't even want to try, at least not now. So where did that leave him?

In a damn awkward spot. He cursed and stabbed a hand through his hair. Then Jenna's stained-glass cove drew his eye, once again evoking the powerful emotions he'd felt that day on the beach. Every moment was engraved on his mind, like the Indian petroglyphs that had survived on cave walls for thousands of years.

And he didn't *want* to forget. He wanted to know the same joy again—with the same woman. Which meant he had to give Jenna some reason for coming to San Francisco and becoming familiar with his life.

Suddenly Adam rounded the desk with decisive steps. Picking up the phone, he dialed an old friend he'd originally met as a client—an old friend who happened to own a small artsy tourist shop located just off Fisherman's Wharf.

"Hello?" Sleep filled the voice on the other end of the line, and Adam felt a flicker of guilt for calling so late.

"Harvey?"

"Yeah? Who is this? Is it morning?"

"It's Adam Durham."

"Durham? As in attorney-at-law? Shit, don't tell me I'm in trouble again."

"You'd know that before I would," Adam said on a chuckle.

Harvey yawned. "What is it, then? What would make a sane man drag a poor working bugger like me out of bed at…what time is it?" There was rustling in the background, then Harvey cursed a blue streak. "Shit, Durham, it's midnight. I've only been asleep for half an hour, and I have to meet a supplier at the store at five-thirty in the morning. This had better be good."

"I need a favor, Harvey," Adam said, then smiled at his friend's resigned sigh.

"Fine. Just tell me what the hell it is so I can get back to sleep."

"YOU LOOK TIRED this morning, dear." Mrs. Durham glanced up from her breakfast as Jenna entered the kitchen wearing her running clothes.

At the end of the table Mr. Durham folded his paper down far enough to verify his wife's words, but didn't comment.

"I didn't sleep too well," Jenna said.

Ryan sat, all dressed and ready for school, across from Mrs. Durham, who still wore her pink bathrobe, bedroom slippers and a net over her hair. "Sometimes moms get sick when they're going to have a baby," he announced matter-of-factly.

He shoveled another spoonful of Rice Krispies into his mouth, then talked through his food. "She'll be better in a few weeks, when the baby's bigger. Won't you, Mom?"

Jenna coughed to hide her panic. She'd planned to tell the Durhams soon, but she'd wanted to wait for the right opportunity. Launching such stunning news on them without any warning didn't seem fair, especially because they couldn't feel free to react honestly with Ryan in the room.

The newspaper crackled again as Mr. Durham folded it and set it aside. Mrs. Durham's spoon hung in her hand, suspended between her bowl and her mouth. Would they still want her to manage the Victoriana? Would she and Ryan be faced with another move in the next few months? A lengthy job search?

"Actually I've been wanting to talk to the two of

you," Jenna said. "I only found out myself a few days ago, but I...I..." She felt tears sting her eyes and blinked them back. "It seems I'm going to have a baby."

Mrs. Durham's jaw dropped so fast Jenna almost moved to catch her dentures. "How can you be sure, dear?"

Sensing the sudden shift in the chemistry of the room, Ryan chewed more slowly and watched the adults. Acutely aware of his presence, Jenna knew she had to be careful to show no remorse, only excitement about the baby.

"I'm sure." She pasted a tremulous smile on her face and skirted the table to take the empty seat next to her son. "Good news, huh?"

The Durhams exchanged a glance. "We're happy about it if you are, dear."

"Great." Jenna ate in awkward silence. Only Ryan seemed unaffected. He gave each of them a quick kiss on the cheek, grabbed his backpack and headed out to the bus stop as soon as he'd finished eating.

"Can Tommy come over?" he called as he left.

Jenna nodded.

"See you after school."

The slamming of the door echoed in the silence of the big house, and all Jenna could think about was how badly she wanted to bite her nails. She stared down at her French manicure, her weekly reward to herself for not succumbing to the old habit, and tried to keep them on the table.

"So." Mrs. Durham pushed her bowl out of the way and reached across the table to take one of Jenna's hands. "Tell us, are you truly happy about the baby, my dear?"

Jenna didn't know what to say. How could she be happy about a child conceived the way this one had been? Then again, how could she not be pleased about having the baby she'd wanted for so long, regardless of the situation?

A tear fell down her cheek, and she quickly wiped it away. She had so much she wanted to explain to these kind people. Yet the experiences she wanted to share were the same ones she wanted to forget.

"I'll understand if you don't want me here anymore," she said. "I can find work elsewhere in town and...Ryan and me, we'll manage. I can teach glass, karate, work at another inn—"

"Nonsense." Mrs. Durham squeezed her hand with surprising strength. "We love having you here, you and Ryan. And we'll love the new baby. I just can't understand how this happened so fast. Adam was only just here. What's more, I can't believe he'd leave you this way."

"Neither can I," Mr. Durham added. He'd remained grim and silent until then, his mouth a straight slash in his face. "But he'll marry you this time or else. He'll not go running off to San Francisco again."

"Adam?" Jenna blinked. The Durhams thought Adam was the father. A logical assumption, in a way. She and Dennis had been divorced for more than six months, she and Adam had a history together, and Jenna hadn't seen any other man since she'd moved in. What else were they to think?

"No." She stared down at the leather tennis shoes she'd worn with her jogging suit. "It's not Adam's. It's Dennis's. He...he came to see me just before I moved here and—" she fought the cracking of her voice and made herself finish "—and I didn't want him to wake Ryan."

"Oh, you poor dear." Mrs. Durham came to stand beside her. Mr. Durham's chair scraped the floor as he stood, too, but he didn't leave his spot. He just shoved his hands into his pockets as if he didn't know what to do with them.

"Everything will be all right. It doesn't matter who the child's father is. It will be yours, won't it." Mrs. Durham said. "It will be all of ours. And there's nothing so fine as having a little one around."

Jenna felt the older woman's arms go around her, and for the first time since the divorce, she let go— and cried for all the sadness that had piled up inside her since the day she'd married Dennis.

CHAPTER TEN

"I'LL HOLD." Tuesday afternoon Jenna sat on the edge of her bed, kneading her forehead with one hand while clutching the phone to her ear with the other. Ryan was at Tommy's house or on his way there by now, and the Durhams were in their bedroom, resting before dinner. No one was around to witness her anxiety. *Thank goodness.*

"County Courthouse. Deputy Hadley speaking."

Jenna cleared her throat. "Deputy Hadley, this is Jenna Livingston. I was hoping you could tell me whether or not you still have an inmate there named Dennis Livingston."

"I just came on. Let me check."

Elevator music filtered through the phone as Deputy Hadley put Jenna on hold again. A moment later his brisk voice came back on the line. "Livingston was arraigned this morning. They set his court date for Thursday. We're holding him until then. If you'd like to visit, our hours are—"

"No, no thanks." Jenna hadn't realized how tightly she'd been gripping the telephone until that moment. Easing off, she drew a deep breath. "That won't be necessary, Deputy Hadley. I don't plan to visit, but thank you," she said, and hung up.

Dennis was in jail for another two days. How that had happened after what Todd had told her and Adam, she didn't know, but she was grateful. Her ex-husband would get out eventually, and she'd have to face all her old fears when he did, but at least Todd or someone else had managed to give her a short reprieve.

Feeling better than she had in months, she stood to go downstairs and finish making the salad she'd started for dinner. Mr. Robertson only worked Thursday to Sunday, so mid-week they were on their own. The ringing of the phone called her back before she reached the hall.

"Hello?"

"Mrs. Livingston?"

"Yes?"

"This is Harvey LeCourt. I own a store called Local Treasures here in San Francisco. A friend of mine visited Mendocino not long ago and acquired a window you made. I was wondering if I might see more of your work."

"You want to see my work?" she repeated, stunned.

"Yes, I'm always looking for local talent, and I like what I've seen so far."

"Wonderful." Jenna's mind groped for the right words. She wanted to sound professional, confident, but she was so excited she couldn't think straight. "When?"

"I'm going out of town for a few days. Could you meet me at the store a week from Thursday, say, eleven o'clock?"

"Fine."

"Let me give you the address."

Frantically Jenna searched through her nightstand for pen and paper and had to settle for the margin of a book she'd just bought and one of Ryan's dry squeaky markers. "Go ahead."

He rattled off a number and a street name Jenna didn't recognize, then said, "See you then."

The phone clicked and he was gone. Jenna stared at the receiver. The owner of a retail store had requested a meeting with her, had said he liked her work. But such things didn't just drop out of the sky to land in an artist's lap. What piece had Mr. LeCourt seen? And who had shown it to him? She'd sold a number of stained-glass pieces the first month she'd arrived, but business had been slow since then....

Adam. Of course. It had to be him. He had *The Cove* with him, and he lived in the same city as this Mr. LeCourt. A little too coincidental for anyone else to be involved. But Adam was back in his own surroundings now. Why was he bothering to help her?

Going into the small office at the end of the hall, Jenna paused to close the door behind her before thumbing through the Rolodex. She couldn't remember the name of Adam's firm, but fortunately Mrs. Durham listed her grandson's home and work numbers under *A.*

"Bernstein and Lowe," a silky voice crooned when she'd dialed the number.

"Is Adam Durham in?" she asked, committing the number to memory without even trying.

"I'm sorry, Mr. Durham's in court all afternoon— Wait, he just walked in. May I tell him who's calling?"

"Jenna Livingston."

"Just a moment."

Jenna played with the twisted cord of the old-fashioned telephone while she waited. Finally she heard Adam's voice.

"Hi, Jen. How are you?"

"Good. Dennis is in jail until his court date on Thursday."

He whistled. "Todd really does have a crush on you. Are you going to have to go out with him for that little favor?"

"He's not my type, remember?"

"Good. I wouldn't want to bust his nose after he helped us out."

Jenna couldn't resist a grin. "Pretty territorial, considering we're not even friends."

"Who says we're not friends? That kiss you gave me last weekend felt pretty friendly."

Growing uncomfortable with the conversation, Jenna changed the subject. "Thanks for contacting Mr. Harvey."

"How did you know it was me?"

"You don't think I'm very bright, do you?"

"Well, you did marry Dennis—"

"All right. Enough of that. Anyway, I just called to thank you."

"Does that mean you'll visit me when you come to town?"

Jenna paused. She was trying to keep an emotional distance from Adam, which was virtually impossible when there wasn't a physical one, as well. "I don't think I'll have time, but if I do, I'll stop by."

"I'll make it worth your while," he promised.

That was exactly what frightened her. The way she felt about Adam, she'd rather spend the afternoon with him than eating caviar and drinking champagne at the finest restaurant in the world. "Mr. LeCourt said he's going out of town for a few days. He wants me to meet him at his store at eleven o'clock a week from Thursday," she said to fill the awkward silence.

"Perfect. We could do lunch. I know some great places."

"Does that mean you're not coming back here this weekend?"

"Did I say I would?"

"Yes."

"Then I'll be there."

"Ryan's been badgering me to go to the Schwinn dealership, but I don't know anything about mountain bikes. What should I buy?"

"I'll pick him up a bike. You worry too much, Jen. And you have no confidence in me whatsoever."

She laughed. "I have more confidence in you than I do in me." *Who knows what I might concede if I'm around you too much?*

"Sometimes you've got to trust your instincts."

"Exactly," Jenna said, and hung up.

She wouldn't visit Adam when she went to San Francisco, she told herself, sitting back in Mr. Durham's leather chair. It was too dangerous. She'd be out of her element and away from Ryan, whose very presence reminded her why she had to be sensible. She wasn't about to turn her life upside down for any man, least of all a guaranteed heartbreaker. Not when she and Ryan had come this far.

She rubbed her abdomen. *And not when they still had so far to go.*

DENNIS LIVINGSTON studied the gaunt face of the district attorney as his public defender conferred with her in a corner of the small Fort Bragg courtroom. Suddenly the hum of their voices stopped, and the skinny bitch sent a meaningful glance his way. Then she nodded. Evidently they'd reached an agreement, but it had sure taken them long enough.

The lawyer the court had appointed to defend him ambled back to where Dennis waited, several rows away from the judge's bench, and leaned over the chair between them. In the background, the judge dealt with another case, and several other unlucky bastards waited for their turn before the bench.

"I've got good news, Mr. Livingston," he said. "Because you have no prior convictions, the DA's willing to go for twelve days' jail time, one-third off for time served, *if* you stay away from Ms. Livingston and have no contact with her."

"Jail time!" Dennis felt a flicker of panic. "You call that good news? I've already been in for five days. You told me violating a restraining order was only a misdemeanor."

The lawyer shrugged. "It's also a court order. Judges can take it quite personally when someone disregards their orders. And the arresting officers filed an affidavit stating that they think you're a serious threat to your ex-wife." He stood and straightened his tie. "I recommend you take the deal. You plead guilty, you'll be out in a week."

Dennis stretched his neck. Since the police had picked him up, he'd had little sleep and less peace, and he wanted a drink so badly he'd have lapped it up from the floor like a dog if he could. Seven days sounded like an eternity, especially when he was certain Adam Durham was screwing his wife. His *wife*, dammit! How could some paper filed by a lousy attorney who didn't know either of them change thirteen years of marriage? How could Jenna leave him and never look back, deny him the right to see his own kid? He'd thought she'd stand by him....

No, he'd always known that in her heart of hearts she loved Adam. She'd denied it for years, had lain beneath him when he'd made love to her and pretended to enjoy it, but Dennis knew how it really was. And now Adam was back and Jenna was gone, and someone was going to pay for destroying his life!

"Mr. Livingston?"

Taking a deep breath, Dennis rubbed his hands against the orange jumpsuit the police had given him when they'd booked him into the Ukiah jail, an hour and a half away from Fort Bragg and Mendocino. "I just wanted to see my kid," he complained.

"That's beside the point, Mr. Livingston. You violated a court order. Will you take the deal? If you don't, you could spend a year in county jail, receive a thousand-dollar fine, or both."

The attorney glanced at his fancy gold watch.

"What? You got somewhere you'd rather be?" Dennis snapped, knowing his lawyer didn't give a shit if he spent the rest of his life behind bars.

"Making an enemy out of me isn't going to help you. Will you take the deal or not?"

Dennis looked at the district attorney, the judge and the face of his own indifferent defender, and wanted to tell them all to go to hell. But it was Jenna's fault. She'd been out to get him for years, and now she had that cop on her side. But her old pal Todd wouldn't do her any good, not in the long run, because they couldn't hold him forever. A week. That was what the man had said.

Then Jenna would be the one to pay.

"I'll take it."

ON FRIDAY AFTERNOON, Adam sat in the parking lot of Bay City Bicycle Works and waited for Cheryl to meet him. He hadn't talked to her since the previous Sunday, the night she'd wanted him to come over and he'd finally called back to tell her he couldn't. She'd accepted the news in silence and hung up, but she hadn't returned any of his calls since. He was hoping she'd respond to the invitation he'd left on her answering machine to come today, as proof she'd forgiven him.

He checked his watch. If he put off his bike-shopping much longer, he'd be stuck in traffic for hours by the time he left his house for Mendocino. Evidently Cheryl wasn't going to soften up and let them continue as friends, which, after ten years, was a pity.

Still, Adam didn't know how he could have handled the situation any better.

Stepping out of his car, he pushed a button on his key ring that locked the doors. He still wore his suit, but he'd loosened his tie, having no intention of returning to the office. He'd already put in a long week, but planned to take a few files with him to work on over the weekend.

"Did you think I wasn't going to show?"

Adam turned to see Cheryl in her white Ford Taurus pulling into the parking lot. "Are you kidding?" he called back. "I knew you couldn't stay mad at me."

She rolled her eyes, parked and got out of the car. She was wearing jeans and a pink sweater, and she was alone. Adam had expected her to bring her son.

"Where's Jason?"

"A friend invited him to stay the night."

Putting an arm around her, Adam gave his old secretary a casual squeeze, hoping to defuse the sudden awkwardness between them. "What made you decide to forgive me?" he asked.

A sheepish smile curved her lips. "I realized you were right. Hearing what you had to say about this Jenna person would have hurt a *lot* more in the morning."

"I'm sorry."

She shrugged. "Things like this happen, or we wouldn't have half the good movies, songs, poetry and books we've enjoyed over the years. What I can't understand is why you wanted me to meet you at a bike store in the middle of the afternoon. Why aren't you at work?"

"The temp the agency sent over drove me away. She cooked fish in the microwave for lunch and stunk up the offices. She clicks her nails whenever we have a conversation. And I don't think she's ever seen a computer. The work is backing up." He sighed. "Are you sure you don't want your old job back?"

"Yes. Are you sure you're not saying all this just to make me feel better?"

"Did I mention she snorts when she eats? I've never heard anyone make more noise over a chocolate-chip cookie."

"Okay." Cheryl laughed. "No one could make *that* up. I should've given you two weeks' notice, but I just couldn't take one more day. And I'm not coming back. I'm going to move closer to my parents and get a job there."

"I'll give you a letter of recommendation, of course." Adam sobered. "In the meantime, do you have enough to get you by?"

"I've put some money aside. We should be all right."

"If you need anything—"

"I know, you'll help me, which is another reason I couldn't stay mad at you. You've got a good heart."

"Don't let that get around." He opened the door for her to precede him inside. "Let me know when packing time comes, and I'll help you move the heavy stuff."

"*If* you're not in Mendocino." She gave him a playful punch in the arm and turned to study a shiny blue bike hanging from the ceiling. "You still haven't told me what we're doing here, but I have a sneaking suspicion it's got something to do with the woman you mentioned on the phone, this Jenna you want a second chance with."

"Nope, not her. Her son. I'm taking Ryan on his first mountain-bike ride tomorrow and he needs a bike. I thought I'd buy Jason one at the same time, as a sort of going-away present to the two of you for giving me ten long years of your professional life."

"You should've told me! I would have brought him."

Adam raised an eyebrow. "You weren't speaking to me, remember?"

She grinned. "I respond to bribes."

A skinny young man sporting bleached-blond hair and four earrings in one ear, a Sex Wax T-shirt and pants big enough to fit the infamous fat man who had to be buried in a piano box, approached Adam. "Help you, dude?"

Adam smiled. Apparently casual fashions had outdistanced him. He could see nothing appealing in wearing his pants belted around his knees. "We're looking for two mountain bikes, one for an eight-year-old boy and the other for—"

"A ten-year-old," Cheryl finished for him. "Are you sure you want to do this?" she asked Adam as the salesclerk directed them through racks of sportswear to a row of smaller bikes along one wall.

"Would you rather have something else?"

"No, Jason's been wanting a bike for a couple of years, and now that we're moving, he'll actually have a place to ride it."

"Then it will serve as the thank-you I want it to be."

Taking Adam's arm, Cheryl pulled him to a stop, regardless of the salesclerk bouncing ahead of them. "This Jenna is one lucky lady. I hope she knows that," she said.

Adam grinned. "Maybe I could use you as a reference."

THE DOOR HADN'T even slammed shut when Ryan rushed in from school and hollered, "Has anyone heard from Adam? Is he still coming?"

On the phone Jenna covered the receiver and called to her son to keep his voice down and to join her in the kitchen. He breezed through the swinging door with a gust of youthful energy, flung his backpack into a chair and went straight to the refrigerator, where he stared inside as though he was seeing his favorite cartoons, instead of several cartons of milk.

"I'm sorry, Todd. Ryan just got home from school. What were you saying?" Jenna asked.

"Todd?" Ryan interrupted. "Who's Todd?"

Jenna put a finger to her lips to indicate silence and turned her attention back to the police officer.

"I said I appeared for Dennis's court date. He got another week," Todd said.

"I'll bet that went over big."

"Actually he looked rather contrite."

Contrite? In fact, Jenna had seen Dennis contrite a number of times. Problem was, his humility only lasted until the next drinking spree. Knowing Ryan was now listening to the conversation and had no idea his father was in jail, Jenna amended what she would have said. "Good. Maybe this situation has given him some time to think."

"We were lucky he had Judge Rubio. He takes domestic violence pretty seriously. As things stand, I'd say a week in jail would give any normal man second thoughts about violating a restraining order."

Should she explain that Dennis had checked out of "normal" more than four years ago?

"Mom, can I have this?" Ryan held up a soft drink, and Jenna shook her head.

"Fruit," she mouthed, then spoke into the mouthpiece. "I called the courthouse in Fort Bragg the day he was arraigned."

"I know. Hadley said you had. That's why I haven't gotten back to you sooner."

"Thanks, Todd. Let's hope our, um, friend has learned his lesson."

"I'm sure he has, but once he gets out I'll drive by the Victoriana occasionally, just to make sure everything's okay."

When Jenna hung up she faced her son's scowl over being denied a soda in favor of an apple.

"Why can't I have both?" he whined.

"Because one is good for you and the other isn't." Jenna put down the pen she'd been doodling with and stood.

"Where's Mr. Robertson? He always has a snack for me on Fridays."

"He's running a little late today, but he'll be here soon. Don't tell me he's giving you soda before dinner."

Ryan frowned. "Only if I eat some fruit or vegetables first."

"Great. Eat some carrot sticks. I'll scrape them for you if you want."

He let loose an exaggerated sigh, relinquished the can of pop to the refrigerator and snagged an apple. "Is Adam still coming?"

Jenna opened her mouth to say she thought so when Mrs. Durham entered the room and answered in more certain terms. "He called this morning to say he'll be here for dinner."

"He did?" Jenna and Ryan spoke at the same time, and Mrs. Durham chuckled.

"It would be interesting to know which one of you is more excited," she said as Ryan dashed outside, no doubt to keep his eyes peeled for the black Mercedes.

"I'm not excited," Jenna protested. "I'm relieved. I was afraid he'd disappoint Ryan."

There was a twinkle in Adam's grandmother's eyes as she started taking food out of the refrigerator and placing it on the counter. "Well, I, for one, am glad to have him back. We haven't seen Adam twice in one week for years, so we must have something new to attract him."

"An endearing eight-year-old boy," Jenna volunteered.

"And his attractive mother."

"Pregnant mother," Jenna corrected, but Mrs. Durham shrugged her words off with a laugh.

"We'll see who interests him more," she said, and started dinner.

CHAPTER ELEVEN

AT TWILIGHT, Adam parked next to a Toyota Land Cruiser in the Victoriana's guest lot, relieved to have left San Francisco before traffic became a problem and more eager than he should have been to be in Mendocino. For years he'd felt like he'd escaped his small hometown in favor of the big city. Now he felt just the opposite—as if he'd escaped the city for the peace and comfort of home. He was changing. He didn't know if all the changes were good, but he did know that his interpretation of personal success was no longer strictly attached to his profit-and-loss statement.

Cutting the engine, he admired the Land Cruiser. Should he trade in the Mercedes for something bigger? He'd bought the car only six months earlier, but a two-seater suddenly seemed so impractical.

"Adam!" Ryan came running from the house.

Adam left his bags and started up the lawn to meet him. "I brought you something, squirt!" he announced, mussing the boy's hair.

Ryan skidded to a halt in front of him and stared, wide-eyed, at the Mercedes. Two bike tires, one large, one small, protruded from the rack attached to Adam's trunk. "Is it a bike?"

Adam laughed. "I would have wrapped it, but a bike doesn't easily lend itself to concealment."

Ryan raced to the car and touched the red frame of

the smaller mountain bike. "Wow, this one's even better than Tommy's!" he breathed as Adam joined him. "Can I ride it?"

"Sure. I've got a helmet for you. Just stay here in the lot and watch for any cars that might turn in."

"I'll be careful."

Adam unhooked Ryan's bike and adjusted the seat to fit him, then retrieved the new aerodynamic helmet from the passenger seat of his car. "Go ahead and get used to the bike now. That way you'll be comfortable with it tomorrow."

"Okay!" Ryan climbed on and began to pedal, his smile big enough to catch flies in his teeth. "This is awesome!" he called.

Adam laughed and retrieved his travel bag. "Bring it onto the porch when you're done. We'll need to lock it up for the night."

Ryan waved and Adam went inside, where several hotel guests were eating by candlelight in the formal dining room to his right. A warm softly lit atmosphere, enhanced by the comforting crackle of a fire, greeted him. He stood in the doorway for a moment, enjoying it, then the smell of steak and mushrooms enticed him to the kitchen. As he'd expected, he found his grandmother and Mr. Robertson there.

"Adam, you made it." The cook greeted him from across the room where he was busy chopping vegetables.

"Safe and sound," Adam told him with a smile.

"How did you get here so early?" Gram turned away from the stove as Adam dropped a kiss on her cheek. "I didn't think you'd arrive until after seven."

"You said you and Mr. Robertson were making my

favorite steak with mushroom gravy. I was so excited, I almost got here for breakfast.''

She shrugged off his words. "You don't need to waste your flattery on us. You can have our steak and mushrooms any weekend. I think this visit is about…other appetites.''

''Don't embarrass me, Gram,'' he teased. ''That kind of thing isn't acknowledged between the generations.''

She laughed. ''Who do you think taught you about the birds and bees?''

Mr. Robertson's knife momentarily stopped its steady thump against the cutting board. ''When you were about ten, I remember answering a few awkward questions myself.''

And Adam remembered asking them. The Victoriana's cook had been almost as permanent a fixture in his life as Gram and Pop. But Adam certainly didn't want to revisit puberty. Feeling a grimace coming on, he stole a morsel of the tender meat Gram was stirring. ''Do we have to go into that?''

''Get your fingers out.'' She smacked the back of his hand with her wooden spoon and reached for a plate. ''Sit down and I'll feed you.''

He smiled, remembering all the meals he'd eaten while watching Gram and Pop and various hired help rush around the inn's kitchen. As a teenager he'd earned money washing dishes for Mr. Robertson. Now the cook stacked dirty plates for the waitress to put in the large dishwasher when she finished out front. ''Where's Pop?'' he asked.

''Fixing a leak under the bathroom sink in the Ocean View room. He'll be coming in search of his dinner any minute.''

"And Jenna?"

"She's in the office, printing up new menus," Robertson answered, going back to his onions. "Nowadays the finer restaurants change all their entrées every couple of weeks."

"And you're not one to be outdone," Adam said.

"No, but I have to admit this new trend is taxing my creative ability to come up with something spectacular and different every two weeks."

"Whatever you make is excellent," Gram told him.

"I second that." Jenna stepped into the kitchen carrying a stack of new menus and wearing a gray jacket and slacks with a white shirt. Simple yet elegant, her clothes looked expensive but probably weren't. Maybe it was the casual way she wore them that appealed to Adam.

"Hi." She sent him a quick smile, then turned to Mr. Robertson. "What do you think? Do you like the new font I used?"

"Very nice."

Adam sat back and listened to the hum of activity in the kitchen while he ate his dinner. He'd driven like a madman to get to Jenna as soon as possible, and now that he was here, he found it difficult to hide his interest.

Her gaze flicked toward him and he smiled. Clearing her throat, she looked at the menus and answered a question put to her by the cook.

Adam could tell his attention was flustering her—which meant she wasn't as indifferent as she pretended to be. Jenna had said she wouldn't wave the white flag, not for him. But Adam was determined to prove her wrong. With any luck he'd have her screaming uncle before the night was through.

FINISHED WITH THE MENUS, Jenna glanced around the kitchen. She'd expected Ryan to stick with Adam from the moment he arrived. So why was Adam here eating alone? "Where's Ryan?"

Christa, the new waitress, breezed into the kitchen to gather the filled plates waiting for her under the food warmer. "He's outside riding his new bike. I can see him through the window. Looks like he's having a blast."

Evidently Adam was serious about taking Ryan mountain biking. Jenna cocked an eyebrow at him but spoke to Christa. "How are you handling your first night?"

"Oh, this is nothing," she said. "You should see how fast I've had to hop in some of the coffee shops I've worked in over the years."

"Well, if you get overwhelmed, just let me know and I'll help."

"Sure." Christa ducked into the dining room, plates in hand, as Adam pushed away from the table.

"Want to go see how Ryan's doing?"

Jenna nodded and followed Adam out, wondering how badly her son's new bike would set her back. Her bank account wasn't too healthy to begin with, but when she was with Adam, practical concerns like money seemed to take on less importance. He'd looked so handsome seated at the table in a denim shirt and jeans, talking and laughing with Gram. The rumble of his voice, the smell of his aftershave and the steadiness of his regard had combined to leave her feeling warm and ready.

Ready for what, Jenna wasn't willing to contemplate.

From the porch she could see Ryan pedaling a shiny new bicycle and smiled at his happy shouts. "Look,

Mom!'' he called and rode up onto the lawn before heading down the opposite side and over a curb.

Jenna held her breath until he made it safely down, then gave Adam a sideways glance, only to find him watching her again. ''That looks like a pretty expensive bike.''

He shrugged. ''Cheap components aren't any good for mountain biking. When you get into mud and water, the gears don't work right. It can be dangerous.''

''But I don't have the money to pay you back for something like that, and it's too expensive to accept as a gift.''

''Then it's a good thing I didn't give it to *you*.'' He moved as close to her as he could without actually touching and leaned against the porch railing.

Able to feel the heat of his body, even through the fabric of her jacket and shirt, Jenna retreated. ''I'll pay you back. When summer comes, the tourists will—''

''Jenna, it's just a bike, for Ryan. It was my idea. I chose to buy it. You don't owe me anything.''

Ryan squealed as he went over the curb again.

''Well…thanks,'' she said. ''I'd better get to work.'' With a final wave to Ryan, she hurried inside.

Adam was different this week, she mused, nervously straightening her jacket. It seemed her refusal last Saturday night hadn't discouraged him. There was no longer any hesitancy in his eyes or his manner. He was pursuing her, cornering her, hoping to conquer, and he was using every weapon at his disposal, all his charm and sex appeal, until Jenna didn't know how most women could withstand him.

Good thing she wasn't most women. She'd been down that road before and didn't like the bumps.

"WHAT YOU IN FOR?" Dennis asked his cell mate. He was long past the point of wanting to keep to himself. The seven days he'd spent inside the beige walls of the county jail had seemed like seven months of living detached from the rest of the world. It amounted to a lot of time to think—and to dry out. He wondered if any of his family had tried to contact him, whether they had any idea where he was, and decided they probably didn't. He'd been on so many binges in the past year they'd never consider looking for him, not even when they hadn't heard from him for several weeks.

His cell mate, a big hairy guy with tattoos covering most of his arms, didn't answer at first. He heaved himself off his cot to take a piss, then ambled to the front of the cell to grip the bars and gaze down the empty hallway. "Assault and battery," he said finally.

"Someone you know?"

"Just a bar fight." With a sigh he moved back to his cot and lay down, propping his great arms beneath his head. "What's your story?"

What did he say? That not long ago he'd had a home, a family, two cars and a decent job? That now he had shit? He remembered the good times with Jenna, before all the moving and fighting and confusion. The years when he'd come home to hot meals, Ryan's exuberance over life's simple pleasures and Jenna, loving, beautiful… He winced at his loss. "Unpaid speeding ticket," he said.

A laugh rumbled from the man's barrel chest. "Yeah, right."

"What are you going to do when you get out?" Dennis asked.

"I'll hit the road again, catch up with my buddies.

I live on my bike, man, just going from town to town. It's freedom in its purest form.''

Drifting didn't sound like freedom to Dennis. It sounded as lonely as his own prospects. God, what had happened to his life? He thought of the rage he'd felt toward Jenna over the past few months and suddenly wondered why—why had he chased her away from him? She'd been the best thing he'd ever had. He'd counted his blessings when Adam walked out on her and he'd been smart enough to step into the gap. But once alcohol caught hold of him...

He eyed his bearded cell mate again. Unless he wanted a similar future, he had to pull himself together. Get rid of the booze. Get Jenna back. He could never rebuild his life without her. She'd always been the strong one.

But how? He had nothing to offer, nothing resembling what Adam could give her. Still, she'd been his wife for thirteen years and had come back to him at least half-a-dozen times. If only he could convince her that he was going clean and sober this time. That spending time in jail had changed him for good. That he was ready to be the dad Ryan deserved.

That was the key, wasn't it? *If only you knew how important a father is to a child...* After what had happened with her own father, Jenna had always been determined to keep their marriage intact, for Ryan's sake.

Dennis smiled as the fear and tension he'd felt during his withdrawal from booze eased for the first time. He'd been ranting and raving and wanting to kill Jenna for leaving him when he already had what it took to get her back.

THE MOON SHIMMERED on the sea, illuminating white foaming waves that splashed up to fling droplets of water in Jenna's face and dampen her clothes. Cold air nipped at her ears and cheeks and fingers until they were nearly numb, but she didn't care. She stood on the farthest rock from the beach she could find and welcomed the embrace of the wind, the sounds of the ocean.

After she'd finished work, she'd found Adam and Ryan curled up together on the sofa, asleep, the movie they'd been watching still playing on the VCR. For a moment she'd tried to figure out how to lift her son and get him to bed without waking Adam, but had finally decided there was no reason to disturb either of them. She knew that Ryan couldn't be safer or more comfortable than he was snuggled against Adam's body. So she'd gone out to walk on the beach.

Feeling a twinge of jealousy that she tried to suppress, Jenna anchored her hair behind her ears. She had to protect herself. She'd been through enough already. A wise woman took control of her life and didn't simply hang on for the ride—not when she had a child to think about.

"Jenna!"

Her name on the wind drew Jenna's attention. Adam stood at the other end of the beach, waving to her, but she didn't budge. What had woken him? How had he found her? Why had he come?

"Jenna, you scared the hell out of me! It's late. Come here!"

Ignoring him, Jenna turned to the vast ocean and sank onto her rock. If she went back, he'd only knock down a little more of the barrier that shielded her heart, a barrier that was starting to crumble already. Just knowing he was so close—knowing they were completely alone in the night—sent her heart thumping wildly against her ribs.

Only the sound of the surf filled her ears during the next few minutes. Had Adam gone back? Jenna hoped so but refused to look, afraid she'd find him waiting for her.

When his arms closed around her, she knew he'd neither waited nor left. He'd come for her. "Let's go back," he whispered against her ear. "You'll catch cold out here."

Still silent, Jenna let him lead her down to the sand, where they paused to stare out over the water.

"It's gorgeous, isn't it?" he asked, clasping her fingers with his own.

Jenna nodded. "How could you leave here so easily, without a backward glance?"

Bringing her hand to his lips, he kissed her palm but didn't answer for a long time. Finally he said, "Aren't you really asking me how I could leave *you* so easily?"

Jenna stared at her feet to hide the hurt, all the while digging the toe of her tennis shoe in the sand. She wanted to say those days were in the past, that they no longer mattered to her, but the words wouldn't come. He was right. Even after all the intervening years, she wanted to know why the boy she'd given her heart and soul to had abandoned her—just like her father had. "Didn't you love me?" she whispered.

He squinted into the darkness. "As much as I was capable of loving."

"Then why?"

He shook his head. "I've asked myself that a million times. I was wrong to hurt you, Jen."

"We were just kids, playing at being adults. I think it's time I realized how young you were when you made that decision," she admitted. "Still, sometimes I wonder how different my life would have been if we'd never met."

A wounded expression flitted across his face before he masked it. "Do you regret being with me that much?"

Jenna paused. Without Adam, she might never have married Dennis. Then again, without Adam, she would never have known the ecstasy of true love.

Rising on tiptoe, she brushed her mouth across his with the lightness of a butterfly's wing. "No. The memories I have of you are some of my very best."

His gaze lowered to her lips, and Jenna held her breath, expecting him to answer her unspoken invitation with a deeper kiss, but he didn't.

"I'm not after a quick tumble in bed for old times' sake, Jenna." His arms went around her, pulling her to him, and his breath was warm on her temple. "I want a second chance."

Splaying her fingers against his chest, Jenna tried to push back and break his hold, but his arms only tightened. For years she'd dreamed of hearing Adam speak those words—and of throwing them back in his face in return for the hurt he'd caused her. Now she surprised herself by finding no pleasure in refusing him.

"Adam, no. It's not that easy. With us it won't be like two people who meet and decide to get to know each other better. We can't start from the beginning, only from where we left off. And the stakes are too high for me to do that. I've just been through a bitter divorce, I'm pregnant and I've got a son who needs some stability in his life. He doesn't need me to get involved with a man right now."

"You mean he doesn't need you to get involved with a man you can't trust."

She stared up at him, trying to measure the sincerity in his eyes, which searched her own. "Why would you want a relationship with someone in my situation? Do you feel responsible for what's happened to me?"

He reached up to keep her hair from flying into her face. "At first I think I did. Maybe on some level I still do, but that's not why I'm asking for this."

"Then why? You've got your practice in San Francisco, probably any number of women who'd love to be with you. Maybe if I wasn't pregnant and was back on my feet and—"

He grimaced. "Listen, Jenna. There's no perfect time to take a risk. Relationships don't come with guarantees."

"From what I've heard, you speak from experience there. Gram and Pop say you haven't dated the same woman for any longer than three months."

"I haven't met anyone in the past fifteen years who's had me clamoring for a marriage license. Does that mean I should stop trying?"

"No, but a long-distance relationship is difficult enough. Add to that children from a prior marriage, especially a new baby, a crazy ex-husband and—"

"And this." His hands slid down her back, pressing her more firmly against him until the curves of her body molded to the hard contours of his. "How will we know if we should be together if we don't go with what feels right?"

Jenna shook her head, consciously fighting the desire to wrap her arms around Adam and never let him go. "I'd have to be a masochist to get into another relationship right now. It's not you I have to learn to trust, it's me. I screwed up so badly with Dennis. Nothing I did worked out right. I couldn't convince him of my loyalty. I couldn't encourage him to succeed in his work. I couldn't—''

''You couldn't stop him from drinking, dammit!'' Adam gripped her chin and tilted it up to make her look at him. ''Dennis is responsible for his own actions. Why are you still blaming yourself?''

''Because I should never have married him. I was still in love with you, and I ruined his life right along with my own!''

Jenna started to sag, and Adam drew her back, supporting her with his strength. ''He knew how you felt about me. He admitted that when I talked to him on the phone. It's not like he went into the marriage blind.''

''The old 'consumer beware' theory, huh?''

''Are my answers that hollow to you now?''

She didn't reply. Closing her eyes against Adam's probing gaze, Jenna turned her face into the hollow of his shoulder.

''We all played a part,'' he said above her head. ''It doesn't help to go around kicking ourselves for the past. We can be together now, Jen. Let's go on from here and see what happens.''

''I know what will happen.''

''What?''

''You won't leave San Francisco and I won't move there. Dead end,'' she said, and this time when she pulled away, Adam let her go.

CHAPTER TWELVE

"SO HE'S BACK?" As Laura's voice blasted over the phone, Jenna flinched and held it away from her ear.

"Yeah, he got here last night," she answered.

"Oh, my gosh! Can I come over? I'm dying to see the two of you together again."

"We're not 'together' and we're not going to be. I've failed in every male relationship I've ever had. Why would I want more of the same?"

"You can't count Dennis."

"Dennis should count more than anyone else. He was my husband! And then there was my father, of course, who left when I was eight and never so much as sent me a Christmas present. My stepfather considered me nothing more than an annoyance, a rival for my mother's love and attention. And Adam took off as soon as he was old enough to leave."

"But what you had with Adam was good."

"While it lasted."

"So what *are* you going to do? Hide out? Nurse your wounds?"

"No, it's called using my head. For now, I'm going to protect myself so that I'll be capable of caring for my children. Maybe when I'm strong enough, in a few years, the right man will come along."

"And how will you know him when you meet him?

I've been thinking the same thing for more than a decade.''

"You've been closeted away, taking care of your father. I can see why you're ready to meet someone. But after living with Dennis, I like being alone. I don't have to answer to anyone. I come and go as I please, with only Ryan to worry about...''

"You're going to have another baby. That's a *lot* to worry about.''

"More than enough. See? You're finally hearing what I'm saying.''

Laura made a noise of frustration and changed tactics. "I understand Adam's rich. Money could definitely make your life easier.''

Jenna tucked the phone between her head and her shoulder so she could continue dusting the bedrooms. "Jeez, Laura, when did you get so opportunistic?''

"It's called practical, and some women are more practical than others.''

"I don't want his money. I want to earn my own. Besides, he lives in San Francisco.''

"So move there. What's wrong with the City by the Bay?''

The smell of lemon sifted through the air as Jenna sprayed wax polish on an Empire-style bureau and began to rub. "What's wrong is it's not Mendocino. I've promised Ryan we won't move again.''

"You said Ryan likes Adam.''

"He does. They're out riding bikes together right now. But what does that have to do with anything?''

"Maybe Ryan'll *want* to move, if it means being closer to his new hero.''

"One week of charm hardly makes Adam a hero. I

want a man who's going to stick around for the long haul, you know what I mean?''

''And you don't think Adam has it in him?''

''I don't know. It's just hard to believe that if we did get together he'd stay very long. He could have been with me before, and he walked away.''

''God, Jenna! People make mistakes. Adam's older now. Maybe this time he'll know what he wants.''

Jenna remembered Adam's words from the previous night and pushed them out of her mind. She wouldn't tell her friend that he'd asked for a second chance. Laura's romantic streak kept her attacking Jenna's resistance enough as it was. ''He knew what he wanted last time. And it wasn't me. Besides, there's got to be something wrong with a man who changes girlfriends almost as often as he changes his underwear.''

''He stayed with you for three years.''

''So he did.''

''And you were happier than I've ever seen you.''

Jenna replaced the dish of potpourri and a hurricane lamp on the bureau she'd been dusting and tried to steer the conversation in a different direction. ''What about you, Laura? What's happening in *your* love life?''

''We're not talking about me.''

Jenna laughed. ''I know, but I'm finished with the Adam subject. I've made up my mind to keep my life simple for the next few years, and that's what I'm going to do.''

''Having a baby without a father isn't simple.''

Mrs. Durham walked into the room and handed Jenna an envelope. ''The mail came while I was on my way back from the store,'' she whispered, and left Jenna to her phone conversation.

"Who was that?" Laura asked.

"Mrs. Durham." Jenna glanced at the letter Adam's grandmother had given her to see who it was from. No return address. Her name, in block letters across the front, was written in a hand Jenna didn't recognize. But the postal stamp indicated it had been mailed in Oregon.

Inside Jenna found a piece of lined paper that had been ripped out of a spiral notebook. One side was filled with Dennis's small printing.

God, didn't the restraining order mean anything to him? He wasn't supposed to contact her, but he had, even from jail. He must have had one of his brothers mail it. They still lived in Oregon; they'd lived there since before Jenna and Dennis graduated from high school.

She tossed the note on the bed as though it had burned her and watched it flutter down with her name staring her in the face. Her ex-husband was getting out of jail. Was he already starting to harass her again? She'd put off thinking about the inevitable approach of Wednesday, but the arrival of his letter reminded her with unmistakable clarity.

"Listen, Laura, I'd better run," she said. "If you'd like to see Adam, feel free to come by. I don't know how long he's staying, but my guess is he'll be leaving in the morning."

Laura paused. "You sound funny. Are you all right?"

"Fine. Just busy."

"Good. Maybe I'll see you later, okay?"

"That'd be great."

After Laura hung up, Jenna stared at the letter awaiting her on the bed. What now? A plea for money? Another threat?

Bending slowly, she retrieved the letter and began to read.

Dear Jenna,

I know you probably don't want to hear from me right now and I can't blame you. I've been such a jerk. I'm so sorry, babe. I've spent almost a week sitting in this cell doing nothing but thinking about how badly I've screwed up our lives. And thinking about my son. You've told me so many times how much he needs a good father. I just didn't hear you.

But that's all over, Jenna. I swear this time I'm giving up the bottle. As soon as I get out of here, things are going to be different. I'm going to prove to you that I can still be the kind of man you thought I was when you married me. If I do that, if I stay sober and show you that I'm capable of living a normal life again, can you forgive me? Will you let me come around once in awhile and see Ryan? Please, give me another chance, for our son's sake.

I'll always love you.

Dennis

Jenna sat on the bed, lips pinched as she read and reread her ex-husband's letter. This was the sober Dennis, the man she'd believed she could build a life with. When she'd married him, she'd known she didn't feel the overwhelming depth of emotion she'd felt for Adam, but she'd thought they had a decent amount of love and respect between them. Their marriage shouldn't have become the hell it had. Ryan shouldn't have lost his father.

And now Dennis was doing another about-face, managing to surprise even her. He'd been so bitter and angry for the past few months, so far from healthy, that Jenna had feared he'd never find his way back to a normal life. Evidently getting picked up by the police had been good for him.

"There you are!" Ryan came bounding into the room with speckles of dried mud on his arms and legs, even his face. "We had a blast!"

Jenna folded the letter and stuffed it back inside the envelope. Maybe now she and Ryan could have some peace and eventually build a healthy relationship between father and son.

And what about the baby?

"It looks like you fell into a puddle," she said.

"Nope. I rode through a creek. I wiped out a couple times, but I didn't get hurt. You should've seen Adam, though. He tried to go down this pile of rocks and flew right over the top of his handlebars. It was awesome."

"That's what I get for showing off." Adam stood in the doorway, grinning from a similarly mud-splattered face. A scrape on his leg testified to the spill he'd taken, along with a matching scrape on his arm and a cut on his elbow. He lifted his torn T-shirt to show her a bruise on his ribs.

"And this is supposed to encourage me to let you go again?" Jenna asked Ryan.

Ryan rolled his eyes. "Come on, Mom. He wouldn't let me try any of the hard stuff, and he's okay. Just look at him!"

Jenna didn't need any encouragement to do that. The lycra biking shorts Adam wore revealed the sinewy muscles of his legs—and left very little to the imagination in other, more intriguing places.

"Next weekend you're coming with us," Adam told her.

Jenna would have tried the excuse that she didn't have a bike, but she was afraid Adam would simply buy her one. "Pregnant women probably aren't allowed."

"I have a friend whose wife biked until six months or so. I don't plan to take you out when you're that far along, but a few trips early in the pregnancy should be okay."

The proprietary tone of his voice said that her words last night hadn't discouraged him. He wasn't backing off. She lifted an eyebrow in challenge, but he only winked at her and headed down the hall.

"I'm going to shower," he called back. "Ryan, you'd better wash up, too, before Gram catches sight of you."

AFTER HIS SHOWER, Adam toweled his hair and body and opened the misted medicine cabinet in search of something to clean his cuts. Rubbing alcohol. Perfect. Uncapping the bottle, he wrinkled his nose at the antiseptic smell, then gingerly dabbed the clear liquid to his injuries and winced at the sting.

As he dressed in a pair of well-worn blue jeans and a long-sleeved jersey with a biking logo on the back, he thought of his morning with Ryan. "Dad" things were fun. Dennis had to be an idiot to let anything stop him from being with Ryan.

Adam wasn't going to be that stupid. He'd nearly lost Jenna for good after his decision to leave her fifteen years ago. But fate—and a rocky divorce for

Jenna—had brought them back together. This time he wasn't going to blow it. Still, he had to admit that the next few months would certainly be easier if she'd co-operate.

He whistled as he remembered the way she'd come alive in his arms the night the police had carted Dennis off to jail. That memory stole his breath away and almost made him regret having done the responsible thing.

Maybe next time he wouldn't be so responsible. Maybe he'd just have to convince Jenna that they were meant to be together—and do it in whatever way he could reach her.

"Adam?" A sharp knock on the bathroom door punctuated his grandmother's voice. "Are you just about finished in there?"

"Be right out, Gram."

"Good. I want you to get some things out of storage for Jenna."

Adam padded barefoot to the door and yanked it open. "Like what?"

"Like your cradle."

"*My* cradle?"

"You were born in this house, you know. Your mother had you right here, with a midwife, and Pop made you a beautiful wooden cradle." A hint of the sadness he'd grown to recognize as a boy filled her voice. He could barely remember his mother, but he knew Gram and Pop still mourned her death, still wondered how things could have gone so terribly wrong. "I think Jenna will feel more optimistic about the baby if she sees that we're with her, that we're all prepared and excited."

His grandmother's mention of the baby brought the

reality of Jenna's pregnancy into sharp focus for Adam. With Jenna's waist still trim and her stomach flat, it was almost too easy to forget about the child. He knew he wanted Jenna—and Ryan. But how would he feel about the baby when it arrived?

"Just let me put on my shoes," he said.

"You know where the storage area is in that old barn," she answered. "I've got to pay some bills. I'll be in the office. I've asked Jenna to help you in case she sees something else she might like to clean up for the nursery. There's an old rocker out there, too, I think."

Adam put on his socks and shoes and laced up his running shoes as his grandmother trudged away. *A baby.* Was he ready to share the responsibility of caring for a squirming helpless bundle? He tried to picture a toddler tearing through his home in San Francisco and couldn't.

When Adam reached the kitchen, he found Jenna waiting for him. Dressed in a pair of jeans and a sweatshirt, she'd pulled her hair into a ponytail and looked so much like the girl he'd known in high school that he almost walked over and slung one arm around her shoulders as he would have then.

"All set?" he asked, keeping his hands to himself.

She finished the glass of water she'd been drinking and nodded. "Do you remember when we were in high school and you tried to convince me this place was haunted? You said the man and woman who built the original house died mysterious deaths, and that their bodies were discovered out in the old barn."

"It's true!"

Jenna rolled her eyes. "I do the advertising brochures now, remember? The couple who built the Victoriana sold it long before they died. It was too much for them to take care of, so they moved to the city and bought a condo. Nothing mysterious about it.''

He grinned. ''I owe a lot to that little story. It got you into my arms every time.''

''Well, scare tactics won't get you what they used to.''

Maybe not, but he didn't for a second believe she was as immune to him as she pretended. If words wouldn't reach her, touch might. Fortunately he was pretty good with body language when he wanted to be.

Just the thought of touching Jenna again fired his nerve endings. He turned abruptly and headed out the door so she wouldn't notice her effect on him.

The chilly morning had crystallized into one of those clear warm days that could belong to spring as easily as autumn. Adam lifted his face to the sun and smiled as he breathed in the smell of damp rotting leaves and wood smoke from a neighbor's chimney.

''Is there any particular reason for the lightness of your mood?'' Jenna asked suspiciously.

''You mean, like, did I win the lottery? No.''

''Someone who drives a $60,000 Mercedes doesn't need to win the lottery,'' she grumbled. ''But it would be just your luck.''

''Do I detect a pang of jealousy?'' They reached the locked garage on the far corner of the property and Adam produced a key.

''No, I'm going to get a new car myself. I've been saving, and if my stained glass does well this spring when the tourists return, I should be able to get one next fall.'' Brushing aside a cobweb, she ducked inside when he held the door.

Adam thought of Gordon Motors, where he'd bought

his last vehicles and knew he could co-sign for Jenna and get her a car tomorrow, regardless of the damage Dennis had done to her credit. He didn't say anything, though. Knowing Jenna, her pride would never allow her to accept that kind of help.

Maybe when she came to San Francisco, he'd drive her to the lot and try to tempt her.

"So where do we start?" she asked, grimacing at the dust-covered collection of stacked furniture, boxes, stuffed black garbage bags, mirrors and lampshades. A narrow path had been made through the clutter, and it meandered crookedly toward the back of what had once been a barn. Gram's storage had grown and multiplied over the years, until odds and ends and recent additions spilled into the walkway, making it almost impossible to move very far very fast.

Adam liked the cozy fit. He could easily detect the light scent of Jenna's perfume and the tantalizing smell of her skin. "I'm guessing the really old stuff will be at the back."

Jenna peered toward the gloomy recesses of the building. "You don't think there are any mice in here, do you?" she asked, picking her way toward the mystery objects along the rear wall.

The farther they moved from the old dirty window at the front, the more difficult it became to see. "Should I give you the answer you want or the truth?"

She shivered. "Just turn on a light."

"Sure." Adam reached around her to pull the chain that dangled from the ceiling in the center of the room, and managed to plaster himself against her backside in the process.

She gave him a warning elbow to the stomach. "Very funny."

"Just trying to accommodate," he told her, and began to survey the items now visible beneath the harsh light of the bare bulb overhead. Several chests of drawers, an old steamer truck, a dining-room table, a piano missing its top... The rocker Gram had mentioned was buried beneath bags of clothes and an orange feather-and-flower arrangement that had to be a relic from the sixties.

Adam grimaced at the musty odor as he dug out the rocker, then nearly choked on the dust when Jenna pulled a sheet off a likely-looking shape sitting on an old coffee table.

"Voilà! One baby cradle," she announced proudly. Running a hand over the painted wood, she added, "Wow, it's beautiful. Look, Adam."

Adam leaned over Jenna to see the cradle Pop had made for him. "The old guy's pretty good with his hands."

"Yeah." She glanced up at him. "I'll be careful with it. I mean, I'm sure you'll want to use it someday yourself—when you marry and have children."

Adam slipped his arms around Jenna's waist. "Doesn't it sound more appealing to get up with the baby during the night from the warmth of my bed than trying to handle this all on your own?" he whispered in her ear.

She hesitated as though unsure, but slowly her body softened and molded to his. "It sounds even better to have *you* get up with the baby during the night."

"That would take an occasional incentive," he said.

"Like?"

"Like this." Adam slid one hand up her shirt and the other down her pants. He'd been achingly aware of her since before they left the house and no longer cared if she knew it.

Jenna moaned as his fingers reached their targets. Her head rolled back onto his shoulder as he nuzzled her silky hair aside so he could kiss the soft skin of her neck.

"Adam, stop," she said, but her voice was thick with the same desire that pulsed through his body, and she made no move to escape him. He could hear the panting of her breath, feel the goose bumps on her body, and thought she had far too many clothes on. Turning her in his arms, he'd just planned to remedy that situation as soon as possible when the door opened with a streak of light and Pop stood at the entrance.

Jenna scrambled a few feet down the aisle, her quick movements and the flush on her cheeks enough to give them away.

"Someone's here to see you, Jenna," Pop said shortly, throwing Adam a disapproving frown.

Jenna darted toward the door. "L-Laura," she said. "She called earlier."

Adam's grandfather caught her by the elbow as she began to skirt past him. "It's not Laura."

She paused, obviously reading Pop's face the same way Adam did: something was wrong.

"It can't be Dennis—" Adam started to say.

"It's not." Pop's expression softened as his eyes locked with Jenna's. "It's your father."

CHAPTER THIRTEEN

JENNA'S MOUTH went drier than dirt. *Her father?* The
same man who'd left her mother almost twenty-five
years ago and never looked back, not even to spare a
kind word for the child they'd created together?

Anger, raw and powerful, ignited in Jenna as she
marched to the house. Damn him! How dare LeRoy
Tottering surprise her now after everything that had
happened? The last time she'd heard from him was
when her mother and stepfather had died. She'd been
staying with Laura and her family, and Laura's parents,
concerned for her, had tracked down her father's number in Santa Rosa and encouraged Jenna to call him. It
was only right he take her in and support her until she
graduated from high school, they'd said.

Feeling helplessly torn between fear of rejection and
hope of acceptance, Jenna had listened to them tell her
that he would come through. He was blood. He was
her father. She just didn't know or understand all the
reasons he'd stayed away. She'd wanted to believe
them, so she'd swallowed her fear and dialed the number.

His wife had answered and coldly informed her that
he'd call if he wanted to speak to her. He did phone
that night, but only to let her know he wasn't the rock
she could cling to. He had another wife to keep happy
and four other mouths to feed. She'd never fit in.

That was it. That was all. She'd never contacted him again.

Jenna tried to suppress the pain that memory occasioned, pain that should have dulled long ago. She wasn't a child anymore. She was an adult with responsibilities of her own, and she didn't need her father. She was no longer vulnerable—so why did the thought of seeing him again scare the hell out of her?

Breathing deeply, she stood outside the door, concentrating on the initial anger she'd felt when Pop had announced her visitor, instead of the confusion and sense of loss that had quickly followed. She didn't hear Adam come up behind her, but she felt his hand close over her cold fingers.

"Come on, Jen," he said. "Let's meet the bastard."

Jenna wanted to scream at him to leave her alone. She couldn't let herself lean on him. What if he withdrew his support when she least expected it? She'd fall without a chance to catch herself, and the hurt would be much worse than if she'd stumbled on her own.

"I can do it," she said, but strength and energy pumped from his body to hers through the contact of their hands and heartened her until she couldn't bear to sever the connection. She'd push Adam away later, she told herself. She wouldn't trust him, wouldn't risk another fall. But for now, for this minute, couldn't she simply be grateful for his support, his presence?

"There's no reason to do it alone. I'm here now, and I'll never again let you face a man who might hurt you without being around to break his jaw if he tries."

She smiled, remembering how good Adam had been to her eighteen years ago. He'd wanted to beat her father to a pulp then—as a mere teenager—and had been the one to support her through the confusion and heartbreak of her parents' deaths. Fortunately, because she hadn't wanted to move away from Adam, anyway, her mother's only sister took her in. Though the widowed Aunt Zelma had been eccentric in many ways, she was kind and lived close to the Victoriana. She'd died of a heart attack five years after Jenna's marriage.

Adam had been there for her once, she thought. And he was here now. She didn't want to think about tomorrow.

"If anybody's going to hit him, I am," Jenna said simply, and headed inside.

The last of Friday night's guests lingered in the front parlor near one window, gazing at the view, but Jenna's attention quickly focused on an uncomfortable-looking gray-haired man in a pair of polyester slacks and a golf jacket. He stood next to the door as though he'd rather bolt than stay, but he stepped toward her when she approached.

"Jenna?"

She nodded, scarcely recognizing this person who was her father. She remembered a man with thick wavy dark hair, like her own, a rather stern face and a slight build. This man, now staring at her from beneath the ledge of a prominent brow, had lost most of his hair. The color of his eyes had dulled to a pale blue, and he seemed several inches shorter than she remembered. But then, she'd been much smaller herself—only eight years old when he left, after all. "Hello."

"You're lovely. All grown up," he said, shaking his head. "How old are you now? Twenty-eight? Twenty-nine?"

Jenna felt Adam's comforting pressure as he squeezed her hand in reassurance, but couldn't keep the chill out of her voice. "I'm thirty-two. This is

Adam Durham, an old friend of mine. Adam, this is…LeRoy Tottering,'' she finished lamely, unable to say, ''my father.''

Her father's gaze moved from her face to Adam's and then down to their clasped hands. ''Can we have a few minutes alone?'' he asked, looking back at Jenna.

Adam spoke before Jenna could decide how to answer. ''I'm afraid anything you have to say to Jenna can be said while I'm here.''

Her father sighed and ran both hands over his bald pate as though combing through hair. ''This isn't easy, is it?''

''That depends on what you want.'' Jenna motioned to the couch as the couple who had lingered at the window strolled out the front door. ''Would you like to sit down?''

He shook his head and clasped his hands in front of him. ''I just…'' His voice broke, and he shrugged. ''I don't know. I just wanted to see you, I guess.''

''After twenty-four years?'' Jenna struggled to control her resentment. ''What makes you want to see me now?''

''Caroline died. Last March.''

Jenna searched for something sympathetic to say, but the memory of his callous reaction to her own mother's death kept her from uttering words she knew would be obviously insincere. ''And?''

''The kids are all gone. You know, what with college and marriages, they're getting pretty spread out. There's five of them. I don't know if you knew that. Pretty big family.''

There'd been only four the last time Jenna had known anything about her father, but it wasn't the number of kids that reverberated in her head. It was his use of the word *family*. Why hadn't LeRoy Tottering wanted her as part of his family? "How fortunate for you," she said. "Big families are nice."

He jammed his hands in his pockets as Adam silently moved to stand behind her, his protectiveness reassuringly familiar to Jenna. Just like the old days. It would be so easy to pick up where they'd left off—but how long would it last this time?

"So you haven't married?" her father asked.

"I'm divorced."

With a bitter chuckle he ran a hand behind his neck. "Then you know marriage isn't a walk in the park."

"Neither is taking care of children, but I'd never abandon one of mine."

He sighed again. "I deserve that," he said with a nod that seemed to confirm the statement. "You've got kids, then?"

Suddenly Jenna wanted this man to see what he had missed, what he had rejected. "Adam, would you go get Ryan, please?" she asked, and felt the loss of his presence the second he left the room.

"I have a son," she told her father. For some reason she didn't mention the baby. It was too much to go into now, in this brief meeting that felt more uncomfortable than Jenna could ever have imagined. "What brings you here?"

LeRoy Tottering seemed old and defeated. He stared at the carpet. "I know it's a bit late. I've been thinking of looking you up for some time, but I didn't know if you'd see me."

If he wanted encouragement, Jenna had none to give him. She was still reeling from the shock of his sudden appearance—and the meekness of his manner. Where was the man who had so firmly set her away from him?

Adam returned with Ryan, and Jenna began to per-
form the introductions. "This is my son, Ryan."

Ryan looked at her, waiting for the other part of the
introduction.

"This is LeRoy Tottering," she told him, knowing
the name would mean nothing to him. He'd heard of
his grandmother, but she had died a Smith, and when
Jenna married she'd become a Livingston.

"Nice to meet you," her son said. Putting a smile
on his recently scrubbed face, he stuck out a hand.

Jenna watched as grandfather and grandson clasped
hands, and her heart contracted. What this man could
have given her if only he'd loved her!

"You seem like a fine boy, Ryan," her father said,
but he didn't try to identify himself any further than
Jenna already had.

"Thank you, sir."

Her father dug in his pants pocket and produced a
card that said, "Tottering Heating and Air-Conditioning," bearing a telephone number and a Santa Rosa
address, and held it out to Jenna. "I know you probably
won't want to use this, but if you ever have need of
anything, you can reach me at that number."

When Jenna hesitated, Adam took the card for her.
"Thank you," he said. "We'll keep that in mind. But
if it's up to me, Jenna won't be needing anything."

Her father nodded. "It looks like she's in good
hands."

Jenna almost screamed that she was in no one's
"hands." She could rely only on herself—but it would
be enough. It had to be.

"Goodbye, Ryan. I hope we can see each other again

someday," her father said before she could add anything else, and left.

"Who was that, Mom?" her son asked as soon as
the door shut behind him.

Jenna sank into the closest chair and nearly said, "A
ghost." Instead, she patted the place next to her and,
when Ryan sat down, put her arm around him. Avoid-
ing Adam's probing eyes, seeking, instead, the comfort
of Ryan's constant love, she said, "That was my dad."

He pulled back, his brown eyes blinking up at her
in confusion. "But you called him LeRoy something."

"That's his name. And it's basically all I know
about him."

Ryan bit his lip, suddenly pensive. "Is that how it's
going to be with *my* dad?"

"So what do you think?" Adam eyed Jenna over
his second piece of pizza while Ryan was still finishing
his first. Music played in the background of Fort
Bragg's Roundtable Pizza, mostly oldies mixed with a
few modern rock songs, and the smell of baking bread
and garlic permeated the air.

"I don't know what to think. I feel kind of weird."
She was sitting across from him in an orange booth by
a window that showed nothing but their own reflections
because of the darkness outside. Ever since her father's
appearance just before lunch, Jenna had withdrawn inside herself. Adam thought it might help her sort
through her feelings if she'd try to explain them, but
he didn't want to push her. Despite the false bravado
she'd attempted at first, because of her tremendous
pride, he remembered how badly her father had hurt
her when her mother died.

"Was your father anything like you expected?"

She shook her head. "He seemed pathetic in a way. I think that's the part I'm having the most trouble with." She took a bite and chewed slowly as Ryan shoved his plate aside. "None of us live forever. I just hope I don't have the regrets he has when I get to his age—if what I saw in his face *was* regret."

"It was regret all right."

"I'm stuffed," Ryan announced.

Adam severed the string of cheese that stretched from the pan to his own plate as he took his third slice. "Already?"

"Maybe I'll have more later." The boy's eyes darted to several video games that gleamed in the corner. He gave his mother a winning smile. "Can I have a quarter, Mom?"

Jenna got out her wallet and handed him a couple of quarters, and Adam tossed him a few more.

They both watched Ryan hurry gleefully away before resuming their conversation. "Do you think you'll ever call him?" Adam asked.

With a shrug Jenna relinquished her pizza in favor of her Coke. "If it were just me, I wouldn't. But I'm half tempted to see what Mr. Tottering's like for Ryan's sake. Ryan doesn't have his father right now, and we were never close to Dennis's parents. Dennis was born several years after their other kids and they were always a little...different. You remember them."

"They kept to themselves. No one knew them very well."

"Well, they still keep to themselves. So it might be nice for Ryan to have some extended family, supposing we could work through the awkwardness of the past. Not that I think my father deserves Ryan."

"He doesn't deserve you, either." Adam studied her,

wishing he could erase the strain he saw in her face. Between her father and Dennis, she'd been carrying a heavy emotional load for far too long. And now there was the baby, which had to weigh on her mind constantly. The protective urge he'd felt as a teenager reared up inside him again, the urge to take care of her. At least until she felt whole.

She gazed at him, her eyes deep and fathomless, then reached into her purse and passed him a letter.

"What's this?"

"The latest from Dennis," she said, nursing her drink. "He claims he's going clean and sober."

Adam unfolded the sheet of paper and quickly read Dennis's letter. "Pretty typical for a man sitting in jail, drying out."

"So you don't think he means it this time?"

"Well, he might mean it, but...has he ever kept his promises before?"

She sighed. "Until he's tempted by the next drink."

"Then chances are you already know how long this will last."

"Maybe going to jail changed him, woke him up to reality. He's never been in trouble with the law before."

Adam had his doubts that a few days in jail could reform the man he'd seen kicking the windows of the police car only a week earlier. And he didn't like Dennis's plea for a second chance. Adam got the impression Dennis had more in mind than just the opportunity to be a good father to Ryan. "You wouldn't go back to him even if he cleaned up, would you?" he asked, keeping his eyes on his food so she wouldn't see how much the answer meant to him.

"I don't think so."

Her voice, flat and somehow subdued, sent a shiver of alarm through Adam, and suddenly the pizza wasn't sitting so well in his stomach. "You don't seem very certain."

She glanced toward the corner, where Ryan was still enthralled with the latest car-racing game. "What Ryan said after my father left really bothers me," she admitted. "I don't want to be selfish about this. I want to give my son what's best for him. And this baby needs a father, too."

"No child needs Dennis."

A devilish smile curved her lips, and for the first time since Tottering's visit, her eyes took on some of their usual sparkle. "You're sounding rather vehement, as though you have a personal stake in all this."

"I do, dammit! Do you think I'm playing around? God, Jenna, do you want me to swear a blood oath that I'll never hurt you again? What would it take to convince you to trust me?"

"You could move back to Mendocino."

The gentle suggestion hit with the impact of a hand grenade. Leaning back, Adam let the rest of his dinner go untouched. "So you want me to raise the white flag instead of you, is that it? Give up what I've worked so hard to achieve? Is this your way of taking revenge for my leaving in the first place?"

She grimaced. "That's a pretty negative interpretation. I just thought maybe Mendocino could use a good attorney. It was a stupid idea really. Of course you wouldn't want to leave your home."

Gathering her purse, she slid out of the booth and went to collect Ryan as Adam stared after her. She didn't understand how much he'd put into his career, how few men attained what he'd managed to achieve.

He couldn't walk away from what had taken fifteen years to build. She had no right to even ask.

But did he have any more right to expect her to move to San Francisco? To uproot Ryan again? And, if she did relocate, what was he willing to promise her? He wanted a relationship with Jenna, wanted to jump in and let the tide of their emotions dictate the future—but he was no less afraid of the undertow than she was.

He had dated some intelligent attractive women, yet he hadn't been tempted to make a permanent commitment to any of them. Was there something wrong with him? Or was it simply the memory of the pain in Jenna's eyes when he'd broken the one promise he *had* made that kept him from venturing down the same path again?

Cursing under his breath, Adam went to get a box for the leftover pizza. Damn Dennis and damn LeRoy Tottering. But most of all, damn himself for hurting any woman who ever got close to him.

JENNA FOCUSED on cutting several small pieces of antique blue glass for the bird window she was making and tried to ignore the emptiness that hung over the house. Ryan had gone to church with Mr. and Mrs. Durham, and Adam had headed home after breakfast. Though she'd rather not admit it, even privately, his going had left her with a lingering feeling of disappointment and regret. She kept telling herself that she and Adam were better off with the hundred miles from San Francisco to Mendocino between them. But then the memory of Adam on the beach or in the storage barn with his arms around her would intrude, and she'd remember how her body tingled every time he touched her.

Why wasn't she one of those women who could have a casual affair? she wondered. Why not enjoy the physical elements of a relationship—the part Adam was so willing and capable of giving her—and turn off her emotional needs?

Jenna blew a wisp of hair out of her face and carefully separated the two pieces of glass she'd just scored. She knew the answer—for her, love went hand in hand with sex. She could no more separate them than she could take the salt out of seawater.

The phone rang, but she ignored it, knowing it would probably be Laura. She, Adam and Ryan had stopped by to visit her friend on their way home from the pizza parlor the night before, and Laura had winked and pinched Jenna until it was all Jenna could do to get Adam out of the house without his noticing. And Jenna didn't want to hear Laura singing his praises now.

"We're home, Mom! We're back!"

Jenna turned to see Ryan burst through the door to her studio.

"How was church?" she asked.

Her son shrugged as if to say church was church, then paused in front of the drawing she'd made for the bird window. "Wow, this one's really great! Are you going to finish it in time to take it to San Francisco?"

"That's the plan. I want Mr. LeCourt to see a good variety of my work. What other pieces do you think I should take?"

Ryan circled the room, biting his lip in serious consideration as Mrs. Durham came through the door, puffing with exertion.

"You didn't need to hike all the way back here. I would have come to the house," Jenna said.

"No. I wanted to see what you've accomplished

since my last visit. I've been bragging to all my friends at church that you're going to be famous once that shop owner in San Francisco sees what you can do."

Jenna laughed. "Thanks for the confidence, but Mr. LeCourt has only asked to *see* my work. He hasn't agreed to sell it."

"If he's got a brain in his head, he'll see what the rest of us see," Mrs. Durham insisted. She joined Ryan in perusing the pieces Jenna had already finished. "It's a good thing you've been working steadily. You have quite an inventory here."

"I want to be prepared for the tourists once the rainy season's over."

"You won't have to worry about tourists. These will all be gone by then." Mrs. Durham put a hand on top of Ryan's head. "You have quite a mother, young man."

Ryan glanced at Jenna over his shoulder. "Do you think Adam likes her?"

Jenna coughed to hide her surprise and pretended to concentrate on making her next cut in the glass beneath her hands.

"Probably more than he wants to," Mrs. Durham replied with a secretive smile. "Why?"

Ryan shrugged again. "Just wondering."

ON WEDNESDAY, Dennis gladly stripped off the orange jumpsuit and donned his own clothes. He hadn't noticed before how filthy they were, but he couldn't miss the worn-in dirt and greasy splotches now. Before his arrest he'd been living out of his car and couldn't remember the last time he'd done any laundry. Somehow he'd lost all perspective on the small everyday processes others took for granted as, more and more, the bottle became the center of his life.

I would have stopped drinking long before now if Jenna hadn't left me. What had they taught him at all those AA meetings? That some people worked as a trigger? Well, Jenna was his trigger. But he couldn't think about that. It made him angry, which made him want to punish her, which only chased her farther away. He could forgive her if she'd take him back. Somehow he had to break the vicious hold alcohol had over him, even when the thought of a drink made him dizzy with desire. Like right now...

Clamping a tight hold on the wayward craving, Dennis told himself he couldn't touch the stuff. It was poison. It had destroyed his life. He'd promised Jenna he was going clean. What other choice did he have, really, unless he wanted to continue living the way he had for the past year?

Following a uniformed police officer from the small changing room, where he'd left the jumpsuit on the floor, he retrieved his wallet, checked for the sixty bucks he had there and shoved it in his pocket.

"Who's going to take me back to Mendocino?" he asked.

"No one," replied the deputy who was handling the paperwork involved in releasing him.

"But my car's in Mendocino!"

"So?"

"That's more than an hour and a half away. You can't cart me clear the hell over here and just leave me high and dry."

A wry smile twisted the man's face, but he didn't bother to look up. "Wanna bet? We do it all the time."

Dennis clenched his fists in anger at the deputy's

indifference. Damn cops! They'd locked him up for ten days like he was some kind of common criminal, and for what? Because he'd tried to talk to his ex-wife? See his son? As if any of them wouldn't have done the same! And now they were throwing him out on the street without so much as a bus ticket.

He needed a drink—just a small one to calm his nerves and help him think. He couldn't expect to go dry without one last beer, one final hurrah. Jenna would never know. He'd rent a hotel room, shower and shave, wash his clothes—in the sink, if he had to—and appear decent and appealing when he went to Mendocino to pick up his car. If he was lucky, his letter had softened Jenna up enough so she'd let him see Ryan, which meant he'd get a few minutes with her, too.

And, if he was really lucky, he'd be able to convince her that this time he was changing for good.

CHAPTER FOURTEEN

AT FOUR O'CLOCK Thursday morning Jenna gave up on sleep. She was too excited to stay in bed any longer. Shoving off the blankets, she pulled on a pair of sweats, laced up her tennis shoes and went to her studio, where she silently considered the few stained-glass windows she hadn't already taped up with bubble wrap in preparation for her trip to San Francisco. Was she bringing the right ones? She'd chosen the lake surrounded by trees—the piece she'd just finished—a large, stone house on a promontory overlooking sea-battered rocks, a red-and-white-striped lighthouse against the backdrop of a raging storm and a Victorian garden. Would Mr. LeCourt like her work? Was he giving her a chance because she was Adam's friend or because he'd truly liked the cove?

The nausea Jenna had struggled with over the past month or so made a weak threat, but she ignored it. For the most part her morning sickness had passed, and the tiredness of the second trimester had not yet set in. Physically she felt better than she had in a long time, especially as Dennis's incarceration and subsequent remorse had left her feeling relatively safe. Perhaps her meeting with Mr. LeCourt would be the start of a new life for her. Perhaps she could now start moving more swiftly and surely toward a promising future.

The ringing of the telephone made Jenna jump. She

scrambled to answer it because the same line rang in the house. Hoping to stop the noise before it woke everyone, she yanked the receiver to her ear for a breathy hello.

"Jenna?"

The tension in her body dissipated like the air from a popped balloon. Dennis had called her so many times at all hours of the night that she was afraid he'd already reverted to his old belligerent self. "Adam? What are you doing awake this time of morning?"

"I was afraid I'd miss you if I didn't call early."

She laughed. "It's four o'clock! Don't tell me you set your alarm just to wish me luck."

"I didn't have to set my alarm. I've been thinking about you for most of the night."

The huskiness of his voice told her he was still in bed, and she pictured him as she'd seen him the night she'd entered his room when the police had come. Something stirred in the region of her belly, but she forced herself to think past it. "I hope it wasn't a nightmare."

"Hardly." She could hear the laughter in his voice. "Are you going to come see me today?"

Jenna hesitated. She'd decided not to visit Adam, but refusing to stop by his office seemed ungrateful, considering that he'd gotten her the appointment in the first place. "You still want to have lunch?"

"If you're interested."

Unwilling maybe, but never uninterested. "I don't know. It depends on how long everything takes. I don't want to drive back to Mendocino after dark. My van hasn't been running very well."

"Maybe it's time to get you a new car."

"I can't afford one yet. I have to save for the baby and—"

"Just come for a quick visit." He sounded irritated, impatient.

"Adam, I don't think our seeing each other is a very good idea."

He swore under his breath. "That's what you keep saying. And that's what I keep telling myself, but..."

"But what?"

"Nothing. Good luck with Harvey."

Jenna sat and stared at the phone for several minutes after Adam hung up. If he wanted her to visit him so badly, why had he waited until now to call her? He'd left three days earlier and she hadn't heard a word from him.

Drawing in a deep breath, she tried to put Adam out of her mind. She had a full exciting day ahead of her, and she wasn't about to let old doubts and longings ruin it.

Frowning at a leaden sky that promised rain, she walked back to the house to shower. But before she stepped beneath the hot spray, she turned to study her naked reflection in the mirror.

She wasn't showing yet. Other than a hard round knot the size of a fist just below her belly button, apparent only when she sucked in her stomach, there was no outward sign of her pregnancy. The dark half-moons below her eyes were nearly gone and her color was healthier than it had been a week ago. She planned to put up her hair and wear her brown suit and tortoise-shell jewelry. The outfit was understated yet professional, and its tailored lines made the most of her slender body.

Would Adam like it?

Jenna frowned at her thoughts. Somehow all roads returned to Adam Durham. But not today, she decided, growing more and more determined to get through her trip to San Francisco without succumbing to the urge to see him.

After her shower Jenna did her makeup, fixed her hair and changed into her suit. Then, with a quick mist of her favorite perfume, she went in to wake Ryan.

"Hey, sleepyhead. You ready to get up?"

Her son blinked against the light streaming in from her bedroom.

"What time is it?"

"Seven-thirty."

"Where's the sun?"

"It's raining."

"Oh."

"I've got to go. Mr. and Mrs. Durham are a little later than usual this morning, but I think they're starting to wake up. They'll help you, but you need to get ready now so you're not late for school."

"Okay. Are you scared about your big meeting?"

Jenna felt the nervous flutter in her stomach and had to admit she was. "A little. It's not every day I have an opportunity like this one. We could have a bright future if Mr. LeCourt likes my stuff."

"Will we be rich?"

"Not quite that fast or that easily. Right now I'd be happy to receive a little positive reinforcement."

"Positive what?"

She smoothed his hair off his forehead. "Never mind. Just kiss me for luck."

He kissed her cheek, then climbed out of bed while Jenna went back into her own bedroom. "I think I'll try to fit the window showing the redwoods into the van, too. I'm going to go grab it while you dress. I'll meet you in the kitchen,'' she called.

Ryan murmured his assent, and she returned to her studio, where she spent twenty or more minutes studying the pieces she'd planned to leave behind. She wanted to take them all—beauty was so subjective that she had no way of knowing which ones Mr. LeCourt would like—but there simply wasn't enough room in the van. Finally she stuck with her original impulse and began to wrap the piece showing the California redwoods.

''Mom?''

Startled, Jenna whirled to see her son standing in the doorway with his hands in the pockets of his jeans.

''What is it?'' she asked, alarmed by the uneasy look on his face. Then she saw a shadow move behind him, and Dennis came into view, holding a single red rose.

''Hi, Jen,'' he said.

It took two attempts at speech to get her voice to work. ''Dennis, you know you shouldn't be here. You know what happened last time.''

''I just wanted to see Ryan for a minute before he left for school.'' He stepped inside and handed her the rose, the scent of which warred with his cheap cologne.

Jenna accepted his gift because it would have taken much longer to refuse it. ''Thank you. You're looking better than you have in a while. I'm glad to see you're taking some pride in your appearance again. That's a healthy sign.''

''Did you get my letter?''

Jenna nodded.

''Then you know I'm going clean. I've got a new handle on life, Jen. I know I can do it this time. And I think I've got a job over in Fort Bragg. My cousin

Joe put in a good word for me at the lumber mill where he works.''

Fort Bragg was only eight miles away. Jenna tried not to blanch. "Wonderful. I hope you can hang on this time, Dennis. You've got a lot to give the world, if you can just stay sober long enough.''

He smiled and dropped a hand to ruffle Ryan's hair. Ryan shifted uncomfortably.

"Are you going somewhere?" Dennis asked, eyeing her suit and the bubble wrap she was holding.

Jenna searched for an explanation she felt she could give him. She hated to mention San Francisco. Dennis would undoubtedly think she was going to meet Adam, and she didn't want to say anything that might set him off. "I have an appointment to show someone my stained glass this morning.''

"Great." He rubbed his face as though he was used to feeling the roughness of whiskers, even though his skin was now smooth and stubble-free. "I hope you don't forget the rest of us when you get rich and famous," he said.

"I don't think you have to worry. I'm not holding my breath on the rich-and-famous bit.''

"If anyone can do it, you can." He glanced at their son. "Champ, could I talk to your mom alone for a few minutes?''

Ryan hesitated.

"It's okay, honey. We'll be right there," Jenna told the boy. "I don't want you to be late for school. Go have yourself a bowl of cereal.''

Dennis watched Ryan leave, then turned back to her. "Jen, I just wanted to ask you—" he shoved a hand through his hair, causing it to stick up in front because of all the hair gel he'd used "—I just need to know what my chances are. I mean, if I stay clean and sober and all that. Would you ever consider coming back to me? Letting us be a family again?''

Jenna thought fleetingly of the baby. She should tell Dennis now. It might help him stay sober to know he had another child on the way. But she couldn't be sure how he'd react, and she had her big appointment today.

"I know I'm asking a lot," he went on. "I just figured if there was a chance, even a small chance, that you'd give our marriage another try, I could do anything."

It hadn't helped him before, but Jenna didn't say that. Instead, she floundered for something to say that wouldn't be too far from the truth. If Dennis kept her here any longer, she'd be late.

"Dennis, I'm sorry, but I can't hold out false hope. You need to get well, but you need to do it for you, not for me or anyone else. Ryan will always be here for you, anytime you're ready to build a relationship, provided you stay clean. But I can't make you any other promises."

"But you loved me once, didn't you? I mean it wasn't always Adam, was it?"

"No, of course I cared about you."

"Then you might still care, at least a little bit, right?"

Jenna hesitated, knowing Dennis would take any positive indication well beyond what she intended and start hounding her again. To avoid that she said, "Not more than I care for any of my other friends."

"You don't love me at all?"

"Not anymore."

He sucked in a breath as though she'd slapped him.

"I know you're angry, baby. You've got every right to be. I've been an asshole—"

"No, Dennis. There's no need for apologies at this late date. I'm willing to be your friend and help you achieve a healthy relationship with Ryan. But I'll never be your wife again. Those days are over."

His jaw twitched and Jenna held her breath, hoping her refusal wouldn't incite his anger. "Is it Adam?" he asked.

Jenna shook her head.

"There has to be someone else. You've never been like this before. So...hard. What happened, Jen?"

Whatever happened had occurred long ago. After everything Dennis had done—and not done—how could he even ask her that? "I've never been this sure of what I wanted before," she said simply.

"And what is it you want? Rich lawyer-boy in your bed?"

Jenna felt a prickle of alarm. "Dennis, I'm not seeing Adam. I've already told you that. I want to be alone, get my feet underneath me. That's all."

Shaking his head, he strode to the opposite wall, then spun around and came back. "That's it, then? No chance? Ever? You can shut me out just like that?"

"Young man, I've called the cops." Mr. Durham stood in the doorway, carrying a bat, eyes implacable beneath gray tufted brows. "If you don't want trouble, you'd better leave now."

Dennis clenched his fists, and for a moment Jenna feared he might try to start a fight. She stepped forward, planning to use her karate training if necessary, but Dennis backed off with a laugh. "I see old Pop hasn't changed," he muttered. "Too bad taking a swing at him isn't worth going back to jail.''

Then he shoved his way past Mr. Durham and was gone.

THOUGH THE ENGINE SPUTTERED and skipped in a temperamental start, the van ran smoothly as Jenna took Highway 128 south to 101. Dennis's visit had upset her, but he'd left without making too much of a scene. And he did look healthier than he had in months and seemed more capable of seeing reason. She hoped his days with the bottle were behind him, for everyone's sake, but she knew only time would tell.

Fiddling with the radio, she decided not to dwell on her ex-husband or his problems. She had enough to think about. Mr. LeCourt could boost her hopes or dash her confidence, but she had to take the risk of meeting with store owners like him if she wanted to establish a name.

Trying to talk herself out of feeling nervous, Jenna wiped sweaty palms on her pants and took a firmer grip on the wheel. Redwoods, intermingled with Douglas fir, towered on either side, surrounding her with a vivid green. The scent of pine wafted through the vents as she snaked through the valley, and that, together with the misty almost surreal quality of the atmosphere, finally succeeded in relaxing her. By the time she reached Santa Rosa, the rain had disappeared entirely, and she was listening to the latest pop hits and enjoying the drive.

Pulling off the freeway and into a station to get gas, Jenna cut the engine and used her ATM card to fill up. She blessed whoever had pioneered the idea of paying at the pump, then slid back into the driver's seat. She was running a little behind schedule, but if she hurried, she might still make it to San Francisco on time.

Turning the key in the ignition, Jenna pumped the gas pedal. The motor coughed and sputtered out. When she tried again, the starter wouldn't even turn over. No clicks, nothing.

"Oh, no! Not now!" She got out to lift the hood.

"Is something wrong?" A heavyset woman carrying a bag of corn chips from the mini-mart to her station wagon paused at the van's back bumper.

"I think I need a jump. The engine was running fine before I stopped for gas."

"Do the lights and radio still work?"

"I know the radio does."

"Hmm." Setting her corn chips on the hood of her own car, the woman returned to look at the van's engine with Jenna. "I've had my share of car problems. Used to expect my husband to take care of the cars, but he's a better cook than I am, so he does dinner, instead, and I play mechanic. Why don't you try starting it again?"

Jenna did as the woman suggested, silently praying that her stubbornness in refusing to borrow the Durhams' car wouldn't come back to bite her. She hadn't had the nerve to leave Mrs. Durham with a battered van to drive to her hair appointment.

When Jenna's efforts to start the car resulted in nothing more than baffling silence, the woman peered around the hood. "It's the alternator."

Jenna let her forehead hit the steering wheel.

"Are you all right?"

"I'm fine. Thanks for the diagnosis. I belong to Triple A, so I'll go call for a tow."

"That's a good idea. Why don't you walk down to that Chevron station down there." She motioned a dimpled hand at the red-and-blue sign only a block away.

"Unlike this one, it's full service, so they'll have a mechanic. See how much they'd charge you to fix it. If they're reasonable, you won't have far to go."

Jenna nodded. "I'll do that."

The other woman retrieved her chips and jimmied herself behind the wheel of her own car, then honked and waved as she drove away. Jenna returned the wave but didn't make any other move, toward the phone or elsewhere.

"Excuse me, are you still using the pump?"

Jenna blinked up at a skinny teenage boy. "I'm finished but I can't get out of here. My car won't start."

"Oh." He looked unhappy about this news because the other pumps were all in use and he was obviously in a hurry.

"Care to help me push it out of the way?"

He shrugged. "Sure."

Once they tried to get the van rolling, two other motorists pitched in, and Jenna steered into a parking spot. She thanked her helpers, grabbed her purse and walked to the Chevron station, where a greasy man with the name "Dale" sewn onto his shirt told her it would cost approximately $200 to fix her car, *if* it was only the alternator, and would take most of the day.

She used the office phone to call Triple A, then sat staring at the floor, wondering what to do next. She'd be wasting her time calling the Durhams to come for her. Mrs. Durham had the car and was getting her hair done, which left Jenna with only one other option—and the secret hope that if she arrived in San Francisco some time today, she could still salvage her meeting with Mr. LeCourt.

Adam's secretary answered on the second ring. "One moment, please. I'll see if he's in."

Jenna bit her lip. ''Please be there. Come on, Adam, I need you. I need you now,'' she muttered.

''I was wondering how long it would take before you admitted that.''

Jenna's heart leaped at the vibrant sound of his voice, even though she denied his offhand remark. ''I'm not admitting to anything. I'm stranded.''

Concern replaced humor. ''What happened?''

''My van broke down.''

''Where?''

''In Santa Rosa.'' She fought the lump rising steadily in her throat, not wanting Adam to know how close to tears she was. She'd been so excited about meeting Mr. LeCourt, and now she was going to miss her appointment.

''But Gram told me she was giving you her car to drive.''

''I wouldn't take it.''

He cursed. ''You and your damn pride.''

''It wasn't all pride,'' she argued. ''The van has a lot more room for my work.''

''That's true. So are you somewhere safe? Off the road?''

''Yes. I'm at a Chevron station. Fortunately the trouble started just after I stopped to fill up, so I wasn't on the freeway or anything.''

''Good. Tell me where you are, and I'll get there as soon as I can.''

''Are you sure? I mean, I don't want to cause you too much trouble.''

''Jen, it's no trouble. Just give me the directions.''

Jenna did, then asked him to call Harvey LeCourt. ''Do you think he'll give me another chance?'' she asked, hating the high pitch of her voice. She'd battled a drunken ex-husband, suffered through the morning sickness of a surprise pregnancy and dealt with seeing her father for the first time in twenty-four years, for the most part without a tear. And now she wanted to cry over a missed appointment!

"Sure. Don't worry, honey. I'll take care of it. Maybe he'll have time later this afternoon."

The gentleness in Adam's voice, and his endearment, felt like a warm embrace, but Jenna tried to ignore the comfort it gave her because nothing worked faster than sympathy to open the floodgate restraining her tears.

"Thanks," she said simply, and hung up.

CHAPTER FIFTEEN

"WHAT DO YOU MEAN, you're leaving? We were supposed to go over the Cavendish case this afternoon." Mike stood in the doorway of Adam's office, his face turning red—as though Adam had given his tie a yank and cut off his air.

"Sorry. A friend of mine is stranded, and I'm going to pick her up," Adam replied.

"*Her?* Is that what's gotten into you lately? A woman?"

Adam retrieved his keys from his desk drawer and grabbed his suit coat from the closet next to the door. "I don't think I like the implication, Mike. I'm pulling more than my weight around here. You no longer have control of my every waking hour, that's all."

"No one's ever been able to control you, Adam, and I wouldn't be stupid enough to try. But neither would I bother to imply anything. I'm saying it straight out: you haven't been the same for the past few weeks. The rest of us are busting our balls trying to build this practice, and you're taking the afternoon off."

Adam shrugged. "And I took the past two weekends off. After nearly ten years of giving this firm everything I've got, maybe I've decided to have a life again. You don't have a problem with that, do you, Mike?"

Making a tsking sound, his partner shook his large

sweaty head. Excessively overweight, Mike could perspire in subzero weather.

"Don't look so ominous," Adam told him, trying to lessen the growing strain between them. "I've never let my clients down and I'm not going to start now. We've got plenty of time on Cavendish."

"It's not Cavendish I'm worried about. There's something going on around here. We need to talk."

The gravity of Mike's tone made Adam pause, but he shook it off. Mike was a control freak and would like nothing more than to bait him into staying. "Whatever it is, it can wait until tomorrow." He slipped on his coat. "I'll call your secretary and set something up."

Adam could feel Mike's glare as he strode past him, but ignored it. Mike had elevated Adam to partner in record time, but he hadn't acted out of kindness or generosity. He'd seen Adam as a rising star and had wanted to gain for himself a reputation of working with a winner, one whose billable hours were very high. Considering the number of cases Adam had already won, he'd given Mike much more than could have been expected. In Adam's mind he owed nothing more.

"I'm going to be out for a few hours, maybe the rest of the afternoon," he told the receptionist. "Do we still have the packaging from those new prints we bought for the conference room?"

"Are you kidding? I save everything. It's in the supply room."

"Thanks."

The telephone rang and she picked it up. He snagged some mints from her desk, then went to the supply room, where he took all the packaging he could find, and left the office.

The drive to Santa Rosa took a little over an hour. Adam called Harvey on his cell phone, then dictated correspondence until he reached the exit Jenna had told him to take. Though he felt bad she'd been stranded, he found himself smiling foolishly at the thought of seeing her again.

Jenna was asleep in the office of the Chevron station, sitting on a gray metal chair with her head resting against the Coke machine and her arms cradling her purse. Adam studied the familiar lines of her face, the thick lashes that dusted her cheeks, the square jaw and full lips, and wanted to bend over and wake her with a gentle kiss. Instead, he hunkered down and took her hands in his.

"Jen? It's Adam. I'm here."

She blinked, then focused her enormous blue eyes on his face, and the temptation to kiss her intensified.

"You all set?"

Nodding, she glanced around as though still trying to recover her bearings.

The buzzer on the door squawked, and the mechanic came inside. "I'm sorry, but it doesn't look like I'm going to be able to get to your car today, after all," he said. "We've been swamped. But I'll fix it first thing in the morning. You can pick it up after noon."

"Thank you," she said, but Adam could tell she wasn't happy with the news. He helped her up and they started out to the Mercedes.

"Are you taking me home?" she asked, squinting against the afternoon sun as they walked outside.

He grinned. "That depends on whether you mean my home or yours. Harvey is expecting you at four-thirty."

"Oh, that's great! But how are we going to take my windows? There's no room in your car."

"I brought some special packaging and my bike rack." Adam popped the trunk. "We're going to have to tie them on the back."

Jenna unloaded her windows from the van and protected them with more bubble wrap while Adam mounted the bike rack on his trunk. After tying the well-padded windows in place, they climbed into the car.

Adam started the engine and shifted into reverse. Then he jammed the gear back into park and looked at Jenna. "You still want to drive this thing?" he asked. And the smile that spread over her face gave him all the answer he needed.

JENNA FOUND NOTHING as exhilarating as speed—except perhaps sitting next to Adam in the confined space of his two-seater car with the CD player pumping out *Phantom of the Opera*'s "Magic of the Night." After passing a slow-moving sedan, she punched the accelerator again, maneuvering the Mercedes back into the fast lane, and couldn't help smiling at the way the sleek little sports car sped along the freeway.

Catching an inquiring glance from Adam, she turned the music down. "What?" she asked, hearing the self-conscious note in her voice.

"Cops don't like people to enjoy themselves quite this much," he said wryly.

For some reason Jenna felt younger than she had in years—especially since she'd refused to acknowledge all the logic and fear that had initially convinced her not to see Adam when she came to San Francisco. Necessity had dictated she call him. No use analyzing it, or second-guessing it, or ruining the fun by thinking this was a mistake.

She frowned. "Don't tell me you've grown conservative in your old age, Mr. Defense Lawyer."

Adam opened the glove compartment and showed her a handful of speeding tickets. "Merely speaking from experience."

She laughed. "I haven't been pulled over since we were teenagers. I can't believe you haven't lost your license."

"There are benefits to being able to defend yourself." He stuffed the crumpled citations back into the glove box and nodded at the speedometer as she changed into the middle lane to pass another car. "You're going to prove me a bad influence by getting a ticket today if you don't slow down."

Reining in her recklessness, Jenna eased off the gas. What had gotten into her? Her van had just broken down, leaving her without a vehicle and at least a couple of hundred dollars poorer. She'd already missed her big appointment, yet all she wanted to do was laugh and speed and enjoy being with her old boyfriend. Almost as though they'd never been apart...

Jenna couldn't help smiling at Adam. She let her hand brush his thigh as she reached for the CD player. "Thanks for coming to my rescue," she said. "I'm sure you had other things to do today."

"Nothing I'd rather do." His car phone rang and he flipped the mouthpiece open. "Adam Durham... Oh, hi, Joan. No, I won't be back today. I'm afraid Mike's just going to have to wait until tomorrow, like I told him... Sounds good... No, not that early." He glanced at Jenna, then twisted toward the window, his voice dropping perceptibly. "I might be busy in the morning. Let's do it later, after one… Sure… Okay, bye."

Jenna stiffened. "You *might* be busy in the morning? Like with appointments or something?"

He shrugged and looked sheepish. "You have to stay somewhere. I thought I'd save you the hotel expense by letting you sleep on my couch. Or in my bed. It's up to you. In any case I was planning to make you breakfast and give you a proper send-off."

"Your bed?" Jenna let her breath go in a rush. "I don't remember you being so direct."

His eyes searched her face, as though he was trying to gauge her reaction. "There's never been so much water under the bridge before. But don't worry, Jen, I'm not some kind of pervert. If you want me, you're going to have to say so."

She cocked an eyebrow at him, thinking she was safe then, because she'd never admit how badly she wanted him. "And if I take the couch?"

"I won't touch you."

"Just laying down some ground rules?"

"I'm saying you can stay tonight and enjoy San Francisco with nothing to worry about."

The sense of freedom Jenna had felt since they'd left Santa Rosa climbed even higher. "So, for instance, if I took a shower and left the door open, you wouldn't look?"

He assumed a supremely confident air. "Not even a peek."

"And if I forgot my towel and you had to bring me one?"

"I'd close my eyes."

"And if I wore a transparent negligee to my bed on the couch?"

He grinned. "Wow, you're really making this difficult. Let's see… I'd avert my eyes and treat you like
a sister."

Jenna pursed her lips, considering. "So if I stayed
at your place, nothing would tempt you to touch me?"

"Only an invitation."

"Do you know how unlikely you are to receive one
of those?"

She caught the crooked smile he gave her, and its
power was almost enough to melt her resistance on the
spot. "I can always hope."

Her stomach did a little flip-flop and her mouth went
dry. "Good thing I'm in no danger."

The scenery outside changed from the low-lying
shrubs, trees and houses of the rolling northern hills to
the skyscrapers of San Francisco, and the Golden Gate
Bridge rose before them, a giant entrance to the city.

"Wow, it's been years since I've seen the bay,"
Jenna said, hearing their tires thrum as they crossed the
bridge. Yellow, red and blue sailboats dotted the water,
and Alcatraz appeared, looking more like a mystical
treasure-filled island than an old prison. "I'd almost
forgotten how beautiful it is."

"There's no place quite like San Francisco," Adam
said as she stopped at the tollbooth.

Almost hating the wistful note in his voice because
it reflected the strength of the city's hold on him, Jenna
stole another glance at his face. "I can understand why
you like it."

He changed the CD to *Les Misérables,* another of
Jenna's favorites, then asked casually, "You don't
think you'd like it here?"

She shrugged, not willing to fully consider the question. Whether she'd like San Francisco or not was a

moot point. She'd promised Ryan and herself that they'd stay in Mendocino, and she planned to keep that promise. "I don't know. Maybe I would. Where to?"

"Why don't we go to the pier? The weather's nice, so it might be fun to eat on the water. And they have a lot of seafood down there."

Jenna thought of the car-repair bill she'd face tomorrow, but she didn't want to be her practical self today. "Crab legs sound great."

Following Adam's directions, she wound through the crowded city streets and eventually angled the Mercedes into a parking garage across from Pier 39. She handed him the keys, which he pocketed, and they got out. "Thanks for letting me drive."

He grinned and came around the car. "What are friends for?"

For sharing their couches, evidently. He took her hand as they walked, motioning to this store or that pier. Street performers played bongo drums, did break dancing or crooned a ballad to the accompaniment of a guitar as they passed. Occasionally Adam tossed a bill into a collection hat. Jenna watched him applaud the buskers and tease the children and, not for the first time, realized what a charismatic man he was. No wonder she hadn't been able to forget him.

"Having fun?" he asked as they stepped into the cool dark interior of a seafood restaurant that jutted out over the water.

She nodded, wishing the day could go on forever. She didn't feel like a pregnant mother who'd just survived a painful divorce. She felt giddy and young and almost in love again.

Quickly snatching back that thought, Jenna told herself she had some unresolved feelings for Adam, nothing more, and moved to inspect an aquarium that held fifty or more live lobsters.

"Seeing them this way is enough to make you lose your appetite, isn't it?" Adam asked from behind her. "Have you ever bought live lobsters and cooked them at home?"

Obviously he didn't understand the meaning of a shoestring budget. The only way she and Dennis could have afforded lobster was if it had come in a box of macaroni and cheese. "I'm not much of a shellfish eater. I've tried crab legs a couple of times, but I've never tasted lobster."

"Are you kidding? Gram and Pop serve shellfish at the restaurant all the time."

Jenna shrugged. "I try not to eat the more expensive items. Your grandparents have been so good to me I don't want to take advantage."

A look Jenna couldn't identify crossed Adam's face, but the hostess arrived just then to show them to their seats, so she turned away.

"There's nothing better than lobster if it's cooked right," he said as they followed the hostess to a table by a large picture window. "I bought some not long ago and cooked them myself, but they came out rubbery."

That conjured up a vision of Adam trying to create a romantic candlelit dinner for some special lady. "Do you think you'll ever marry, Adam?" she asked as she took the seat opposite him.

"Is that a delicate way of telling me I'm getting too old for the singles scene?" He ran a hand through his hair and grinned. "Should I catch a woman before I go bald or something?"

Jenna wished she could touch the glossy locks that

fell across his forehead. "No, I just can't see you playing the field forever. You like children too much."

He handed her one of the menus the hostess had left. "I guess I've just been waiting for the right time."

"Not the right girl?"

"That, too. Should we order the lobster?"

"You're trying to change the subject. But your personal life isn't any of my business, so I'll shut up and look at the menu."

Silence fell as they both hid behind heavy booklike menus, then Adam asked, "What about you?"

"I'll stick with the crab legs." Jenna was afraid to learn what "market price" was, but she knew Adam would question her if she played it safe and ordered the chicken.

"I meant, do you think you'll ever remarry?"

Jenna set her menu aside and gazed out the window at a string of bobbing vessels tied to the pier and a colony of seals, farther off, sunning themselves on a fenced-off portion of the jetty. "I hope so. Someday."

"But not for a while?"

She patted her stomach. "Can you imagine anyone wanting to take this on?"

"What about the baby's father?"

"What about him?"

"Do you think you'll ever see him again?"

Jenna shifted uncomfortably at Adam's reminder of her falsehood. "There are times when I hope not."

"And other times?"

"It's unavoidable."

Adam's cheek twitched. "So he lives in Mendocino? Where does he work? Where did you meet him?"

Oh, what a tangled web we weave… Jenna sighed. "I'm sorry, I really don't want to talk about this."

"Just tell me one thing. Have you told him about the baby?"

"No."

"Are you going to?"

"At some point I'll probably have to."

"Why? I mean, why complicate things?"

Jenna blinked at him in surprise. "Don't you think he has a right to know?"

"No. I don't think he has any rights at all. I could break his face for even looking at you."

"What?" Jenna laughed, realizing Adam was jealous of a fantasy man. As she considered telling him the truth, in spite of how pathetic it would make her seem, the waitress approached, and Jenna decided to put her worries aside for the moment.

"What can I get you?" the waitress asked.

"Two live Maine lobsters." Adam returned the menus to the waitress and frowned at Jenna as if daring her to contradict him.

Because she really had wanted to try the lobster but knew the price would be even higher than the crab, she held her tongue.

The waitress left and Adam gazed at Jenna, looking uncharacteristically angry.

"What's wrong?"

"Why won't you tell me anything about him? Do you still have feelings for him?"

"Who?"

"The baby's father!"

Jenna dropped her head in her hands and groaned. "No feelings, at least not the kind you think, but grilling me like this isn't fair. I'm sure you haven't lived a celibate life since we broke up."

He opened his mouth as if he'd like to deny any

sexual encounters or justify them in some way, then pressed his lips together again. "You're right. I just can't imagine anyone making you lose control like that. It's driving me crazy to think another man could make you forget everything, even birth control, especially when you won't let me get close."

"Adam—"

Adam's cell phone chirped, and Jenna waited for him to answer it. He spoke to someone who sounded like a client, then set the phone on the table. By the time he turned his attention back to her, he was in control again. "I'm sorry. I was way out of line."

Jenna nodded. "No problem."

"You're still safe on the couch."

"I know."

Her answer seemed to bother him as much as their earlier conversation about the baby's father had, but their salads arrived just then, distracting them both.

While they ate, Adam turned into the charming man who had entertained her earlier, and soon Jenna was laughing and talking again. But the lobster, when it came, looked a little daunting. She'd expected the fluffy white tail she'd seen at the Victoriana's own restaurant, not the entire creature, eyes, antennas, claws and all.

Adam laughed at her hesitancy to touch it. "I'll show you how to eat it. Trust me, you'll love this."

Using a metal cracker, he broke through the hard shell. When he'd made a small pile of white meat on one side of her plate, and a big pile of red shell on the other, he pushed a bowl of melted butter toward her. "Now you're all set."

Jenna stared at the black eyes that seemed to gaze back at her from the top of the shell pile and wondered who first thought of eating these creatures. The sight of them didn't exactly inspire thoughts of dinner.

She realized Adam was waiting for her reaction, so she took her first bite. The salty butter combined with the sweet tender meat nearly melted in her mouth. No wonder people paid such high prices for lobster.

"Good, huh?" Adam seemed more eager to watch her enjoy her meal than to eat his own.

She felt her smile grow. "You'd better hurry or I'll eat yours, too."

He laughed. "I knew you'd like it."

When the bill was presented, Jenna tried to snare it, but the waitress left it on Adam's side of the table and he grabbed it first. "Let me take you out, Jen, for old times' sake."

At first Jenna thought she didn't want to feel she owed Adam anything. But then she decided she was already so deeply indebted—for the ride, Ryan's bike, his help with Mr. LeCourt and his offer to put her up for the night—that she might as well add this meal to the list. Nodding, she slid from the booth to visit the rest room. "Thanks." She paused before walking away. "It was wonderful."

When she returned, Adam was waiting for her by the door. "Where to now?" she asked.

"Local Treasures. It's time to visit Harvey."

CHAPTER SIXTEEN

HARVEY LECOURT was on the telephone when the elegantly dressed saleswoman showed Adam and Jenna into a small square room at the back of his shop. It obviously served as part office, part storeroom. He smiled and made a welcoming motion with his hand, but was clearly in the middle of something that would take a few minutes to finish.

Jenna leaned the two framed stained-glass pictures she carried against a green vinyl chair, and Adam did the same.

Photographs on the walls and desk showed various people standing next to the storefront, shaking Mr. LeCourt's hand. Evidently Adam's friend had been in the business for many years, judging by the number of such pictures and his own physical appearance in them. The older photographs showed Harvey LeCourt as a slender young man with a full head of straight dark hair; the more recent showed him as he looked now, just beyond middle age and slightly overweight, with a receding hairline.

Perching on the edge of the chair, next to her work, Jenna tried not to fidget as they waited. From what she'd seen in the shop, Local Treasures sold a mixture of expensive antiques, paintings from local artists, hand-thrown pottery and weaving. There was also a wall of cameras and video equipment, as well as a counter of jewelry and watches. The eclectic merchandise was tagged with a wide range of prices, most high enough to make Jenna's eyes widen, but she could see how her work would easily fit in—if Mr. LeCourt liked it well enough to buy it.

As if reading her mind, or at least her agitation, Adam reached over and squeezed her hand.

Jenna gave him a brave smile, grateful for his presence. With him—and only with him—she didn't mind revealing her anxiety; it was a legacy of their former closeness.

"I've got some people in my office, and this is taking longer than I expected. I'll have to call you back," Mr. LeCourt said into the phone, and a moment later hung up.

"Sounds like you've been keeping busy," Adam said.

"Busy is good. Busy means I'm selling merchandise and making money. Can't complain." Standing, Mr. LeCourt came around the desk and shook Adam's hand. Then Adam introduced him to Jenna.

"I hadn't expected the artist to be as beautiful as her work," he said.

Jenna smiled, hoping he wouldn't notice the iciness of her fingers as he took her hand. "Thank you. I appreciate the opportunity to be here."

"Well, I hope it'll be an opportunity for both of us. I admit that when Adam first called me, I was reluctant to get involved because I didn't want to be in the uncomfortable position of disappointing a friend. But after seeing the window in Adam's office, I started to feel very enthusiastic. Why don't you show me what you've got?"

Tucking away the knowledge that Adam had hung

her window in his office, Jenna removed the protective packaging from the red-and-white lighthouse.

Mr. LeCourt settled one hip on the corner of his desk. Turning the window so he could see it, he narrowed his eyes, then held the frame in his own hands. "The glass seems to glow from within. How incredible."

Jenna took the compliment as a good sign, but her stomach still knotted as she reached for the Victorian garden. "I've done a lot of the more traditional Victorian themes, like flowers and birds, but I've tried to modernize them, stylize them somewhat. I draw all my own designs."

LeCourt grunted as he set the lighthouse aside and studied the garden. "What else do you have?"

Jenna showed him the rest. The stone cottage overlooking the promontory held his attention the longest.

"These are unique." He smiled. "I don't doubt there's a market for such work."

"Really?" Jenna glanced at Adam and noted his satisfied expression as her fear and skepticism turned to cautious hope. "And what, exactly, does that mean?"

"It means I'd like to carry your work in my store. It'll be on a consignment basis—at first, anyway. That'll give you a chance to test the market."

While Jenna was tempted to take Mr. LeCourt's offer at face value, she didn't want to waste her time or her hopes on someone who was merely helping out a friend. Her stained glass had to stand on its own merits, preferably sooner than later. "This isn't because of some feeling of obligation to Adam, is it? Because if that's the case, I'd rather—"

LeCourt's sharp laugh interrupted her. "I like Adam, but you overrate his charm. And Lord knows I don't owe him anything." He slapped Adam on the shoulder. "That firm of his charged me a small fortune once upon a time."

"Believe me, Jen," Adam said, chuckling, "if this guy didn't like your stuff, he'd have said so."

Jenna finally let her excitement grow. "So you're serious?"

"Completely."

Provided Mr. LeCourt was honest in his motivation and accurate in his assessment—and his percentage wasn't too high—what did she have to lose? She looked at Adam, then nodded. "As long as we can agree on sale prices and the split and all that, I'll do it."

"I take fifty percent, which is pretty standard. But you'll still end up ahead because I plan to charge a lot more than the amount Adam told me you sell them for in Mendocino. I'm not sure exactly where I'll set the price just yet. We'll discuss it after I've had a chance to do some research and to figure out what the market can bear. Of course, you'll have to raise your prices to match mine, or at least come close. It wouldn't do either of us any good to have you selling your work for a fraction of what I'm charging. Especially since you're only three hours away."

Jenna nodded, more than a little overwhelmed. She hadn't expected Mr. LeCourt to make a decision so fast and wasn't sure her brain was taking in all the significant details.

"When can I get more?" he asked.

"I have some other pieces at my studio, and I'm making new ones all the time."

"Good. This is enough to get us started. I'll let you know when you need to send replacements." He motioned to the windows he'd just seen. "Can you leave these with me so we can get them on display this week?"

Jenna glanced at her work and couldn't think of any reason to delay. "All right."

LeCourt clapped his hands. "Fine. I'll walk you through the paperwork."

Adam put his arm around Jenna and smiled proudly. "Fortunately she's got her attorney here to read over the fine print."

SHOES AND JACKET removed, Jenna propped her feet on the dash and reclined in the passenger seat, chattering exuberantly as Adam wove through traffic toward his house. It was only six-thirty, but already the city's lights glittered against a black backdrop, creating the night skyline plastered on everything in tourist shops, from mugs to sweatshirts to postcards—the same skyline engraved in Adam's heart. Turning to Jenna, he approached a subject he'd been wanting to address ever since they'd left Local Treasures.

"So now you'll probably be visiting the city occasionally, don't you think?"

"What?" Jenna blinked up at him. "Oh, yeah, I guess. I'll definitely have to see my work on display." She breathed a whimsical sigh and shifted in her seat belt. "There were times I thought I'd never see the day."

Adam was equally pleased that everything had gone so well with Harvey, but he tried to steer her back on course. "It's probably pretty hard to send glass through the mail or even by courier, which can get costly. By the time you get it packaged right and all that, you might as well drive down here. It's only three hours."

She frowned. ''Three hours doesn't sound like much unless you're driving the van. Even after the alternator's fixed, there's still a dozen other things ready to go out on that heap.''

Reaching over, Adam pulled one of Jenna's feet into his lap and massaged it with one hand as he drove. He expected her to protest, but she didn't. ''What about getting a new car?''

''After I sell a few windows, I might have the money for a down payment...oh, that feels good. Where did you learn to massage?'' She closed her eyes as a satisfied smile curved her beautiful mouth, and Adam was tempted to let his hand creep up her leg. He wanted to make her quiver until she called out his name and begged for more. But he'd promised he wouldn't touch her without an invitation, so he kept his attention on the massage. Rubbing her foot could hardly be construed as an attempt at seduction.

''What if we traded in your van for more reliable transportation?''

She opened one eye. ''We?''

He pressed on a particularly sensitive spot just below her toes and elicited another soft moan. ''I could co-sign for you.''

Obviously torn between wariness at his words and the pleasure of his touch, she didn't answer for a moment. ''Why would you want to do that?''

''Because then you'd feel obligated to come and see me when you were in town.''

She laughed. ''You want me to feel obligated?''

''If that'll work.''

''But what if I couldn't make my payments? You'd be stuck with the bill. I could never take that risk.''

''Come on, you're going to do great in LeCourt's

store. You'll be able to make the payments. And if not—'' he shrugged ''—what would be the harm in letting me help you out a little?''

Pulling her foot away, she put her seat in the upright position. ''I'm not going to let you co-sign for me. We're not even friends, remember?''

He rolled his eyes. ''We're more than friends, Jenna.''

''What does that mean?''

''It means I don't see anything wrong with admitting we still care for each other, at least a little bit. With our history it's only natural. It would be stranger if we felt nothing at all.''

''I don't know if lust can be classified as 'caring.'''

Adam felt her words like cold water dashed in his face. What was she trying to say? He'd been speaking for himself and assuming she felt the same, but maybe she merely hungered for a physical satisfaction she could never achieve with Dennis. Dennis had been a selfish son of a bitch. Maybe that selfishness extended as far as the bedroom, which would certainly explain what had driven Jenna to the one-night stand that had left her pregnant.

''Are you saying that's all I feel for you, or that's all you feel for me?'' he ventured, not sure he wanted to hear the answer.

Jenna shook her head. ''I'm only saying that I'm not going to let you help me get a car. It's not your responsibility. I can take care of myself.''

''Then, for God's sake, take care of yourself and make the payments, but I don't want to worry about you driving that piece of junk back to Mendocino or anywhere else.''

Her lips thinned, and she turned to stare out the window.

"What about Ryan?" he continued. "I know you'd die before you let anything happen to him. Surely you can lower your pride long enough to accept my help if it means a safe car for your son to ride in."

Jenna's unhappy reflection in the glass made Adam sorry for ruining her earlier excitement. He'd been so eager to relieve his own anxiety about her welfare—and to hear her say she'd come and see him—that he hadn't been sensitive enough to her fierce independence. "Just think about it," he said, easing off. "We don't have to decide right now."

"Okay," she murmured, but her earlier carefree attitude didn't return, and she didn't speak again until he turned into his drive—and then it was only to express further doubts about staying with him.

Adam shoved the car into park, feeling frustrated and angrier than the situation merited. "You coward! You're afraid to stay with me even though I've promised not to touch you. You're afraid to take my help for fear it'll hurt your precious pride. And you're afraid to admit that what you feel for me is more than lust. But dammit, Jenna, you're not the only one who's scared to take another chance! Do you think it feels good for me to know you'd never have married Dennis if I hadn't left you?"

"If you loved me you wouldn't have left, and I certainly don't want to be an obligation, Adam. Poor Jenna screwed up her life. Poor Jenna married a loser. Pity Jenna who—"

"Pity, my ass." Slipping a hand around her neck, Adam pulled her toward him. He needed her to appease some sexual primitive instinct; he needed her in other less-obvious ways that ran far deeper. Combined, they created a powerful hunger that demanded he claim her as his own, regardless of the fears and doubts that plagued them both.

At first Jenna tried to pull away, but once his mouth descended on hers, the power of her response astounded him. Her lips parted and her hands entwined in his hair. The small sounds she made in her throat urged him on until he would have given anything for a bed to replace the console that separated them in his Mercedes.

"Admit you still feel something for me," he insisted, hearing the hoarseness of his voice as he drew back just far enough to gaze into her eyes.

"You said you wouldn't touch me."

"You want me to touch you."

"But I didn't ask you to."

"No." Taking a deep breath that did nothing to slow his pounding heart, Adam released her. Maybe it really would be better if Jenna returned to Mendocino tonight, he thought. If she stayed, he doubted he could keep the promise he'd given her—which wouldn't improve his track record any. And moving from friendly conversation and teasing to anger and distrust and finally raw passion couldn't be easy on either of them. "If you want, I'll get you a rental car."

She closed her eyes and rubbed her forehead. When she looked up again, a scowl had replaced the flush on her face. "I'm not a coward."

"You're not afraid of me?" He felt like smiling at the stubborn tilt of her chin and the defiance in her eyes, but didn't want her to think he was laughing at her.

"No. I'd like to see your house." Jenna got out of

the car and started up the drive. Adam felt a disquieting mix of tension and excitement, fear and happiness. His first lover had come back into his life, and it was like a tidal wave, burying him in memories and carrying him away with the desire to be with her again. But he was beginning to feel very vulnerable where Jenna was concerned. As a matter of fact, he'd never felt so open and unprotected in his life. And he wasn't sure he liked the sensation.

EQUIPPED WITH A FULL gourmet kitchen, breakfast room, comfortable living room, an office set off by glass double doors, a small library adjoining the office and four bedroom suites, three of which looked as though they'd never been occupied, Adam's house lacked for nothing. Jenna wandered around, marveling at the pristine cleanliness and expensive furnishings, while Adam brought in his car phone, briefcase, laptop computer and a stack of files. She could scarcely believe that he lived in such opulence—and that he seemed to accept it all so casually.

Raising one hand above her eyes to reduce the glare of the inside lights, she pressed her nose against the back wall of the living room, which was mostly glass. A large deck and patio with a Jacuzzi and what looked like a small waterfall filled the backyard, along with a variety of trees and flowering shrubs.

Coming up behind her, Adam flipped a switch and flooded the yard with light. "What do you think? Do you like it?" he asked, eagerness in his voice.

Jenna dropped her hand and turned back to the leather chairs, big-screen TV and glass coffee table in the living room. "It makes me unreasonably angry."

"Angry?" Shoving his hands in his pockets, he

lifted his brows in surprise. "Anger is hardly the re-action I was looking for."

"I know. It means I'm jealous of course, just like you once accused me of being." With a sigh she sank into the supple softness of his leather couch. "I haven't wanted to admit it, but there it is."

"There's no need to be jealous." He studied her. "You could come here on weekends and enjoy it with me. Actually you could come as often as you wanted to."

Jenna chuckled. "No, thanks." She picked up a *Sports Illustrated* from the coffee table and thumbed through the pages before tossing it aside. "I need to tell you something, Adam, something I should have said long ago."

He loosened his tie, but the tautness of his muscles told her he was far from relaxed. "What's that?"

"You were right to follow your dream. Look at this place! You've done so well. You started with nothing and overcame all the odds. Part of me is so darn proud."

His smile was tentative but wary. "And the other part?"

She held her head in her hands, not wanting to see him when she admitted the truth. "The other part hates your success because, by contrast, it magnifies the mess I've made of my own life."

Jenna felt the couch shift as Adam sat next to her. "Jen, when you marry someone, you have no way of knowing how he or she will behave through the coming years. You take a leap of faith and entwine your life with the other person's. And that takes courage—more courage than I've had."

She shook her head. "Marrying Dennis had nothing

to do with courage. It was the most cowardly thing I've ever done.''

''That doesn't matter. You were eighteen, Jen. All you can do now is close the door and move on.''

''I know.'' She gave him her best imitation of a smile. ''I just wanted you to know that you should never feel guilty for leaving Mendocino...or me. There've been times when I've blamed you for everything that's happened to me, but it's not fair to hold you responsible. You took nothing I didn't freely give. Then you chose to build a future, alone, and you had that right.''

''Jenna... '' He started to reach out to cup her chin, but she stood up and moved away. It was time she forgave him, but relinquishing the hurt and blame she'd laid at his doorstep meant letting go of him completely—which was probably why she hadn't done it before. ''I'd better call Ryan and tell him how my meeting went,'' she said.

Adam looked as though he wanted to say more. Instead he directed her to the office, where she could talk in private. By the time she returned, he'd changed into a pair of worn jeans, running shoes and a golf shirt and was on the phone. Two glasses of bubbling golden liquid waited on the table.

''What's this?'' she asked when he hung up.

''It's apple cider. No alcohol. Someone brought it to my open house just after I moved into this place. And it's perfect for a pregnant lady who has something to celebrate.''

''My deal with Harvey?''

''Exactly. Are you hungry? Should I call and order a pizza?''

''We had such a late lunch I don't want any but we could eat the leftovers for breakfast.''

''No, I'm not hungry, either, and I have other plans for breakfast. I'm going to make you my famous sourdough waffles.''

''*Famous* sourdough waffles?''

He grinned. ''Okay, so not many people have heard of them. It's a recipe I learned from a friend of mine.''

Jenna cocked an eyebrow. ''A woman who used to make you breakfast in bed, no doubt.''

He didn't answer and Jenna guessed her words had hit too close to the truth to be denied. She stifled a flash of jealousy.

''How was Ryan?'' he asked, handing her a glass of cider.

''Good. He wanted to know how soon we could start spending money, now that my things are actually in a regular store. I told him it wouldn't make any difference to our budget for a while.''

''Is he okay with you staying away overnight?''

''Yeah. I talked to Gram, too. She said not to worry about anything, that she'd take good care of him. She's so great. She and Pop were playing checkers with Ryan when I called.''

He took a sip of his own cider. ''Does Gram know you're staying here?''

Jenna nodded. ''I wanted her to be able to get hold of me if she or Ryan needed anything. I hope you don't mind her knowing we're together.''

''Of course not.'' He paused. ''I'm glad you've told them about the baby.''

Jenna grimaced. ''Actually Ryan blurted it out during breakfast one day last week.''

He laughed, and she considered telling him that

Gram and Pop had both jumped to the conclusion that the baby was his, but then decided not to. Emotions had leveled out since their kiss in the car, and she was beginning to relax and enjoy herself again.

"Want to get into the Jacuzzi?" he asked. "It's a beautiful night."

"I don't have a suit."

"You could wear one of my T-shirts."

Jenna sent him her best "get real" look, but he raised his hands in a defensive gesture. "It's dark outside. I won't be able to see anything."

Drinking mock champagne and soaking in hot water surrounded by ferns and fragrant trumpet vines sounded appealing. She hadn't done enough things like that in her life. "Okay," she said. "Find a shirt you don't mind me dousing in chlorine, and we'll get in."

He went to the master suite and returned carrying a white T-shirt with "Hawaii" written across the front.

"You don't have anything that's a darker color?"

"Do you want to ruin all my fun?" he teased.

Jenna groaned in exasperation, then held up the shirt; it should cover her well enough. "Have you ever been to Hawaii?"

"Not yet. My secretary brought that back for me. Her parents took her there a year ago. I'd like to see the islands someday, though."

"What's stopping you? Certainly not a lack of funds."

"Time," he said with a wry smile.

T-shirt in hand, she headed to the bathroom. "Well, then, you'll just have to find yourself a client in Hawaii."

WHEN JENNA RETURNED, Adam had a difficult time keeping his gaze from wandering up and down her shapely legs.

"All set?" he asked, retrieving their glasses and the bottle of sparkling cider.

She nodded, and he started out ahead of her so she wouldn't see his physical reaction to the knowledge that she was naked underneath his shirt—except, perhaps, for a pair of panties. For a moment he imagined stripping off those panties and cupping her bottom in his hands as the water swirled around them. He shook off the vision because it was wreaking the kind of havoc with his body that, in a swimsuit, was virtually impossible to hide.

Setting down the cider, he threw back the cover and tested the water. "Just right," he said, getting in.

Jenna stepped in behind him. "This feels great."

Adam seated himself at a safe distance from her and leaned back as he waited for his eyes to adjust to the darkness.

"How long have you lived here?" she asked.

"About two years. I used to own a condo near the office. I spent so much time at work that it didn't make sense to drive very far, but a couple of years ago I decided it was time to buy something I'd enjoy, at least when I *was* home."

"This place is incredible."

"What's inside that T-shirt is incredible," Adam said, hopelessly distracted by the clinging fabric.

She smiled, but it was a perfunctory smile. "Tell me about the past fifteen years," she said in an obvious ploy to change the subject.

So Adam launched into the story of his crazy college days and how he'd met Mike and started with Bernstein and Lowe. Then he told her about some of his clients and court experiences. As he talked, she surprised him by inching toward him. He kept his recitation light and funny, wanting to draw her even closer with his voice, since he couldn't use his hands.

A gentle breeze stirred the branches overhead and a ray of moonlight peeked through, highlighting Jenna's face. He almost leaned over to give her a gentle kiss, hoping to coax her to open her heart to him again. But remembering his promise, he kept his hands and lips to himself.

"What about you?" he asked when he'd finished regaling her with lawyer stories. He was feeling a little overheated—because he'd stayed in the water too long or because of Jenna's proximity, he didn't know—but he didn't want to get out and break the quiet companionship they were sharing.

A pained expression crossed her lovely face. "I worked to put Dennis through school. He could never decide what he wanted to be, kept changing his major and then, just after we had Ryan, dropped out to be a cable installer. He didn't make enough for us to get by, so I started working for a doctor friend we'd met at church. Dennis started hanging out with the guys after work and drinking more and more heavily." She shrugged. "Things went downhill from there. Not a very engaging story."

He felt her leg brush his, slick and satiny soft, and flexed against his instinctive response. "Did you love Dennis initially?"

Jenna gazed up at him, finally dropping the guarded look she'd had since they'd come back into each other's lives. "I think we both know who I loved."

Her leg touched his again, and this time Adam had to grit his teeth not to take her in his arms and crush her to him. She had loved him without reservation once. Had she been too deeply hurt—by him, by Dennis—to give that much of herself again? Maybe, if he took things slowly enough, he could convince her he wouldn't make the same mistake twice.

But was it true? Was he finally ready to give Jenna forever?

Yes, he realized. He wanted it all, marriage, Ryan, her unborn child—and his own babies.

He felt her shift in the water, now close enough that he could easily have touched all the alluring parts of her body. The past few weeks she'd held herself aloof, avoided physical contact with him whenever possible, but now she was acting curiously different. The way she'd moved closer to him, the way she leaned toward him when she laughed, sent subtle signals telling him she'd changed her mind about the ''hands off'' edict. But why? Adam didn't understand what had finally melted her resistance, but he couldn't be satisfied until he knew she was offering her heart, as well as her body.

Taking her hand, he lifted it to his lips and took her fingers, one by one, into his mouth, tickling the sensitive pads with his tongue.

She closed her eyes and let her head fall back, leaving him free to enjoy the curve of her long neck and the sight of her breasts rising and falling as her breathing grew shallow. Finally he let her go. ''Like I told you before, Jenna, I won't take this any further without a verbal invitation,'' he said softly. Then he held his breath, hoping that, this time, she'd give him one.

CHAPTER SEVENTEEN

JENNA WANTED to tell Adam the truth, to admit she'd been thinking about him almost constantly for the past two weeks, but for some reason the words wouldn't come. She'd closed the distance between them in the water because she couldn't remember why she'd wanted to stay away. Their day together had been so perfect, so right. She wanted to take the opportunity to be with Adam again, even if it was only for one night.

Unfortunately he wouldn't accept that. He wanted more than her body. He was trying to capture the part of herself she'd learned to protect, to hold well beyond a man's reach. And after fifteen years spent building barricades, one night couldn't tear them all down.

"I'm sorry, Adam," she said. "I'm not the same person I used to be." Moving away, Jenna got out of the Jacuzzi, toweled off and didn't look behind her as she headed back inside. She needed to close her eyes and sleep and forget how Adam made her feel, how he tempted her away from her carefully laid plans for the future.

She stripped off his wet shirt and wrapped herself in her towel, waiting for him to come in and lend her something to sleep in. But she couldn't forget the way he'd looked at her in the Jacuzzi, as if the whole world hung on her answer.

He left me, dammit. This is not my fault!

It always seemed to come back to this—the years of hurt and betrayal.

Adam didn't say anything when he came in wearing a towel around his waist and holding his swimsuit in one hand. He simply walked past her, looking like a dark Adonis. His naked chest and legs, crafted as beautifully as any statue, made Jenna's heart trip over itself. And still she couldn't make herself utter the words that would bring her into the comforting circle of his arms.

A moment later he returned from his bedroom wearing a pair of pajama bottoms and holding out the matching top, along with a new toothbrush.

"Thanks." Accepting the articles, Jenna closeted herself in the bathroom, showered, changed and brushed her teeth. Then she blow-dried her hair, hoping Adam would be in bed asleep by the time she finished. When she stepped into the hall, however, she could see him sitting in the living room. The television droned in the background.

Apparently he'd only been waiting to do the polite thing, because the moment he saw her, he stood and flipped off the TV. "You can take your pick of the bedrooms. They're right this way."

"You don't have to show me. I know where they are." Jenna bit her lip, reluctant to allow the night to end at such an impasse. Physical intimacy was far more than she'd been willing to give him even hours before. Didn't he know when to quit? Wasn't an affair what he'd wanted in the first place? Certainly he wasn't interested, couldn't be interested, in anything more permanent, especially with someone who was pregnant with another man's baby. "I appreciate your letting me stay here."

"It's no problem." His face looked grim. "I'll see you in the morning."

He disappeared down the hall, entered his bedroom and closed the door. Jenna heard his shower go on. After a few minutes the house fell silent.

She chose the room decorated in denim contrasted with yellow plaid, because it was farthest from Adam's. Jenna climbed into bed; the sheets felt crisp and smelled new, as did the fluffy goose-down duvet, but she couldn't get comfortable. The aching need to be close to Adam kept pulling at her, tempting her to go down the hall, and even when she did finally doze off, she awoke only minutes later.

"Damn," she grumbled, throwing back the covers and getting up to pace the floor. She'd seen how rigidly Adam had held himself in the hot tub. He'd been aroused at other times during the day, too. She'd felt his intense regard, seen his pupils dilate and his body grow hard. He had to be as tormented as she was. So what was he trying to do? Was he truly after her heart?

Jenna let her breath go on a long sigh. She didn't want to give her heart to him or anyone else, at least not now. Not yet. She only wanted things to feel the way they used to, when she and Adam were in love. For just a little while...

Shutting out logic and any thought of tomorrow— when she'd have to go back to being a responsible parent—Jenna padded down the hall and slipped into Adam's room.

He wasn't asleep. At the soft click of the door, he angled his head up but didn't say anything.

"Are you going to send me away or will you take what I can offer?" she asked.

The covers fell down to his hips as he sat up in bed.

Judging from his bare chest and the pajama bottoms in a heap on the floor, Jenna knew he was naked between the sheets.

She ventured closer, until she stood within reach of his arms.

"What are you offering?" he asked.

"Tonight."

He hesitated, as though considering. "You know me too well to think I'll settle for less than what I want."

Why was he making this so difficult? "Problem is, I don't know what you want, Adam. Or what I want."

His teeth gleamed in a smile. "It's simple for me, Jen. I want it all—your heart, your soul, your body. But I'm not an idiot. For now, I'll take what I can get." Reaching out, he pulled her swiftly down on top of him, and their mouths connected in a fierce passionate kiss.

JENNA AWOKE in the morning with a smile and a contented yawn. She was now alone in Adam's bed, but every inch of her body still tingled from his touch, and his scent lingered in the room. He'd aroused her and satisfied her again and again throughout the night, in a variety of ways. But it was the memory of his gentleness and the murmured endearments that had moved her the most. He seemed to take their intimacy more seriously than she'd anticipated and openly expected something to grow from it.

Jenna wanted the same thing. She couldn't deny it any longer. She didn't remember a time when she *hadn't* wanted to spend her life with Adam. But how many days would pass before he realized that a long-distance relationship was too difficult for a busy lawyer? That she and Ryan would only get in the way?

Rolling over, Jenna buried her head in the pillow, trying to shut out the inevitable intrusion of rational thought as it once again asserted itself in the ongoing war with her emotions. She wanted to enjoy the relaxed aftermath of their lovemaking, not face hard realities. But the night was gone, and in the cool light of day she could see that they'd never make their relationship work. She couldn't expect Adam to stand by her while she had another man's baby. Besides, the everyday life of a mother had more to do with loyalty and devotion than it did with sex or excitement. Such routine days would eventually bore someone as vital and charismatic as Adam, a man who hadn't been able to make a commitment in all the years they'd been apart.

He'll leave, just like he did before, Jenna decided. She'd been a fool to let her guard down. The memories of making love with him would only make things awkward when he came to Mendocino to see his grandparents. She'd blush whenever one of them mentioned his name, and Laura would tease her unmercifully.

"Dumb, dumb, dumb," she muttered, getting out of bed, hoping she could throw on some clothes before Adam returned. She couldn't find her panties in the tangle of bedding, but she managed to don Adam's pajama top just before he came striding into the room, wearing a pair of sweats and carrying a white wicker breakfast tray.

"Why are you getting up? It's still early and I brought you my sourdough waffles like I promised." His boyish smile nearly melted her heart, but Jenna steeled herself against it.

"It looks great, and I'll have a few bites, but then I should be getting back."

His smile disappeared, and his eyes narrowed. "Something's wrong."

"No, nothing. Last night was…well, last night was fantastic, but I have a son waiting for me in Mendocino, and—"

"Jenna, what aren't you telling me?"

"I don't know what you're talking about. I just have to get back. I have some things I need to do for Gram and Pop. I do most of their bookwork, you know, and some of the extra cleaning. Pamela's had to take a lot of days off, and Gram's getting too old to do the heavier stuff and—"

Adam slammed the tray down, rattling the silverware and sloshing juice over the sides of the glass. "Cut the bullshit, Jenna. You told me Dennis could never really reach you, not deep down, in here." He thumped his chest. "You're shutting me out, too. Or is this just another one-night stand?"

She shook her head. "No."

"Then what are you doing?"

Leaving you before you can leave me. "Adam, I have a lot going on right now. I can't devote myself to a relationship that'll probably never work. I've told you that before."

His jaw clenched, with anger or pain, Jenna didn't know. "And what if I said you're not getting rid of me that easily?"

"I'd say of course not, because you're better at walking out when it suits *you.*"

He stiffened as though she'd slapped him. "So we're back to that. This is some kind of get-even, turnabout-is-fair-play game, isn't it?"

Jenna pinched the bridge of her nose and tried to gather her fractured thoughts. "No, I didn't mean that.

I've already told you I don't hold the past against you anymore. It's just that…it's just me. I'm broken, somehow, Adam, and I don't know how to fix myself.'' She swallowed hard, trying to ignore the tightening in her chest and fighting the tears burning behind her eyes. ''Don't you understand? I just can't *believe*,'' she said softly.

The telephone rang and Adam sent it an irritated glance. ''Then I'll teach you how to believe again, how to believe in us.''

Resisting the tenderness of his words, Jenna focused on the phone. ''That might be Gram or Ryan.''

With a frustrated sigh, Adam strode to the nightstand and snatched up the receiver. ''Hello.''

Jenna was tempted to flee the room so she could shower and dress. With luck she could avoid finishing their argument. But she paused long enough to see if the caller really was Gram or Pop or Ryan, and then she couldn't move because the look on Adam's face froze the blood in her veins.

''What's wrong?'' she whispered as Adam's hand tightened on the receiver until the muscles of his arm stood out. He extended his other hand to her, and she went to him, feeling her heart start to pound until the sound of its beating seemed to echo off the walls. ''Is it Ryan? Tell me!''

''We'll be right there, Gram. Calm down. It'll be okay. I've got Jenna and we're leaving now.''

Tears filled Jenna's eyes and streamed down her face. She stared at Adam, terrified to hear what his grandmother had said, yet too desperate not to ask. *''What happened?''*

Quickly replacing the receiver, Adam pulled her into

his arms and pressed his lips to her temple. "Jen, it's Dennis. He's taken Ryan."

ADAM FELT JENNA sway as though she might collapse and tightened his grip.

"Oh, God. I never should have left him," she sobbed. "Dennis came to the house yesterday. He was angry, but I thought...I thought... *What* was I thinking?"

"Jen, you couldn't have stopped Dennis, anyway. He snatched Ryan from school. Ryan forgot his lunch this morning and Gram drove it over, but when she got there, Ryan was gone. Some kid on the playground saw him getting into a beat-up old car with a man who fits Dennis's description."

"That bastard!" Jenna's tears continued to flow, but now her body grew rigid with what Adam could only imagine to be white-hot rage. "If he hurts Ryan..."

"He won't, Jen, because we're going to get Ryan back. I promise you that."

Pulling away, Jenna closed her eyes and made fists of her hands. "I can't go to pieces," she said with a stifled sob. "Ryan needs me. We've got to go."

"Get dressed and meet me in the garage," Adam told her. "I'm going to call Todd."

She nodded and ran from the room. The phone rang again, and he grabbed up the receiver, hoping to hear that his grandparents had already found Ryan. "Gram?"

"Who?"

Adam nearly cursed when he recognized his partner's gruff voice. "Mike, I'm going to have to cancel our meeting today. And I can't talk right now. I've got an emergency."

"Damn right! We all do. You get your ass down to the office right away, or there's no more partnership! Roger's in trouble. The police have arrested him, and now they're investigating the rest of us."

"What?" Adam shook his head. Somehow he'd known it would come to this.

"You heard me! I don't know exactly what's going on—the bastards won't tell me anything. But from what I can figure, someone tipped them off that Roger manipulated Whitehead's records, and now we're all under suspicion. Especially you, since you had the case before Roger."

"I tried to warn you, Mike. Roger was too ambitious for his own good."

"I thought you were just being uptight. I never dreamed—"

"What? You're the one who coached him, Mike."

"I only told him to win. And I've told you the same thing often enough. Regardless, we all need to be here to put on a united front."

"I can't be there. Give the police a key to my office and let them dig through whatever they want. I don't have anything to hide."

"I'm depending on you, Adam. It's time to defend yourself and the firm and—"

"And Roger? Sorry, Mike. He's a big boy. He knew what he was doing."

"I don't care what you think of Roger," Mike barked, "he's one of us. You have to come in."

"And if I don't?"

"Then it's over. I'll dissolve the partnership. You know I can. It's in the agreement."

Adam closed his eyes. His career. Fifteen years of

blood, sweat and tears. He had to go back and defend his little empire.

But he couldn't abandon Jenna again, not now, not ever.

"Then I'll be in to pick up my things when I can," he said. Feeling a door close somewhere in his heart, he hung up.

"What did Todd say?" Dressed in the clothes she'd worn the day before, Jenna stood in the doorway, looking drawn and pale and more fragile than Adam had ever seen her.

"I haven't been able to get hold of him yet. Grab my keys and get in the car. I'll be right there." She hesitated and Adam wanted to take her in his arms and croon softly in her hair that everything would be all right. He wanted her to nod and look up at him with trust shining in her eyes. But she didn't believe in him. She'd said as much, and her lack of faith kept them as separate and alone as though an ocean stood between them.

"I can't expect you to…" Her words dwindled away and she tried again. "I mean, he's my son. I know you probably have to work today. I'm too frightened to take the time to get a rental, so if maybe you could rent a car and let me use yours… I'll pay all the charges, of course…"

How could she be so formal after everything they had shared last night? "I'm going with you," he said in a voice that brooked no argument. "Get in the car."

This time she obeyed without question, and Adam paused only long enough to call the Fort Bragg police department. Gram had already reported the kidnapping, but Adam wanted to make sure Todd knew what had happened to Ryan in hopes he'd take a personal interest.

Todd was out on patrol, but Adam asked the dispatcher to give him the message. Then he grabbed his day planner, which contained his money and credit cards, and dashed out to the garage.

Jenna was waiting for him in the car, staring straight ahead with her hands knotted in her lap. Adam got in and covered her hands with one of his own, noting the coldness of her fingers. "You okay?"

She nodded, but Adam guessed she was seeing all sorts of unpleasant things in her head—things he cringed to even think about. He started the car and backed out into the street.

Mendocino was usually a three-hour drive, but he had no intention of letting it take that long.

CHAPTER EIGHTEEN

RYAN SAT IN THE PASSENGER SEAT of his father's old car and felt Dennis staring at him as he ate a Happy Meal. They were parked outside a McDonald's, in some town Ryan didn't recognize.

"What surprise did you get?" his father asked.

Ryan hadn't even checked. He was eight, almost nine, and much too old for such small toys. He couldn't summon much joy over it, not when more than anything he wanted to be home with his mother. To avoid making his father mad, however, he dug through the wrapping his hamburger had come in and pulled out a small metal car. When he held it up, Dennis whistled.

"That's nice. McDonald's beats the hell out of school lunch, huh?"

Ryan's stomach twisted with longing at the thought of school, but he nodded because he didn't dare disagree.

"You okay here for a minute?" his father asked.

He looked around at the other parked cars and the drugstore across the lot. People came and went, but no one seemed to be paying them any attention. "Sure."

"Good. Shouldn't be too long."

The door squealed as his father climbed out. Then Dennis ducked down to talk through the crack in the window. "Don't go anywhere," he said. "I don't want to have to punish you on our first day together."

"I won't."

"Promise?"

Ryan nodded, then turned to watch his father walk toward the glass-fronted McDonald's. He went back to eating and quickly finished his lunch, but a long time passed without any sign of Dennis.

Growing more and more frightened, Ryan unbuckled his seat belt and got up on his knees to gaze through the dirty back window. Where had his father gone? He'd spent the morning telling Ryan how they were going to live together now and what great care he was going to take of his boy, but it wouldn't be unlike him to change his mind and simply disappear.

There was a light dusting of snow on the ground outside. Ryan had on a coat, but cold air seeped into the car and numbed his hands and feet. He waited for Dennis a little longer, then got out to check for his father inside McDonald's.

Raising a hand to shade the glass, he peered into the brightly colored room. He was afraid Dennis would catch him out of the car, but he was equally afraid of being abandoned.

It was crowded inside, so it took a few minutes to decide his father wasn't there. Biting the skin around his nails, Ryan checked the parking lot behind him and began to circle the building.

Dennis's voice, coming from around the corner, froze Ryan's tennis shoes to the concrete. Peeking around the beige-painted brick, he saw his father standing with his back to him, clutching a paper cup that he held out to the people who entered and left the restaurant.

As Ryan watched, Dennis approached a man and a woman. The man took some money from his pocket and stuffed it into the cup. Dennis thanked him, and the couple ambled away.

Didn't his father have any money of his own?

Remembering Dennis's search through the car for the coins he'd used to buy the Happy Meal, Ryan decided he must not. That would explain why his father had said he wasn't hungry and why they weren't driving anymore.

Blowing on his hands to warm them, Ryan turned around and headed back to the car. His father would give him a beating like the kind he'd seen his mother take if he got caught disobeying. But before he wedged his door open to climb back onto the cracked vinyl seat, he glanced at the drugstore, and a longing so sharp it stung rose up inside him. He wanted his mom. He wanted to be home where it was warm and where he knew he was safe.

Fighting the tears that threatened to make him sob like a girl, he studied the pay phone glinting in the sun in front of the store. It was clear across the parking lot, but if he ran...

Could he call for help? Would his mother be able to find him? He shoved his hands all the way to the bottom of his pockets. A pay phone cost thirty-five cents. His mother had taught him how to use one at the mall once, but he had no money.

Climbing into the car, Ryan dug through the wadded clothes, empty bottles and fast-food wrappers that flooded the back seat, looking for change. If he could only find a quarter and a dime... Evidently all the quarters had been spent on the Happy Meal, but he did manage to find three nickels and two dimes. He knew the coins added up to the right amount of money— they'd done math problems like this one in school—

but he wasn't sure nickels would work in a pay phone. His mother had used a quarter.

Leaving the car door slightly ajar because he couldn't bear to hear it slam, Ryan checked to make sure Dennis was still standing on the other side of the restaurant, then began weaving his way through the parking lot. His mother had always told him not to run where cars were moving, but he was too frightened to go slow. His brisk walk turned into a trot and then a full run as he neared his goal.

"Be careful, kid," someone called from a truck as he darted across its path.

Ryan didn't even look up. The sidewalk shimmered before him, and he leaped to safety, grabbed the hand-held part of the telephone and dropped in his money. He dialed the Victoriana's number and waited, hoping he'd dialed it right and his father wouldn't catch him before someone answered.

"Mom…Mom…Mom…" he begged under his breath, but heard no ringing, nothing. Just then an old lady got up from a bench in front of the store and with the help of a cane tottered toward him.

"That silly phone doesn't work, dear," she said. "It just took my money. I told them inside. It's good to report things like that, you know. Otherwise, it doesn't get fixed. You might want to do the same."

"No need. He's just playing around, anyway."

Ryan whirled at the sound of his father's voice and saw Dennis coming toward him. Gripping the side of the phone pedestal as his stomach dropped to his knees, he wondered if he was going to throw up the hamburger that churned in his stomach.

Dennis gave the old lady a polite smile, then turned to him. "Ready to go, son?"

Ryan glanced at the woman. He wished he had the courage to run to her and beg for help, but she looked so old and frail. He knew she was no match for his father. "Yeah…um…I'm sorry. You were gone so long I thought you weren't coming back."

Dennis raised his hand and Ryan flinched. Instead of striking him, however, his father took him by the neck and started guiding him back to the car. "I'm sorry," Ryan told him again, and sent another pleading glance at the old lady.

She stood and peered after them. "Wait a minute," she called. "Who are you? Does that boy belong to you?"

Dennis ignored her and increased their pace until they were nearly running. "Now look what you've done," he hissed. "I told you to wait in the car."

Too breathless to speak, Ryan nodded.

"And you promised you'd obey."

The old lady was yelling at them, but Ryan could no longer turn around to see her.

"I expected better from you, Ryan," Dennis snapped. "I can see your mother hasn't taught you anything, but discipline's a father's job, anyway. It's a good thing we're together now. I'll get you shaped up in a heartbeat."

"I'll be good," Ryan promised, willing his wobbly knees to support him as his father dragged him along. He wanted to yell for help, but fear clogged his throat. He'd really done it this time. His dad would beat him for sure. "I didn't mean to do anything wrong."

"Then why did you leave the car? You'll have to face the consequences, you know."

Ryan blinked rapidly as he searched for an excuse his father might accept, something to diffuse his anger.

"I know. I'm sorry. It's just that Mom's pregnant and she's been sick, and I wanted to call and check on her, that's all."

It worked. As soon as the words were out, his father froze. But his eyes took on a dangerous glittery look, and the hand clamped on Ryan's neck eased.

Ryan could no longer hear the old lady. Had she gone for help or had she given up? He jerked, breaking his father's hold, but before he could run, Dennis grabbed him again, this time by the arm. "Whose baby is it?"

Wishing the old lady would hurry if she was bringing help, he said, "It's Mom's—"

"Who's the daddy?" His father's nails bit so painfully into his arm that Ryan couldn't hold back the tears.

"She said you're the daddy!" he cried.

Dennis finally loosened his grip but didn't let go. "No kidding!" Suddenly he laughed and dragged Ryan the rest of the way to the car. "Well, that's all the more reason for us to be a family again, don't you think, son?"

Then he shoved Ryan in and shut the door.

JENNA SAT ALONE in the Durhams' office, battling the panic that had threatened to immobilize her since she'd heard about Ryan's disappearance. She and Adam had arrived at the Victoriana in record time. But she'd spent the first hour at the police station, providing a more recent picture of Ryan than the one Gram had taken from her room, filling out forms, answering questions about the color and make of Dennis's car.

Now it was nearly one o'clock. Ryan had been missing for almost five hours, which seemed a lifetime to

Jenna, an eternity for her child to be at risk. Trying to ignore the ominous ticking of the clock on the desk, she focused on the names and telephone numbers in the tattered address book she'd retrieved from a box at the bottom of her closet. This book, with its dog-eared pages, belonged to the years she'd been married. Jenna had thought she'd never need it again. If not for Ryan's blood connection to Dennis's relatives, she would have thrown it away.

Thank God she hadn't. Dennis could be anywhere, and contacting his friends and family, anyone who might hear from him, was her only chance of getting her son back quickly.

Because Dennis had mentioned his cousin Joe, Jenna had tried him first. But something about the earnestness in Joe's voice led Jenna to believe him when he said he hadn't heard from Dennis since Wednesday, the day they'd talked about getting him on at the mill.

Reaching for the telephone, Jenna took a steadying breath and dialed Kim and Meredith Livingston, Dennis's parents. It had been three years since she'd spoken to either of them. They'd moved from Mendocino more than ten years ago and, last she knew, lived a peaceful, quiet life in a mobile home on the outskirts of Elko, Nevada. Jenna hadn't really kept in touch. They'd never wanted to be bothered by Dennis or his little family. Especially after the problems started.

At one point, when she and Dennis were going for counseling, Dennis had admitted that his father had been an alcoholic and had sometimes beaten up on him and his mother. But this news had come as a complete surprise to Jenna. When they were kids, Kim had seemed strict but not violent, although Mr. Durham had once mentioned that he'd had his suspicions.

From all the evidence, Kim Livingston had kicked his habit and learned how to control his anger, but now Meredith would tolerate no more pain resulting from alcohol. If she didn't hear from Dennis, it was easier to believe her son was well and happy. She had her daughters and several grandchildren living close by and seemed to dote on them. There was a time Jenna had resented the Livingstons' treating her and their youngest son so differently, never reaching out to Ryan. But in the end, she'd given up trying to build a relationship between them.

"Hello?" The quaver in Meredith Livingston's voice made her sound much older than Jenna remembered.

"Meredith? This is Jenna."

There was a long awkward pause.

"Dennis's ex-wife."

"I know who you are. What do you want, Jenna?"

"It's about Dennis—"

"Whatever he's done, I don't want to know about it."

In the background Jenna heard Kim Livingston ask who was on the phone, then a low hum in her ear as Meredith covered the mouthpiece to respond.

"I wouldn't have bothered you without good reason, Meredith," Jenna continued. "Dennis has taken Ryan—"

"He called 'bout a month ago. Said you wouldn't let him see his kid. Maybe if you'd treated him fair in the divorce, he wouldn't have had to resort to doing something like that."

"Fair, Meredith? Dennis is abusive. I had to do what I could to protect Ryan and myself."

"I don't think Dennis will hurt him." Her voice was

dismissive, as though she didn't want to face the possibility that maybe he would.

"You don't know that. He could have an accident while driving under the influence, or he could leave Ryan in an unsafe situation. You obviously don't know that Dennis is in really bad shape."

Another long pause. "I stuck it out with my man and he came around. You could have done the same."

Jenna put a hand to her forehead, refusing to let this woman's probing of her deepest pain bring fresh tears. "Maybe you're a better woman than I am, Meredith. I tried to hold our marriage together, but our problems were bigger than I was. Dennis became too violent. I wasn't willing to risk the safety of my son."

Silence greeted this statement, and Jenna wondered what Meredith was thinking. The woman seemed to feel that staying with Dennis's father and letting him vent his anger on her and their children was the right thing, the self-sacrificing thing, to do. And maybe it was, although Jenna doubted it. More likely Dennis wouldn't have traveled the road his father had if he hadn't experienced the same kind of abuse in his youth. If Meredith had left her husband, maybe the cycle would have been broken. Who could say? Jenna had no intention of placing herself in the lofty position of judge. She only knew that sometimes it took greater courage to leave, and to live with the failure of a marriage, than to stay.

"We haven't heard from him," Meredith said at last, but her voice had softened ever so slightly, and Jenna hoped that in some small way she'd reached her.

"Will you take down my number and let me know if you hear from him?"

In the background Kim's voice intruded again. "Let

me talk to her. I'll tell her what we think of a woman who leaves her husband and then refuses to share their child—''

''No.'' Meredith sounded surprisingly forceful. ''I'm taking care of it. Hand me that pencil.''

Evidently Kim did as he was told, because Meredith cleared her throat and said, ''I'm ready.''

Jenna gave her the number, then the phone clicked and Dennis's mother was gone.

''Any luck?''

Jenna glanced up to see Adam leaning against the doorjamb, looking as tired and worried as she felt. The sight puzzled her in a vague way, but she was too preoccupied to examine it. ''I was talking to Meredith, Dennis's mom.''

''I remember Meredith.''

''I'm not sure, but I think she'll call me if she hears anything.''

''And his brothers?''

''I've only talked to his cousin, who hasn't heard from him. His brothers are next on the list.''

Turning back to the faded writing in her address book, Jenna found Gary's number, the brother who'd lived just across town from them for most of their marriage, and dialed. Three beeps and a recording played in her ear.

''The number you have dialed is no longer in service....''

She frowned at Adam and hung up, wondering if Gary and his family had moved, then tried his work number.

''Henley's Autobody.''

''Is Gary there?''

''Just a minute.''

Jenna tapped her foot as Adam crossed the room to sit on the corner of the desk. Finally Gary came on the line.

"Gary? This is Jenna, Dennis's ex-wife."

"Shit. What's he done now?"

Jenna had occasionally called Gary, when things with Dennis had gotten really bad. But she'd soon realized there wasn't anything he could do to help her, not really. By the time he arrived, Dennis had usually stormed out. The one time he hadn't, Dennis had broken Gary's nose, along with a window and two doors. Jenna had never called Dennis's brother for help again. He had a wife and three kids of his own. It wasn't fair to involve him.

"He's taken Ryan from school," she said simply.

"God, he's a mess. Will he ever quit?"

"I don't know. I'm terrified, Gary. I'm afraid he'll hurt Ryan."

"Where are you living now, Jenna?"

"I'm back in Mendocino. Dennis followed me down here, making all kinds of threats. He went to jail for a week for violating his restraining order. As soon as he got out, he took Ryan."

"When?"

"This morning, before school started. Do you ever hear from him?"

"Not often. Every once in a while he comes by here asking for twenty bucks, but the last time I wouldn't give him any money. I tried to get him back into AA, even got him a job here with me. And what does he do? He takes his first paycheck and goes on a drunken binge and gets fired for not showing up at work."

The story didn't surprise Jenna. She'd heard it many

times before. "Will you call me if you hear from him? For Ryan's sake?"

"Sure."

Jenna gave him her number and hung up as Adam rounded the desk and started to knead her tense shoulders.

Dennis had one other brother, Russ, but he'd always taken Dennis's side, and Jenna had much less confidence he'd help her, even if he could. She dialed him next, anyway, and an answering machine picked up. She left the Victoriana's number and the number of Adam's car phone, then called Dennis's sisters, both of whom treated her distantly but promised to call if they heard anything.

"Do you think any of them will really contact us?" Adam asked when she slumped in the chair.

"I think Gary would. The others? Who knows? Dennis is a convincing liar when he wants to be. If he told them he'd gone clean and I was being vindictive in not letting him see Ryan, he could probably sway their sympathy."

Adam's strong hands continued to smooth the knots out of Jenna's shoulders and neck. But her head still throbbed with the pressure of tears, both shed and unshed.

"Well, I finally got hold of Todd," he said after a moment, and Jenna could tell he was trying to infuse some positive energy into his voice. "He said Dennis has no address down here. My guess is that he's on his way back to Oregon, trying to put some distance between us and him. He's got to get back to familiar ground where he might be able to lay hands on some money. If he couldn't post bail, he doesn't have much."

Jenna winced. "Which means he might not have what it takes to feed Ryan or get them a place to sleep at night."

"You can't think of that, Jen. Only of finding them. I'm going to head up to Oregon and see what I can dig up, ask a few questions along the way. Give me the numbers of his family, and I'll contact each of them again once I get there. You call me if you hear anything on this end, okay?"

The telephone rang and Jenna snatched it up. "Hello?"

"Jenna? This is Todd. I think I've found something."

CHAPTER NINETEEN

JENNA STARTED to shake so badly she could hardly keep her grasp on the phone. She felt Adam's arms go around her, felt him give her a kiss on the top of her head, and his warmth and calm helped to bolster her. "What is it?"

"Since I talked to Adam, I've been checking with different police departments between here and the address you gave me as Dennis's last known residence. Just across the Oregon border, in Medford, an elderly woman reported seeing a man drag a little boy away from a pay phone outside a drugstore. She said the boy seemed frightened, reluctant. She insisted the man had to be some kind of sexual predator, but the uniforms up there didn't take the incident too seriously because she calls in so often. Most of what she reports turns out to be nothing. But in this case the description of the man's car matches the one Dennis was driving."

Jenna's heart beat faster with hope. "Medford is on the way to Portland."

"Yep, right off Interstate 5. I think we've got a start. At least we know what direction he's taking. I just wanted you to know we're doing something about this, Jenna. We'll get your son back."

"Thanks, Todd. I can't tell you how grateful I am." After stoically withstanding the coolness of Dennis's family, Jenna felt the kindness of Todd's voice slip beneath her resistance like smoke beneath a door. Tears started streaming down her cheeks again, tears she couldn't hold back. She hung up quickly so Todd wouldn't hear the wobble in her voice, but there was no hiding what she felt from Adam.

"So he is on his way to Oregon," Adam said. Pulling her up and against his chest, he stroked her back while she cried. "I'm going after them."

Jenna straightened, collecting her thoughts. "I'm going with you."

"But what if we're wrong and the sighting's a fluke? Don't you want to be here in case—"

"No. I know Dennis. He's running back home. His family acts like they don't care about him, because they're so disappointed in him, but his brothers have tried to help him a dozen times. He'll use Ryan as an excuse to get some money out of one of them, probably Russ, and claim he's going sober and getting a job."

"All right. Gram and Pop will be here. They can call us the minute they hear anything."

As if Adam's words had conjured up his grandmother, Mrs. Durham knocked softly on the open door to announce her presence. "What have you learned?" she asked, hobbling into the room.

Adam helped her to a seat, evidently sensing, as Jenna did, that the crisis had stolen her energy for the day. He told her what Todd had found out and what Jenna suspected, then asked, "Are you holding up okay, Gram?"

"Fine," she said, but her eyes filled with tears. She self-consciously wiped them away with fingers slightly bent from arthritis, but it was then that Jenna understood how much the Durhams cared for Ryan. Over the previous months he'd become their grandson in every way that mattered, and at that moment they became Gram and Pop to her, too.

Pop came in and stood behind his wife. Somehow that unity, that common bond of love for her son, helped calm Jenna's frantic heart. They were all searching for Ryan, praying for his safety, drawing close in their worry and fear. Dennis's parents might be uninterested in Ryan, and her parents were gone, but in the Durhams, her son had the very best grandparents in the world. Together they would get him back.

But did that *together* include Adam? Jenna eyed him and tried, once again, to keep some emotional distance between them.

Don't depend on him, no matter how tempting his strength. He won't be here forever. He won't last.

She decided to think about Adam later, except that later didn't exist. While Ryan was gone and possibly in danger, there was only *now,* which made it so damn easy to lean on him when he put his arm around her.

ADAM TURNED the radio down when he noticed that Jenna had nodded off. They'd had little rest with which to confront the emergency that had greeted them this morning, and the motion of the car had eventually put Jenna to sleep. They'd have to stop at each town they came to once they crossed the Oregon border, to ask after Dennis and Ryan, but he wanted to give Jenna as much time as possible to get her strength back before he had to wake her.

A gentle rain fell and beaded on the windshield as Adam drove. He automatically flipped on the wipers, and their rhythmic slap, combined with the steady hum of his tires, began to ease the tension that cramped the muscles of his back. Memories of Jenna's son—Ryan's gap-toothed smile the day they'd ridden bikes together, the feel of the boy's skinny arms locking around his neck the night of his bad dream, Ryan's trusting young chatter when they'd gone out for burgers—threatened to bring the worry back with a vengeance, but he refused to give it audience. Telling himself they'd find Ryan soon, he forced the fear of what might happen if they didn't to the back of his mind. Then he turned his thoughts to Mike, and Bernstein and Lowe, and the decision he'd made on the phone that morning—and waited for the devastation to hit.

Surprisingly enough, what he felt fell far short of devastation. He wasn't even sure it was regret. Concern for his clients seemed to be chief among his emotions. He'd called the office to tell the secretaries to reschedule all his appointments and appearances, and to send someone else to those that couldn't be postponed, but he needed to follow up and make sure every client was given to a competent colleague.

And then what? Did he go out on his own? He'd given Bernstein and Lowe more than a decade of his life. Why didn't he feel—

"What are you thinking?"

Adam glanced over to see Jenna watching him. "You didn't sleep long."

She rested her head in her palm and propped her arm on the door, but didn't look away. "You didn't answer my question. What's going on inside that head of yours?"

"Nothing in particular," he lied. "Why?"

"You had an odd smile on your face."

Adam supposed his expression probably *was* odd. Who would have thought he could cut himself loose from Bernstein and Lowe so easily and feel...what?

Free? Free from Mike's demands and expectations, and the grueling all-consuming pace he'd set for himself?

Briefly he considered telling Jenna what had happened, then decided against it. He didn't want her to feel responsible for his decision. And he sure as hell didn't want to frighten her by making her think their relationship was more serious at this moment than she felt it should be. He needed to lull her along, become part of the fabric of her life again, slowly convince her that he belonged there.

Her gaze didn't waver. "So you're not going to tell me?"

"Are you sure you want to know?" He gave her a wicked grin and raised his brows. "I was thinking about last night."

A reddish stain darkened her cheeks, and she glanced out at the passing greenery. "Men," she groaned, then turned back to him, and he could tell by the pensiveness in her eyes that she had something to say.

"What's that look about?" he asked.

She scowled. "It certainly has nothing to do with sex. Being female, I can think of other things."

"Not last night, you couldn't." He laughed, unable to resist the opportunity to remind Jenna that she was the one who'd traipsed through the hall to reach *him*.

Suddenly she laughed, too, and it did Adam's heart good to see her smile again. "You should be used to that," she said. "Don't you drive all the women crazy?"

Her voice was almost flippant, but Adam sensed there was something deeper underlying her words. "Are you asking me if you're only one in a crowd, Jen?"

"No." She fiddled with the jeans she'd put on, along

with a sweater, before they'd left the Victoriana, and Adam reached out to stop her before she could put her fingers in her mouth to bite her nails—nails that had already sustained considerable damage since they'd learned of Ryan's disappearance. "I mean, yes," she admitted with a frustrated sigh.

He gave her a sideways glance. "Jenna, I told you while I was making love to you that you mean something to me. My feelings haven't changed with the rising of the sun." He'd told her that he'd never been able to forget her, that he never could, but he hadn't said he loved her. The words had nearly escaped him a dozen times. He *knew* he loved her, had always loved her, but each time he'd been tempted to make the declaration, he'd choked it back, determined to wait until she gave him some indication that she might return his feelings. Or at least that she wouldn't throw the words back in his face.

She didn't answer for a long time. When she did, she surprised him by saying, "What are you doing here, Adam? This is my problem, my nightmare. You should be in San Francisco, at work. I heard you on the phone earlier, telling whoever it was that they had to cancel all your appointments and…and everything. You don't have to do this."

"You're right. I don't have to be here," he said. "That should tell you something."

"What? What does it tell me, Adam?"

"You'll figure it out when you listen with this—" he pressed a hand to the soft swell above her heart "—and not this." Pulling gently on her ear, he grinned, knowing the real question was whether or not she'd let herself trust what her heart was telling her.

"WHERE DID YOU GET this?" Stunned, Jenna stood behind Adam in a dingy service station only fifty miles from the Oregon border and gazed down at a flyer with her son's picture. Across the top in big block letters it said MISSING.

Adam tacked one up on the wall. "What did you think I was doing while you were at the police station? Enjoying a leisurely lunch?"

Jenna barely heard him. The fact that he'd made up hundreds of flyers wasn't so surprising; the fact that he was offering a $25,000 reward for information leading to the recovery of her son was. "How could you do this?"

He shrugged. "It was easy. I typed the body of it on my laptop, used the copier at the Victoriana to add Ryan's picture, and there you are."

"You know what I mean. I don't have this kind of money."

"Which is why I'm the one who's offering the reward." He stepped back to study Ryan's picture. He'd placed it right in the middle of the wall, surrounded by photographs of other lost or stolen children, and it was the sheer number of those small faces that frightened Jenna. How many of them were ever found?

"But..." She didn't know what to say. How could she thank him for such a grand gesture? Money motivated people, and only the promise of a large reward separated her kid's picture from all the others. Surely they'd get Ryan back now.

As her gratitude overwhelmed her, she felt tears prick behind her eyes, and she didn't bother to fight them. Nothing, least of all her pride, mattered more to her than getting Ryan back.

"Come on, don't cry," he said, lifting her hair off

her neck and kissing the groove beneath her ear. "You can work it off as my love slave."

His joke relieved the intensity of the moment, and she laughed in spite of her jumbled emotions. "How much did I earn for last night?"

He whistled. "If I had to put a monetary value on last night, I'd say I owe *you* money."

"God, you know how to break a woman down." Jenna's worry for her son had twisted her stomach and her heart into such a painful knot that she wondered how other parents lived through the ordeal. But laughter helped ease some of the rawness of her feelings. She doubled her hand into a fist and gave Adam a playful punch, and he used the gesture to pull her into his arms.

Sobering once he got her there, he gazed down into her eyes. "You're putting up a good resistance," he said before his mouth quirked into another smile. "Have you ever seen *Fatal Attraction?*"

"No."

"Some people can be pretty tough to get rid of."

"What's that supposed to mean?"

"That I'm not going anywhere."

Jenna stared at him, wishing she could believe him, but experience had taught her too memorable a lesson. He'd stay until the novelty wore off or he met someone new in San Francisco. As long as he worked and lived there, it would be all too easy for him to walk away.

Shifting, she looked beyond him to the flyer, hoping she sounded calm and detached as she said, "The reward is really something, Adam, way above and beyond the call of duty. Ryan isn't even your son."

"How do you know he won't be?" he asked, his voice soft but finally serious.

Jenna felt light-headed as his words sank in. "Because you know that would take a serious commitment, my attorney friend."

He smiled. "I guess it would. But you know what? Losing you again is the only thing that really scares me."

Until you have me back and the challenge is gone. Jenna kept her gaze on her son's picture and tried to edge away from the emotional precipice that yawned before her. "I guess you're putting your money where your mouth is, huh?"

DENNIS SAT ON THE HOOD of his car holding a sign he'd made from the flap of a cardboard box. It read, "Trying to get home. Please help," but the patrons of the rest area mostly ignored him. They shuffled into and out of the cement washrooms, got a drink from the pebbled fountain and hurried on their way. The few he'd approached had shaken their heads and circled wide if they had to pass him again. And now that it was dark and getting late, Dennis doubted his luck would improve. Ryan had fallen asleep in the back of the car. Without him, strangers had no trust and even less sympathy.

"Screw 'em," he muttered and pocketed the few bills and some odd change he'd managed to collect when he'd forced Ryan to hold the collection bucket. Standing, he stretched and thought how good a beer would taste, then circled to the driver's side of the car and got behind the wheel.

At the squeal of door hinges, Ryan peered over the seat. His face was swollen from sleep, his hair mussed and sticking up on one side.

"Where are we?"

"After that little phone trick, you don't need to know," Dennis barked. His patience was wearing thin, not only with the boy but with life in general. After Ryan's stunt in Medford, Dennis had cuffed him a time or two—nothing like the beating *he* would've suffered for such disobedience when he was a kid—but his son had barely spoken a word since. When Dennis tried to draw him out, Ryan had answered in monosyllables and kept his gaze firmly fixed to whatever he saw flying past his window.

But his son's behavior hadn't been the worst part of the day. They'd had to stop for long periods of time to beg for enough gas money to make the next town, and because of the stingy assholes they'd met, it was taking forever to get to Portland.

"Do we have enough money for dinner?" Ryan asked, rubbing his eyes.

"What do you mean? I just bought you a Happy Meal, and you didn't even appreciate it." Dennis started the car, hearing the foreboding sputter of the engine, a noise that had been getting louder all day, and backed away from the curb.

"That was lunch. Aren't you hungry?" Ryan persisted.

Dennis *was* hungry—for a beer. And for a little peace. When he'd taken Ryan, he'd thought only of punishing Jenna, of showing her that he was every bit as good as she was and capable of raising their son. But the reality—constant bathroom breaks, recurring hunger, thirst and moodiness—was far different from what he'd envisioned. With his car acting up, his pockets empty and his son crying at any mention of his mother, Dennis doubted he could survive the rest of the night without a drink.

"Dad, my stomach hurts. Can't we get something to eat? Please?"

"Shut up!" Dennis growled. His hand flexed at the impulse to hit Ryan, but the boy flinched and ducked behind the seat before he could move. Gazing at his fisted hand in surprise, Dennis shook his head. Ryan hadn't done anything wrong this time. It was after ten o'clock and his son hadn't eaten since noon. Of course the boy was hungry.

Forcing himself to relax, Dennis shook out his hand and left the concrete oasis of the rest area behind as he again headed north on Interstate 5.

"We'll get you something at the next stop," Dennis muttered, but the weight of the change in his pocket felt far too light to purchase everything they needed: gas, food, beer.

More than anything, beer.

No. Dennis took firm hold of himself. They'd eat, put the rest in gas and forget the beer, he decided—until his craving grew so strong he broke out in a cold sweat. Then he decided to feed Ryan a cheap bean burrito, skip his own dinner and buy the beer, leaving the problem of gas money till tomorrow.

But by the time they reached Winston, Dennis had changed his mind. Ryan had fallen asleep again. The kid wouldn't die if he had to wait until morning to eat, Dennis thought, because he already knew he was going to spend every cent they had at the liquor store—and on something far stronger than beer.

ADAM STRETCHED OUT on the motel bed, wondering if Jenna would allow him to hold her. She was curled on her side, facing the wall, and hadn't spoken since they'd finally given up their search for the day. Though they'd hired kids in every town and city to post flyers and had received numerous calls because of the reward, they hadn't learned anything that would lead them to Ryan.

"How are you feeling, Jen? Okay?"

She nodded.

"All this worry can't be good for the baby."

"It's hard to think about the baby right now. All I can think about is Ryan."

"Have you been to a doctor yet?"

"I have an appointment next week."

"Good."

He watched her for another minute, resisting the urge to gather her close. "I'm going to call Dennis's brother, Russ."

"I've tried a dozen times. The last time was just a few minutes ago. All I get is an answering machine," Jenna said, turning toward him.

Adam vaguely remembered Russ and Dennis's other siblings. At least a decade older, they'd left home before Adam and Dennis reached high school, but he'd seen them around town occasionally, when they'd come back to visit. "It can't hurt to try again. Unless he's out of town, he has to get home sometime. Isn't he married?"

"Divorced."

"Still…" Adam had transferred the information in Jenna's old address book to his day planner and quickly found the number. Picking up the phone, he dialed, expecting to leave another message, when a male voice came on the line.

"Dammit, Jenna, this sure as hell better not be you again, or I'll call the police and tell them you're harassing me!"

"Is that any way to respond to the news that your nephew's been kidnapped?" Adam asked.

Jenna sat up and climbed onto her knees, a hopeful look on her face. "Is he there? Is that Russ?"

Adam nodded as silence stretched between him and Russ Livingston. Then Dennis's brother asked, "Who is this? The police?"

"No. This is Adam Durham—" Adam held Jenna's hand away from the phone "—an old friend of Jenna's. I'm helping her look for her son, and I'm calling to see if you've heard from Dennis."

"I've heard your name too many times. Why the hell would I tell *you?*"

"Because you know your brother's a drunk, and if anything happens to Ryan, you won't want it on your conscience."

"Dennis would never hurt his son."

"He hurt his wife. Who knows what he might do if he really tied one on?"

Russ Livingston sighed. "He loved Jenna. She should've stayed with him. It's her fault he's the way he is."

"That's easy for you to say. You weren't the one he was beating."

"It wasn't that bad. He only hit her once or twice."

Adam tried to distance himself from the emotions that would have him arguing with this guy. "Look, I wasn't there. I don't know how bad it was, but then, neither do you. So let's cut the bias and the loyalty rhetoric, and get down to what really matters now— Ryan. Dennis just got out of jail for threatening Jenna's life—"

"What?"

"It's true. You can call the Mendocino County

Courthouse if you don't believe me. He's angry and he's probably shaking from withdrawal and he's broke. Where do you think he might go?''

Another long silence. ''I don't know. I haven't heard from him in three weeks or more.''

''Do you have a pencil?''

''Yeah.''

''I'm going to give you my number. I think deep down you're a decent guy, Russ, who wouldn't like to see a little boy get hurt. I'm going to ask you to call me if Dennis contacts you. Will you do that?''

Another sigh. ''Yeah.''

Adam put a calming hand on Jenna, who was staring at him with frightened eyes. ''Thanks, Russ.''

''What did he say?'' Jenna asked as soon as Adam had hung up.

After plugging his car phone into its charger, Adam lay back and pulled Jenna down beside him. With her head on his shoulder he idly stroked her hair and said, ''He hasn't heard from Dennis, but if he does, he'll call us.''

''You're sure?'' she asked, her voice full of hope.

And though he wasn't, he knew Jenna needed the reassurance enough to say, ''I'm sure, sweetheart. I'm sure.''

THE FACE STARING BACK at him from a blue flyer posted on the wall of the twenty-four-hour liquor store looked surprisingly like Ryan. Dennis hadn't seen it when they'd arrived several hours ago, shortly after eleven o'clock. But then, he'd been thinking of only one thing—getting a drink. It was only after he'd finished the bottle that he'd gotten up and stumbled from the back of the building to the front, where he'd left

Ryan asleep in the car. He'd approached the liquor-store entrance, blinking at the bright light spilling through its glass front, wishing he had the money for another bottle—oblivion didn't come as cheaply or easily as it used to—and that was when he saw it.

Tearing the flyer from the painted cinder-block wall, Dennis squinted to improve his blurry vision. He still carried the empty bottle because it felt good in his hands, but now he set it down and moved closer to the light.

Missing: Ryan Livingston, 4'5'', 75 pounds, blondish-brown hair, brown eyes, eight years old...

The flyer went on to give a description of himself, too, but it was the reward that sent his temper soaring.

"$25,000! Shit!" He whirled and kicked the bottle he'd left standing on the cement. It crashed and broke on the pavement not far from the car.

The clerk inside the liquor store must have heard the disturbance because he came to the door and told Dennis it was time to move on. "No loitering here," he insisted, and stood waiting to make sure Dennis disappeared. "I'll call the cops if you don't leave."

But Dennis paid no attention. Jenna was offering a $25,000 reward for the return of their son. Where would she get that kind of money? The whole thing reeked of Adam Durham. Worse, if a flyer could be posted here, at a run-down liquor store, there could be flyers everywhere. Everyone in Oregon would be looking for him, hoping to cash in!

"Son of a bitch!" he ground out, but the store clerk had already headed back inside, probably to call the police, and Dennis didn't dare linger. The shock had left him nearly sober. He jumped into the Escort and started the car, hoping he had enough gas to get to some out-of-the-way place on the fringes of the city, some field or parking lot, where they could wait for morning. He was a sitting duck now, thanks to Jenna and Adam. If he wasn't careful, he'd go back to jail, this time for kidnapping.

"Shit, oh shit, oh shit," he muttered as the car rattled along. What now? He couldn't go to Portland. He'd be stopped long before he got there, if not right afterward. He had to do something unexpected. But he had no money and was almost out of gas.

"What's wrong, Dad?" Ryan's voice came from the backseat.

"Nothing. Go back to sleep!"

"But I can't. I'm cold and I'm hungry. Can't we eat, please? You said we'd get something."

"I said go back to sleep!" Dennis hadn't meant to yell as loudly as he had, and regretted it the instant Ryan started to cry. He couldn't think while the kid was blubbering in the back seat, mumbling about his mom and Gram and Pop Somebody, and how bad he needed to eat.

"Shut up or—"

Dennis caught himself before he finished the threat, not wanting to make the situation any worse. Ryan's sobs died down, but the soft gasps that emanated from the back seat maddened Dennis almost as much as the outright crying.

Trying to ignore the urge to pound Ryan until the sounds stopped completely, Dennis decided he had two choices. He could abandon his son and take off on his own. The police probably wouldn't waste their time searching for him if Ryan was back with his mother.

Or he could surprise them all by striking out across country and taking Ryan with him. With no job and no home, he might as well live in Carolina as Oregon. If he chose back roads and avoided any of the places his family lived, he had a good chance of slipping away, provided he could beg enough for gas and food or come up with money some other way.

And wouldn't it just serve Jenna right if she never saw her son again!

CHAPTER TWENTY

THE CALLS FROM THE FLYER continued through most of the night. Sometime after two o'clock, Jenna had grown so exhausted from experiencing the emotional highs and lows of hope and disappointment whenever Adam's cell phone rang that she just didn't hear it anymore. She felt as though she couldn't take one more vague sighting of Ryan that contradicted the previous caller.

Jenna shut out all sound except Adam's deep voice as he sifted through the leads, reporting the ones that seemed legitimate to the police. She retreated into a dark safe place in her head where she could sleep.

Periodically, when there were no calls and only the hum of the television broke the silence, Jenna would start awake, afraid that Adam had fallen asleep and left no one standing vigil for her son. But she would find him staring at the television, a frown of concentration on his face, or sitting against the headboard, jotting notes in his day planner. He would shift on the bed and tuck the blankets around her again or smooth the hair off her forehead. Sometimes he'd murmur, "It's okay, Jen, I'm here."

"Anything?" she'd ask.

He'd shake his head, but add, "We'll find him."

She'd shudder at the knowledge that it was colder and later than the last time she'd asked, then say, "I

need to give you a break.'' And he'd insist he felt fine
and couldn't sleep even if he had the chance, which
was the greatest kindness of all. Then the exhaustion
that still weighted her limbs and hovered at the fringes
of her mind could take over again and pull her back
into the darkness of sleep. There she felt Ryan's absence only in a vague subconscious sense that something was wrong, instead of the poignant longing that
wracked her soul every time she opened her eyes.

Finally a call came that changed everything. Jenna
sat up the moment the phone rang, somehow knowing,
before Adam even answered it, that she would need to
hear what this caller had to say.

Taking her cold fingers in one hand, Adam smiled
reassuringly as he retrieved the phone from its place
on the nightstand and pushed the talk button.

A moment later his smile vanished and white lines
of strain appeared around his mouth and eyes. "I know
where it is. We'll be right there," he said, and hung
up.

Jenna stared at him, completely vulnerable, no
longer capable of shielding herself. "What?"

Adam put his hands on her shoulders, and the com-
passion in his eyes terrified her even more. "There's
been an accident," he said. "A single-car collision or
something. The description fits Dennis's Escort, but the
police don't know if it's his yet."

"And Ryan?"

"There's been no report of victims or injuries. It
happened back in Camas Valley on a rural road. A
farmer reported seeing something burning that turned
out to be the car."

"But Camas Valley is south of here."

"It's about an hour away. We don't know how fast

Dennis and Ryan were traveling. Maybe we passed them in our hurry to get to Portland. A woman who called said she saw a man and a boy matching their descriptions at a rest stop in the same general area.'' He rubbed the whiskers that had sprouted on his chin. ''Or it's possible that this is completely unrelated, someone else's accident, someone else's sadness.''

Numbly Jenna nodded. Though she'd tried not to lean on Adam or depend on his emotional support, at that moment she'd never been more grateful for another human presence in her life. She doubted she could have faced this nightmare alone, was glad she didn't have to. ''Thank you, Adam, for sticking it out with me,'' she whispered.

Closing his eyes, he drew her toward him and kissed her cheek. ''I'm not going anywhere, Jen. I've already told you that. We'll get through this together, okay?''

She nodded, somehow beyond tears. ''Let's go.''

The sun stained the east pink, purple and finally blue, as they drove south to Camas Valley. Jenna refused to dwell on the worst possibilities, telling herself that Ryan would be all right, but from the first moment she saw it, the charred Escort forged a lump as hard and heavy as iron in her stomach. It was Dennis's car. She knew it, deep in her bones.

Adam pulled off to the side of the road, where several police cars were already parked. After giving her a silent look of reassurance, he jumped out and she scrambled to follow him, bracing herself against the smell of smoke and burned rubber that hung in the air. A barrel-chested police officer came to meet them before they reached the wreck.

''You the man I talked to on the phone?''

"Adam Durham," he said. "This is Jenna Livingston, Ryan's mother."

"Well, we have good news for you folks. There's definitely no bodies in there, and there was no accident, either. From what we can tell, the car was torched." He motioned to Jenna. "I suspect your ex-husband did it to destroy the evidence that he'd been here."

Jenna realized she hadn't been breathing only when the fear squeezing her heart and lungs finally eased enough for her to manage a breath. "You're sure?"

"We're sure."

Adam's brow furrowed. "The farmer saw the fire about an hour ago, isn't that right?"

Hooking a thumb in his pocket, the officer used his other hand to scratch the back of his head. "That's right, which means Dennis Livingston and his son can't be far away, if Mr. Livingston is indeed the one who set the fire. They were probably on foot when they left, unless someone picked them up and gave them a ride."

Jenna squinted at the rolling farmlands surrounding them, noting the early mist that capped the tops of the hills. "Have you started to search the area?"

"We just determined the cause of the fire, but we're on it now. We'll let you know when we find something."

Jenna thanked the officer and urged Adam back to his car. "We've got to call Russ," she said.

"You think Dennis has contacted him?"

"Dennis wouldn't burn his car to cinders unless it wouldn't run anymore, or he had plans to get around some other way. In either case he'd need money."

"And Russ is the likely benefactor."

Adam had carried his cell phone with him to the

burned car. Jenna watched him dial Russ Livingston's number, then took the phone.

Russ answered on the first ring.

"You're up early, Russ," she said. "Any particular reason?"

"Certainly not to talk to you."

"What's the matter? Were you expecting Dennis?"

Silence answered her question, and Jenna feared Russ would hang up. "Look," she said, hoping to forestall him, "I'm not out to get Dennis. I know you don't believe that, but if you don't help us, your brother's going to be in a lot of trouble."

"What makes you think you're any better a parent for Ryan than my brother is? My ex pulled the same shit with me—"

"This is different. You know that, Russ. And it's not going to help anybody to fight our old battles again. I'm here with the police right now. Dennis just set fire to his car and abandoned it. He must be looking for some money or another car." She paused. "I think you know what he's up to."

"That's bull. I haven't heard from him."

Jenna squeezed her eyes shut and prayed she could get through to Russ. He was her only hope. "Too bad," she said, "because the police know he couldn't have left the car more than an hour ago, which means he isn't far. They're going to find him, and when they do, he's going to jail."

"For taking his own son?"

"It's kidnapping, plain and simple. Dennis doesn't have the legal right to take Ryan across the street, let alone out of the state. He lost that right when he broke my arm." Not knowing how much Russ had heard about the physical abuse Dennis had inflicted, or how much he was willing to believe, she let that sink in, then offered her ex-brother-in-law a bone. "But I'll make you a deal, Russ. If you help Adam and me, if you tell us where they are, we'll intercept them. We'll take Ryan and leave Dennis alone. Without Ryan, Dennis can slip away. I doubt the police will bother to keep searching for him."

Adam squeezed her arm. "Jen—"

Jenna waved him to silence.

"And how do I know you'll keep your word? Just last week you had Dennis put in jail," Russ said.

"You'll have to trust me. My way is Dennis's only chance."

Russ Livingston sat on the other side of the phone for almost a full minute without speaking. Jenna could hear his steady breathing, felt him weakening, prayed he would give way altogether.

"Russ, please," she pleaded, ignoring Adam's frown. "Do it for Ryan. Help me get him home safely. Then see what you can do for your brother. He needs to go into detox."

"I know." Russ groaned. "Okay, okay, dammit. Dennis called not more than fifteen minutes ago. He's at the bus station in Roseburg waiting for me to wire him the money for two bus tickets to Indiana. There, are you happy now?"

"Not yet, but if I find Ryan I will be. And I'll keep my word, Russ, I promise you that. Just get Dennis into detox."

She disconnected and stared up at Adam. She knew he didn't agree with what she'd just done. If she were Adam, she'd probably feel the same way. "I know where they are," she said hesitantly.

"Jenna, you promised Russ you'd let Dennis go. He's broken the law. We can't do that."

Jenna searched Adam's eyes, hoping he'd understand why she'd done what she had. How could she explain the unique blend of nostalgia, pity and guilt she felt toward Dennis? "I'm angry with Dennis, just like you are. But he's still Ryan's dad. He'll always be Ryan's dad, and that makes me want to do what's best for him."

"You feel partly responsible for why he is the way he is."

"I've admitted that to you before."

"And I'm saying that's crap. It's also a hell of a reason to let someone escape justice."

"Do you think going to jail will help Dennis?"

"It might teach him to obey the law."

"It didn't do him any good the last time." She paused. "What Dennis needs is to get some counseling, Adam. His alcoholism is at the bottom of everything. I'm sure that in your line of work you've seen what prison can do to a man, how rarely it changes behavior. Is that really where Dennis belongs? You grew up with him, too. You know he's a weak person but not really a bad one."

Adam sighed and his expression softened. "I remember riding bikes with Dennis when we were kids. He had a gap-toothed smile for most of fourth grade, always wore a 49ers baseball cap and chewed an entire pack of gum at the same time." Adam took Jenna's hand and gazed down at it, but she knew he wasn't seeing it. He was busy remembering. "The same details could have been used to describe me at that age."

"We've all been through a lot since then."

"I know. Maybe you're right. Dennis needs a dif-

ferent kind of help than he'd get from the judicial system.''

Jenna smiled and brushed a quick kiss across his lips
because it was the most natural thing in the world to
do, and started running to the car. ''Let's go get my
boy.''

THE BUS STATION smelled of cigarettes and stale sweat.
Adam scrutinized the tired faces in the old building,
the ones bloated from alcohol, the eyes that glittered
through the smoke of an endless chain of cigarettes,
the bewhiskered vagrants who loitered at the entrance,
the nervous mothers struggling to control small children. But he saw no sign of Dennis.

Her fingers laced through his, Jenna walked beside
him through the large echoing lobby with its high ceil-
ings and dirty tile floor. She gripped his hand with the
same fear and nervousness he'd sensed in her since
Ryan's disappearance, but this time he felt something
more in her touch, a kind of confidence that had not
been there before.

He could sense the subtle change in the way she
looked at him, too. He found it strange that he'd never
felt happier at the prospect of getting so close to a
woman. In every other relationship he'd reached a
point where he became uncomfortable and unsettled
and wanted to back off. Why things were different with
Jenna he didn't know. He was just glad they were.
Maybe now he could have the family he'd always
wanted and experience the type of commitment other
men did.

''There!''

An announcement over the loudspeaker, about the
departure of a bus heading to Las Vegas, nearly

drowned out Jenna's voice, but her hand tightened in
his, and Adam knew instantly that she saw Dennis or
Ryan or both. His eyes flickered over the rows of chairs
that faced nothing more interesting than a beige wall
with vending machines, until he, too, spotted Dennis.
Jenna's ex-husband sat slouched in a chair, his mouth
gaping open as he slept.

But there was no sign of Ryan.

"Damn." Adam let go of Jenna to reach Dennis in
a series of long strides. Grabbing the other man by his
stained and wrinkled shirtfront, he hauled him out of
his chair without giving him a chance to wake up first.

"Where is he?" he ground out.

Dennis blinked in bewilderment, then his face red-
dened as recognition dawned. He started to struggle
and tried to take a swing at Adam, but Adam neatly
blocked the blow and twisted Dennis's arm behind his
back. "If it's a fight you want, I'll be happy to give
you one, but first I need to know where Ryan is."

Jenna had had to run to keep up with Adam. She
stood staring at the two of them with both fear and
hope shining in her eyes, but did nothing to intervene.

Dennis cursed. "I don't have him! Let me go!"

Adam tried to keep his voice from attracting any
more attention than his actions already had. "And
where would you go, Dennis? I'm the one with the
money you need to get on the next bus. You tell me
where Ryan is, and I'll give you the money before the
police get here to haul you off to jail."

Dennis's eyes darted around as they scanned the
lobby. "He was here. I don't know where he went."

"Are you sure?" Adam shoved his arm higher up
his back, causing Dennis to curse again.

"I swear it. Where else would he be?"

Mumbling Ryan's name like a prayer, Jenna turned in circles, searching the lobby. Suddenly she stopped and her eyes went wide as she gazed at a circular bank of pay phones. Following her gaze, Adam saw the jeans and tennis shoes of a small boy extending below the pedestal on the far side.

"Ryan!" Jenna called his name and closed the distance between them in a matter of seconds.

Hearing his mother's voice, Ryan ducked around the pay phones and ran to meet her. "Mom! How did you get here so fast? I was just trying to call you."

Cautiously Adam freed Dennis, half expecting him to run away, but he didn't. They stood and watched a laughing Jenna swing her son up into her arms. She staggered beneath the boy's weight, but didn't let him down until the two of them had kissed and hugged and cried together.

"You're safe," Jenna said. "I'm so glad you're safe."

"I thought I'd never see you again," Ryan said.

"I would never have stopped searching for you, you know that, Ryan? Never," Jenna told him.

The boy nodded. "You just seemed so far away. Hey, that's Adam!"

When Jenna finally let him go, Ryan raced over to Adam, who hunkered down and returned the boy's fierce hug.

"Hey, Ryan," Adam murmured. "Are you okay?"

"I am now. I'm so glad to see you!"

"Take him, then!" Dennis snapped. "I don't want him, anyway. Jenna's poisoned him against me, just like she'll try to do to the baby. But when I get my life together, I'll be able to get partial custody of both my kids."

Noting the sudden chalkiness of Jenna's complexion, Adam slowly released Ryan. "What are you talking about?"

"I know all about the baby. Ryan told me."

"But the baby isn't yours," Adam said. "You have no right—"

Dennis turned on him, a triumphant gleam in his eye. "Oh, yeah? How do you know it's not mine? Jenna and me, we had a grand time together, a right memorable occasion. What's it been, three months or so, honey?"

The way Dennis's hooded eyes moved to take in Jenna's body made Adam's hand flex into a fist. "Be careful," he warned. "I don't want to hit you in front of Ryan, but I won't allow you to talk about Jenna like that again."

"Adam." Jenna covered his right fist with her hand, keeping it at his side, and something about the look on her face told him the truth. There had been no one-night stand, no stranger capable of sweeping Jenna away into unspeakable passion. She'd lied to him. Jenna had slept with her ex-husband three months after the divorce, and it was he who had fathered her baby.

"A paternity test should prove it easily enough, if you want to push it that far." Dennis smiled. "Or maybe we can strike a deal."

Adam studied his old buddy, wondering what had induced Jenna to be intimate with him again. A weak moment? Loneliness? The hope of keeping her family together? "What kind of deal?"

"You were offering a $25,000 reward for Ryan's safe return. I don't think that's too much to ask in exchange for both my kids."

"No! Dennis, please!" Jenna put out a beseeching

hand, visibly shaken that her ex-husband could put a price on his own children.

"You heard me, rich boy," Dennis said to Adam, ignoring Jenna altogether. "You give me the money and I'll leave the two of you and the kids alone."

Jenna's brows drew together as she worried her lip. "Dennis, you could go to jail for kidnapping. Adam doesn't have to give you anything—"

"Jenna, would you please take Ryan to get a candy bar out of the machines over there?" Adam turned to her, willing her to trust him. If for no other reason, he hoped she'd comply with his suggestion because no son should have to hear what Dennis was saying.

"Adam, don't. This isn't your problem," Jenna hissed, but she finally took Ryan's hand and led him away.

When they were out of earshot, Adam said, "If you want something like this, Dennis, you're going to sign papers that will permanently relinquish your rights to both children."

Dennis paused and something flickered in his eyes that said his show of nonchalance wasn't as easy as he made it look. Pride was doing his talking now, along with an innate sense of survival. But Adam knew there would be times throughout his life, probably many of them, when Dennis would regret this moment.

Finally he shrugged. "Why not? I might as well get *something.*"

"Then I'll buy you a ticket to Portland. Your brother's expecting you. When I get back to San Francisco, I'll have adoption papers drawn up so that all Jenna has to do, if she ever marries again, is fill in the blanks."

Dennis laughed. "Who're you kiddin', Adam? You

want the name in those blanks to be yours. I've never been able to compete with you, and I can't now.''

"The ironic thing is that until you started drinking, you'd already won.''

Dennis glanced at Jenna and Ryan and rubbed the whiskers on his cheek. "Just take good care of 'em, okay?''

Adam watched Jenna bend closer to her son, pointing to something in the vending machine. "I will," he promised. "And when I receive the papers back, properly signed and notarized, you'll get your money.''

Dennis nodded, and with that, Adam handed him two hundred dollars, gathered Jenna and Ryan, and walked away.

AFTER STOPPING at a fast-food restaurant and ordering Ryan enough breakfast to feed three grown men, Jenna drove them back to Mendocino so Adam could sleep. Although she wondered how he could rest while holding a wriggling eight-year-old on his lap in the cramped space of the Mercedes, he seemed to be having no trouble.

Adam had phoned his grandmother as soon as they'd left the bus station to tell her they had Ryan back safe and sound. But Ryan wanted to call her now just to talk and, Jenna suspected, to play with Adam's cell phone. Knowing Adam wouldn't mind and not wanting to wake him to ask, she gave her son permission, as long as he kept his conversation brief. She smiled at the warmth in Ryan's voice when Gram answered the phone.

"I'm okay. It wasn't so bad," she heard him say. "Yeah, it's all over now and I'm on my way home…

No, my dad wouldn't dare try that, not with Adam around.''

The pride in her son's voice emphasized how important Adam had become to him. Jenna leaned forward to see around Ryan, wondering if Adam had noticed, but his eyes were still closed, his head propped against a bunched-up coat. Even with his hair tousled and dark beard shadowing the lower half of his face, Jenna thought she'd never seen a more handsome man. Nor had she met a finer one. His strength and resourcefulness in the face of her desolation over the past two days had convinced her it was hopeless to barricade her emotions against him. He knew every path, every angle, possessed all the keys to her heart. He had from the beginning.

But ever since Dennis had blurted out the truth about the baby, Adam had seemed remote. Jenna longed to explain to him why she'd said what she had about the baby's father, but they couldn't talk in front of Ryan. So she contented herself with the hope that they'd have some time together once they reached the Victoriana.

"That's enough now," Jenna cautioned when Ryan had had a chance to talk to Pop after his conversation with Gram. "Every minute costs money, and we don't want to take advantage."

Reluctantly Ryan said goodbye and hung up, then leaned over and nuzzled her shoulder. Putting her arm around her son, Jenna kissed the top of his head. "I'm so glad to have you back," she whispered.

He grinned up at her. "Does that mean I don't have to make my bed every day?"

"Only if you want to make mine and Gram's and Pop's, instead, and eat spinach every night for dinner."

As her son heartily, and wisely, rejected this less

than even trade, Adam shifted. Jenna wished he'd awake and reach across to take her hand, but after moving Ryan to his other knee, he settled again and slept until she drove into the Victoriana's parking lot.

"We're here," she announced, touching Adam's arm.

Adam blinked awake, but when he met her eyes, he didn't smile, and Jenna again wished she could talk to him about the baby. He helped Ryan climb out to meet Gram and Pop, who were already standing on the front porch waiting for them. Then, with a yawn and a stretch, he got out of the car and headed across the lawn, too. Jenna collected the wrappers from Ryan's meal and followed.

Gram and Pop hugged Ryan and told him how happy they were to have him back. Then Pop surprised them all by turning to Adam. "It's good to see you again, son," he said gruffly, and gave him an awkward embrace.

As if embarrassed by this uncharacteristic display of emotion, Pop immediately retreated into the house, but Gram gave Adam a radiant smile. "This terrible experience with Ryan has taught us a thing or two," she admitted.

Adam gaped at her. "Like what?"

"Like how devastating it would be if something happened to you. You've been our baby, our own son since your mother died. We've been wrong to chase you away with guilt."

Feeling as if she was eavesdropping on a private conversation, Jenna edged away. She wanted to go inside so she could leave the two of them alone, but Gram's portly body blocked the entrance.

Adam ran a hand through his unruly hair. "Maybe

I feel guilty because I should. You're my only family. I should probably have stayed and taken care of you.''

"Nonsense! We've always known you'd take care of us if we really needed you. You merely wanted to build a life that was different from the one we envisioned for you. And we didn't want to let you go.''

Adam shook his head. "I keep telling everyone that San Francisco is only a couple of hours away. You've visited me a few times—come more often. It's not like I live in France.''

"Speaking of San Francisco,'' Gram said. "That partner of yours has called and called. He says he needs to talk to you as soon as possible. You should go in and phone him.''

Adam sighed. "I know. He's been trying to reach me on my car phone every few hours, but I have caller ID and haven't been answering. I'm not ready to talk to him yet, but I've got to get back. I left things in a mess. I just came up to say goodbye.''

Gram patted his arm. "I'll tell Pop you had to go. Thanks for helping Jenna and—''

Before Gram could finish her sentence, Ryan's excited high-pitched voice carried out to them through the open door. "Gram! You made my favorite chocolate cake!''

Mrs. Durham chuckled. "Goodbye, Adam.'' She turned and went inside, and Jenna heard her tell Ryan that she had to bake something special for her favorite grandson.

When they were alone, Adam glanced back at his car. "I'd better get going.''

Jenna was reluctant to let him leave. Especially before they'd had a chance to talk. "What did you and Dennis work out?'' she asked.

He raised his hands. "Jen, I'm beat and I have a mess to take care of. Can we talk about it later?"

She nodded.

"I'll call you," he promised, but he made no move to touch her before walking quickly to his car.

Jenna stood on the porch and watched him start the Mercedes and back out of the drive. "Goodbye, Adam," she whispered.

CHAPTER TWENTY-ONE

"JENNA? YOU STILL AWAKE?"

Jenna glanced up to see Gram standing in the open doorway of her room. Ryan lay beside her, asleep, along with the pile of books they'd read together.

"How is he?"

"He seems fine. Dennis frightened him, but no more so than when we were living with him." Jenna smiled down at her son's sleeping face. "I think he's already bounced back, and it hasn't even been a day."

"Children are pretty resilient. He might need to talk about what happened later, but we're all here to support him. I think he knows we love him."

Jenna nodded. "Thanks for being so good to him."

Gram moved farther into the room and handed her a small piece of paper. "I found that in the office a few minutes ago. Pop took the message, but with you being gone and all the worry over Ryan, he forgot to mention it to anyone."

"What is it?" Jenna squinted to read Pop's chicken scratches.

Gram's eyes sparkled. "Mr. LeCourt called. He told Pop you need to get him more stained glass. The other windows have sold already."

Excitement tingled through Jenna. "Really?" Ryan stirred, as though unconsciously aware that something had changed, and she carefully removed her arm from beneath his head. "But it's only been a few days. And he never told me what he was going to charge."

"I can't give you the details. You know Pop. Getting words out of him is like prying rusty nails from a thick board, so you'll have to call in the morning to find out what happened. But it can only be good news, right?" She smiled. "After what's happened, I thought you could use it."

She *could* use it. The stress or the pregnancy—probably both—had taken its toll on Jenna. She felt like she could sleep for a week—if only she could stop worrying about the way Adam had turned so cold and distant after he'd learned that Dennis was the baby's father. She kept seeing his closed face, hearing his curt goodbye, and trying to figure out what he was feeling underneath it all. But there was no way to tell for sure, not until he was ready to talk to her.

"It's only nine o'clock, but I'm going to bed," Gram said, moving back into the hall. "I think we could all benefit from a little extra sleep tonight."

"Good night." Jenna returned the older woman's smile, but her thoughts were on Mr. LeCourt. If she established a name for herself, she could probably make a good living at her stained glass. She could sell her windows in just a few exclusive shops. Or maybe she could even take on apprentices and expand her little company until her designs were sold all over the country. The possibilities were endless. And this was just the beginning.

Too excited to stay still, Jenna got up and headed down to the kitchen to make herself some hot tea. She'd met Mr. LeCourt because of Adam. She wished Adam was still here so she could tell him the good news. She had Ryan back, unharmed. Her business was showing promise. Her morning sickness was behind her, and she was starting to look forward to holding a newborn. And Gram and Pop were there to love and support her little family. Her future seemed bright at last, but she had a hard time looking forward to any future without Adam.

Jenna eyed the phone and considered calling him. Adam had done a lot for her, and though her reasons had seemed valid at the time, she'd lied to him. At the very least she owed him an apology.

THE RINGING of the telephone pulled Adam into the house before he could even get his keys out of the lock. By the time he picked up the receiver, the answering machine had already started its spiel. He told his caller to hang on and hurried to the office, where he clicked it off.

"Hello?"

"Adam, it's me."

Jenna. Just the sound of her voice was enough to escalate his pulse, despite his anger toward her. "Jen, how's Ryan?"

"He's good. Everything's good. You got home okay, then?"

"Just walked in the door. I've been at the office all afternoon and evening."

"Did I catch you at a bad time?"

He leaned back in his chair and propped his feet on the desk, feeling his anger give way, despite the memory of Dennis taunting him about the baby. "No."

"Mr. LeCourt called. He's sold all my windows already," she said, obviously brimming with delight.

Adam sat up again. "Wow, that's fast! How much?"

"I don't know yet. Pop took the message."

"That can be scary."

She laughed. "I know. I can't even read Pop's hand-writing. Gram interpreted—that's how come I know as much as I do."

He chuckled. "Those two make quite a pair. Any word on Dennis?"

"Russ called to tell me he found a great detox pro-gram for Dennis. He goes in tomorrow."

"How long does he stay?"

"Six months. Russ told me what you and Dennis agreed to do about the papers and the money. He said to send anything you need signed to him, and he'll take care of it and get it right back to you."

"Good."

"Can you have someone sign something like that, Adam? I mean, is it legal?"

"Acting as private citizens, Dennis and I can cer-tainly make this agreement. Whether or not it would ever hold up in court, I don't know. I don't know enough about family law."

"But the money, Adam. That's a lot to risk on some-thing you're not sure of."

"It's worth it to buy peace, even for a short time. And maybe it'll actually do Dennis some good."

Silence fell between them, then Jenna cleared her throat. "Adam, I...I'm sorry for what I told you about the baby's father."

Adam pinched the bridge of his nose with a thumb and forefinger. "Evidently you didn't feel you could trust me with the truth. Trust is a real issue with us, isn't it, Jen?"

"Yes and no. I mean, that's not why I said what I did."

"Then why did you?"

He heard a soft sigh. "I told you what I did because...because I didn't want you to know how the pregnancy really came about."

"I think I can imagine how—"

"No. I don't know if anyone can imagine it." Her voice was clipped, as though she was angry, too. "Dennis came to the house, drunk, about three months after the divorce was final. It was late on a school night and Ryan was asleep. He'd seen so much ugliness between Dennis and me, so much I'd rather he hadn't seen, that when Dennis started pressing me, I..."

Her words dropped off, and Adam's stomach tightened. "It was easier to give in than to fight him. Is that what you're saying?"

"I just wanted peace, you know? I wanted the violence to end, and I knew Dennis would go away without disturbing Ryan if—"

"It's okay, Jen." Adam felt like a jerk. If not for his ego and his unreasonable jealousy, he might have understood sooner. "You don't have to say any more."

"I'm sorry."

"No, I'm the one who should apologize. I know you better than to believe you got carried away with some guy you met at a bar. You've never been like that."

"Adam?"

He had no idea what Jenna was going to say, but what he heard pierced him to the core. "I love you."

He sat, telling himself to breathe, to believe he'd heard her speak those words—at last. Finally he said, "Again, Jenna? You love me again?"

"No, still," she admitted, then the line clicked and he heard only a dial tone.

ADAM SAT IN MIKE'S OFFICE, toying with the glass globe paperweight from his partner's desk. He'd tried to arrange a meeting with Mike when he'd first arrived in San Francisco yesterday afternoon, but his partner had been in court. So Adam had spent the past twenty-four hours packing up his office and making sure his clients were in good hands. Now it was after five. The telephones had died down, along with the foot traffic, creating the perfect opportunity for him and Mike to speak in private.

"You've been wanting to talk to me," Adam said, gazing across the desk.

Mike loosened his tie and his shoes before sinking into his chair, which groaned beneath his weight. "Listen, Adam, I owe you an apology. I flew off the handle the other day on the phone, but I didn't mean what I said. I was frantic, what with the Roger thing and all that. Now that he's gone and none of the rest of us have been implicated—"

"He's gone?"

Mike wiped away a trickle of sweat that had begun to roll down his heavy jowls. "They've got him, Adam. Even Whitehead admits that Roger destroyed the records. Without that evidence the DA probably can't get a conviction on Whitehead, unless they come up with better witnesses than they have now. But Whitehead seems to think that pointing the finger at Roger will help get him out of the mess he's in."

Adam shook his head, disgusted as much by the ease with which Mike sacrificed Roger as he was by Roger's illegal actions. "Stupidity and blind ambition don't mix."

Mike agreed, even though he was the one who'd hired Roger and, on a number of occasions, had insisted Whitehead was a model citizen. "Exactly, but I really don't see any reason why we should break up the partnership. I mean, our working together has always been good for both of us, hasn't it?'' He chuckled and rubbed his hands together. ''We've sure made a lot of money.''

''The money's not important,'' Adam said drily.

''What?'' Mike looked as though Adam had just said something absurd.

''Never mind. Just my way of saying I'm out of the partnership.''

''But I said I was sorry. What more do you want? A bigger share of the profits?'' Mike cackled. ''You wily fox, Adam. I thought you might hold out for something like that. You've been around the block a few times and you can tell when you're holding a good hand. 'The money's not important.' All right, then. I'm willing to deal. What if I make you my senior partner? What do you say?''

Since an equal partnership had once been his most driving ambition, Adam tested Mike's words, holding them in his head, spinning them around as carefully as he'd sample wine, until the full flavor burst upon him. He waited several seconds, expecting the lucrative offer to entice him. But in the end it didn't, at least not enough to tempt him away from the decision he'd made after Jenna's call last night.

Returning Mike's paperweight to the desk, Adam stood. ''I'm sorry, Mike, but I have other aspirations,'' he said, and he hid a smile because he knew the other man wouldn't believe it if he knew how humble those aspirations were.

But Adam didn't care. He would have what he'd been missing. At last, he would have what meant more to him than anything.

"No word from Adam?"

As Gram entered the kitchen, Jenna threw off the trance she'd been in. It was early yet, the sun barely over the horizon, but Jenna had been up long enough for her tea to grow cold. They'd had Ryan back for more than a week and had returned to their calm peaceful routine, but she hadn't talked to Adam since the night Jenna told him she loved him. He'd called once, while she was helping at Ryan's school, but he hadn't been home when she'd returned the call, and he hadn't tried to contact her since. She was beginning to think she'd scared him away, that he wouldn't call at all, even though tomorrow was Thanksgiving.

At least they had no guests booked for the weekend. Jenna could relax, work on her stained glass and finish up the Victoriana website.

"He's probably too busy," she said, hoping to sound indifferent. But her voice was just high enough to betray her.

Gram patted her shoulder. "Why don't you call him?"

Jenna shook her head. She *had* called him, and she wasn't about to do so again. If Adam wanted her, if he felt the same way she did, he knew where to find her. *I'm such an idiot. I tell myself not to trust Adam, not to love him again, and here I am feeling as weepy as a jilted bride.* She stifled a sigh and rose. "Can I make you some coffee?"

Gram stood with her back against the counter, frowning and looking as though she had something on her mind. "No, thank you. How was your appointment with the doctor yesterday?"

Jenna smiled in spite of herself. "I heard the baby's

heartbeat. It's so incredible to realize I'm bringing another life into the world.''

"Did the doctor give you a due date?''

"April fifteenth.''

"Spring's a wonderful time to have a baby! We'll
have a shower and get you some nice things. If you
have an ultrasound, are you going to let them tell you
if the baby is a boy or girl?''

Jenna could tell Gram was doing her best to cheer
her up, and she tried to respond with the appropriate
enthusiasm, but her heart was too heavy. "I think I'll
let it be a surprise.''

"That will be exciting.'' Gram studied her for a moment. "Jenna, Adam…''

Jenna looked up from washing her cup in the sink.
"What?''

"There's something I should tell you, dear,
but…never mind. After all, today's the day.''

She set her cup in the drainer, wondering what Gram
was talking about now. "The day for what?''

Opening the cupboard that contained the breakfast
cereals, Adam's grandmother quickly located the round
tub of oatmeal and brought it down. "The day to buy
a new rug for the dining room, I guess. There's a wonderful little shop that just opened next to the health-
food store. I've been meaning to get down there. Will
you go with me?''

"I appreciate your trying to get me out of the house
and all, but I talked to Mr. LeCourt again yesterday,
and he's pressing me for more windows. If I'm to keep
up with him, I need to get busy.''

Fortunately Gram didn't know she had just wasted
an hour doing absolutely nothing besides staring

glumly into her tea. "But that's wonderful news, dear! Aren't you excited?"

Jenna shrugged. She would have been ecstatic if she could have thought beyond how badly she wanted to hear Adam's voice.

"I think that grandson of mine should be ashamed of himself for putting you through this. He should have called."

Feeling guilty for not doing a better job of concealing her disappointment, Jenna said, "Don't be mad at him. He's been great, really. I don't know what I would've done without him last week."

"Well, forget Adam and come shopping with me today."

The phone rang and Jenna snatched it up, but it wasn't Adam. It was Laura.

"Hi. I thought I'd swing by and see you today. Okay?"

Jenna contemplated an hour spent in Laura's company, trying to avoid her friend's pointed questions—and decided to accompany Gram to buy the rug. "I'll be out for a while," she said, knowing she was in no emotional shape to deal with Laura. "Gram and I are going to do some shopping. Why don't I call you when I get back?"

"Great. You all right?"

"Yeah."

"I got your message. The baby's due April fifteenth, huh? Maybe I'll knit you an afghan."

"I didn't realize you know how to knit."

"I don't, but I could learn."

Jenna laughed. "I'll call you when I get back."

"Bye."

She smiled at Gram. "When do you want to leave?"

"I'll make breakfast while you get Ryan up for school. We'll leave as soon as the stores open at ten."

JENNA FOLLOWED GRAM down Ukiah Street, mildly surprised when the older woman passed, without pause, the pretty window displays that normally drew her attention. Handmade jewelry, handblown glass, chocolates and truffles and antique linens sparkled in the mellow sunlight, but today Adam's grandmother seemed too intent on her destination to admire such shopping delights.

"Well, he said it was right here," she muttered when they came to the end of the block and found no store selling rugs.

Assuming it was the salesclerk who had given Gram the store's location, Jenna said, "If it's not on the next block, maybe we should stop and ask somebody."

Giving her an absentminded nod, Gram started across the street. When she reached the other corner, she turned back with a gleam in her eye and announced, "I think I see it."

Two stores down, Jenna noticed a large white flag hanging over the sidewalk, rippling softly in the wind, and wondered what type of store hung out such a thing. An American flag, she could understand. But a plain white flag that looked like it had seen better days as a sheet?

To her surprise Gram motioned her toward that very store. "There it is. Take a look."

"At what?" Mystified, Jenna stepped closer. The building was rather plain but in good repair and looked more professional than its Victorian neighbor. Despite the cool weather, the door stood ajar. Fancy gold lettering covered its one large window:

Adam Durham, Attorney at Law
Wills
Divorce
Personal Injury
Contracts

The implication of the words took a moment to sink in, but when it did, all the pain and disappointment Jenna had felt in the preceding week disappeared. She stared at Adam's name, tracing the upswing of the *A* with an imaginary hand over and over again before she felt Gram at her side, prodding her toward the entrance. A glance at the open doorway revealed Adam, leaning against the jamb with his hands in his pockets, watching her.

"So what do you think?" he asked. "Can Mendocino support another attorney?"

The soothing tenor of his voice and the sight of him standing there so close sent Jenna's pulse into high gear. "What happened to your practice? To San Francisco?"

He shrugged. "I closed up shop."

The breeze carried the barest hint of his aftershave to her, making Jenna want to close her eyes and simply breathe in the scent of him and revel in his being there. "But…why?"

"Because the woman I love is in Mendocino."

His voice, his words, caressed her, and before Jenna knew it, she was in his arms, only half-aware that his sweet grandmother was watching them with a look only a few degrees short of the rapture Jenna felt.

"I love you, Jen," Adam murmured, holding her tight. "I have always loved you." Putting his hands on her shoulders, he drew back, and the intensity of his gaze felt like the sun on her face. "Will you marry me? We'll buy a little house here, any one you want, and raise Ryan and our new baby where they can be close to Gram and Pop. You can make your windows in a little studio I'll build off the back, one that'll give you plenty of light. And while we both live and love and work, we'll make more babies, maybe a dozen, because I already know I'll never be able to keep my hands off you."

The white flag snapped in the wind overhead, and suddenly Jenna understood the significance of it. "Uncle," she said.

"What?" He followed her gaze to the flag. "That's right, my love. I surrender my heart to you now and forever."

"My only complaint is that forever could never be long enough," she whispered, and his lips brushed hers, softly and gently at first, then with an urgency that made Jenna feel as though he'd just flung her heart up in the air, to fly freely and joyfully through space. Only this time, she had no fear of a hard landing.

EPILOGUE

LeRoy Tottering had just returned home from his heating and air-conditioning shop when the invitation arrived. Puzzled by the heavy white paper and elaborate scroll print, he shoved the rest of his mail aside and squinted to make out the return address, thinking he must have gotten his neighbor's mail by mistake.

But the envelope was clearly addressed to him. Hmm… He didn't know anyone who was getting married.

Relinquishing his easy chair and the TV remote lying in his lap, LeRoy searched the kitchen counter for his reading glasses. Finding them beneath a section of newspaper, he slid them on and tore open the seal. As he pulled the invitation from its envelope, a picture fell out and fluttered to the ground.

Bending down to retrieve it from the worn shag carpet, LeRoy gazed at the pink and wrinkled face of a newborn. On the back was written, "Alexa Lauren, April 19, 7 lbs. 2 oz."

Whose little girl was this?

He went back to the wedding invitation, which also sported a picture, and stared down at his daughter Jenna. She'd been a skinny little girl, but she'd turned into one of the most beautiful women he'd ever seen. Next to her stood the man he'd met at the Victoriana, both of them smiling as though they'd found heaven.

"Well, she deserves it. It's not as if I did anything to make her life any easier," LeRoy muttered. There was no one around to hear him. Now that all the kids were gone, he lived alone with only his memories and his regrets to keep him company.

Removing a delicate sheet of tissue paper, he studied the inside of the card. In the formal manner of a wedding invitation, Adam Durham and Jenna Livingston requested the pleasure of his presence at a wedding reception to be held in their honor three weeks from Saturday, the weekend after the Fourth of July, at the Victoriana. But LeRoy had a hard time believing they really wanted *him* to come—until he read the neat handwriting at the bottom.

Dear Father,
May the sorrows of the past be lost in the happiness of the future. Please come and meet your new granddaughter.

Jenna

And though LeRoy hadn't shed a tear since he was a boy, he cried like a baby.